Hidden Book Two

COLLEEN VANDERLINDEN

Broken: Hidden Book Two
Colleen Vanderlinden

Published in the United States
by Building Block Studios LLC

ISBN 0615941443
ISBN-13 978-0615941448

http://www.colleenvanderlinden.com/hidden
http://www.buildingblockstudios.com

DEDICATION

For Roger

Partner in crime,
love of my life,
my rock.

.

CONTENTS

ACKNOWLEDGMENTS

I could not do what I do without my amazing family. You guys are my everything. Emily, Sarah, Elizabeth, and Alex – you guys are the best kids ever, and I am stunned every single day that I'm lucky enough to be your mom.

To my husband. You are wonderful in every possible way. You made me believe that there are such things as soul mates, and you are most definitely mine. Thank you for always having my back, for making sure things get done to make these books happen. I love you.

To my readers. You make this whole writing gig fun. Thank you for reading, reviewing, encouraging me. Thank you for loving Molly and company. It really means the world to me. Thank you!

CHAPTER ONE

My name is Molly Brooks.
Vigilante.
Demon.
Mindflayer.

I killed the man I love. Ended the lives of every enemy he'd had, in one fiery, bloody night.

It did not bring him back to me.

My friends, the team of supernaturals who followed the demon they knew as the Nain Rouge, tiptoe around me. They want me to eat. They want me to tell them what to do, where to go, the way he used to. They want me to feed.

I will never feed from another.

I will keep this city safe, in his honor.

I will die trying.

I can only hope that it happens sooner, rather than later.

My wrath is absolute, my lust for death, pain, fear, unending.

I have lost myself.

I have been lied to, used, left behind, by the being I loved most in this world.

And this thing I have become…this is exactly what Nain always knew I would be.

Damn him for making me do this without him.

♦♦♦

Six months, exactly, since the day I lost Nain. The day I destroyed him. The day I realized how far he would go to get what he wanted. I'd be lying if I said I didn't hate him. I'd also be lying if I said I didn't love him, didn't miss him so much it hurt.

I'd spent the first two months like a zombie. I stayed in his room, surrounded by his scent. I didn't speak. I didn't eat. I didn't feed.

And, yet, here I am.

Death would not come for me, the way I hoped it would. So I did the one thing that would make me feel better: I hunted. My imps found demons, warlocks, vampires for me, and I destroyed them. Each kill momentarily made me feel better.

But they didn't ease the pain I felt when I laid in bed at night, alone.

The gaping wound in my soul, the one left when our

marriage bond had been severed at his death…well. It never stops hurting. It is eternal pain. This is the cost of the marriage bond between demons.

I am living a half-life.

That night, I fed, took powers by force. I truly became a mindflayer, a nightmare among nightmares. Power flows through my body, and I can kill in dozens of ways with little more than a thought. But it wasn't just my mind, my powers, that changed under the stress of losing Nain.

I changed.

I am afraid of myself. I will not use my powers anymore. The temptation to do more of what I did that night is overwhelming.

But I still hunt. I go back to the way I used to do things: blades and fists. The only difference now is that I have no qualms about killing my prey. I destroy those who would cause harm to the people of his city.

Tonight, six months after Nain's death, I hunt werewolves. I revel in their pain and fear, and their deaths fill me, for a time. Their blood stains the ground around me, bodies litter the street. The Guardians arrive and claim their souls, even before I've left the scene.

And then I go home, and I am alone, hungry, and afraid again.

Sleep is not the friend it once was.

It won't come easily. And when it does, I am not granted the deep, dreamless sleep of the peaceful.

There are the nightmares. Nain dying, over and over again in slow motion as I realize what I've done. Brennan rips my limbs from my body. My friends stare, mutter "murderer" over and over again.

But I'll take these nightmares over the sweet dreams.

The dreams in which I am wrapped in his arms, my legs tangled with his, and it feels so real I swear I can smell him. And then I wake up. For just a moment, I am happy. And then reality sets in, and I've lost him all over again.

I finished hunting werewolves, and retreated to the

roof of the loft. Ready to spend quality time with my punching bag. Another thing that always made me feel better.

I don't know how many hours I spent whaling away at the punching bag Stone installed for me after Nain's death. When I wasn't beating up on bad guys, this was my place.

My knuckles bled, healed, cracked, and bled again. My arms were tired, but not tired enough to make me stop. Constant motion, hitting, was the only thing keeping me sane. I stopped punching, looked up at the sky. It was probably a little after three A.M. I'd been at it since I got home from taking out the werewolves a little after midnight.

I punched the bag again. Harder. I would not cry.

Before Nain, I'd been so good at avoiding feeling things. I had managed to keep emotions, mine and others, in their own compartment. I recognized them, but they didn't affect me.

He changed everything.

I stopped punching for a minute, rested my forehead against the punching bag. The air around me was frigid. It didn't matter. My breath formed clouds in the dark night.

I tried to remember to breathe. I wished I could stop. Stop breathing, stop feeling, stop living. Just, stop.

I felt Brennan's presence nearby. Shook my head, tried to pull myself together, and started punching again. Sure enough, within seconds, the roof door was opening, and he strolled out, dressed, as usual, in jeans and a flannel shirt. I glanced at him, continued whaling on the bag.

"Are you going to sleep at some point tonight, or spend all night up here, hitting things?" he asked, leaning against the wall.

"Am I keeping you up, Bren?" I asked, well aware of the snarl in my voice.

He shook his head, watched me for a while in silence. I kept punching, hoping he'd go away.

"You've been up here every night for weeks. You're

busy the rest of the time with meetings and keeping this place running and fighting big bads. Everyone has to sleep sometimes."

"I sleep when I need to." This, along with everything else in my life, had changed with Nain's death and its aftermath. Meeting Nain had helped me tap into my powers, and losing and avenging him had taken them a step further. Or, a few hundred steps further.

I barely felt human at all anymore.

"You're going to eventually lose your temper and incinerate that one," he said, gesturing at the bag I was hitting. "And then Stone will put another one up for you, and he'll be happy because it gives him something to do for a while and he can feel useful again."

"He's busy enough. He's still out there kicking ass."

"But you're keeping him away from the really bad stuff. That's the stuff he lives for, and you know that. You take all the bad shit, and you leave him and the rest of us with the supernatural equivalent of traffic stops."

I stopped punching and looked at him, finally. "I'm not in any hurry to lose anyone else right now. I'm sorry if that offends you, Brennan. And if you're here to lecture me again, you need to leave. Because I'll be honest," I said, hitting the bag so hard it swung, creaking on its chains. "I'm really not in the mood tonight."

"Six months," he said quietly. "You're not the only one who's been keeping track." We stood in silence for a few minutes. "Sometimes it feels like we lost both of you that night. Those first weeks afterward, you were a zombie. Now, you're like a machine. We all understand. We're mourning him, too."

"Did you strike the blow that killed him?"

Brennan just looked at me.

"Then you have no goddamned idea how I feel."

"You know as well as I do that he knew it would happen that way," he said quietly. I sensed nervousness in him. "He knew it would kill him, and he told you to do it anyway."

I turned away. "How did you know that?"

"He left me a letter. Father Balester delivered it, after. He knew."

"I know he did. I got to hear his thoughts as he died."

"So maybe you should stop blaming yourself. Maybe you should blame him for putting you into that situation. Or maybe you should blame whoever was ordering Astaroth to capture you. But you can't keep blaming yourself for something you had no control over." He paused. "And that last part is something I do have experience with, and you know I do."

Of course I did. I still had the nightmares when I did manage to doze off. "And have you stopped feeling guilty yet?"

"No."

"And you didn't even manage to kill me," I said, meeting his eyes, then turning back to the punching bag.

"Molly, I think, maybe you should talk to somebody," Brennan said.

I scoffed. "Yeah? Who am I going to talk to, Bren? Who is going to give me the magic words to make all of this okay?"

He bristled. He hated the tone I used at times like this. I knew it. I just didn't especially care.

"You could talk to Father Balester," he said. I rolled my eyes.

"Yeah, a priest who turns into a tree is going to be a great help in this situation," I said.

He was quiet for a while. Frustrated. "You could talk to me." I didn't answer. A few seconds later, he continued. "You could let me help."

"Yeah. Are you going to charge in on your horse and save me, Bren? Are you going to make it all better?" I laughed, and I knew how I sounded.

He was angry now. "I'd try, Molly. I know I can't do much–"

"No, You can't. You need to take your white knight complex, and your desire to fix me, and go back in the fucking house."

"This is not you," he said, shaking his head.

"This is me. And you are not him. You are not even close."

He stared at me. "I know I'm not. And I have no desire to be him, in any way."

I buried my face in my hands, wishing he would just go away. "That was bitchy. I'm sorry."

He waved it off, shook his head. Worked at putting a wall up between us again. "Okay. Well. You have another full day of meetings tomorrow. I had to start making appointments, because too many were showing up here hoping to see you. Is that okay?"

"As long as Ada is around to maintain the wards, it's fine with me." I was relieved at the change in subject. Tired of going over the same shit over and over again.

Brennan nodded. "She'll be here. Also: that Shanti girl showed up here again today. She said she really needs to talk to you. I'm pretty sure she's manifested some type of powers."

"Can we fit her in tomorrow?"

"If you can stand one more meeting after listening to warlocks and shifters bitch all day long, sure."

"Tell her she can come. Final meeting of the day so I don't have to rush her out. It'll probably be late."

"Won't matter to her. She'll be relieved."

He stood there a while longer, watching me hit the bag. "Try to rest, Molly. I know you think you don't need to. But you don't sleep, and you haven't fed since—"

"I will not feed from another," I said, stopping and meeting his eyes, making it dead clear.

"You're not eating food, either. Saltines and coffee do not count."

"I. Am. Fine." I said, well aware of the threatening growl in my voice.

7

"Obviously," Brennan said, heading back toward the door. "You can't do this forever, you know."

"Don't shifters mate for life?" I asked. He stopped and turned toward me. Nodded.

"And if a shifter's mate dies, they feel empty. Like part of them is missing. Yes?"

He nodded again.

"Okay. When demons bond, it is for life, and death. Imagine, for just a second, being bound to someone, and then losing them and feeling like your soul's been ripped to shreds. And then imagine that you can still feel that person inside you, their blood running through your veins. And they're with you, every second, but also not. He's so close, and yet, he's gone. Try to imagine how much that would screw with your head before telling me how I'm supposed to handle this."

"Molly," he said, and he held his hands up in a gesture of helplessness, regret.

"I won't have this discussion again. I'm doing things the only way I know how."

He nodded, opened his mouth to say something, then turned and headed for the door.

"Just, remember that you have people who care about you, who want to be here for you, okay?" Then he turned and went back into the loft. I was alone again. I settled onto the glider, and stared into the nothingness, waited for the sun to rise again. One more night without him by my side.

♦♦♦

Time to face another day. Time to stumble along, trying to save the world without destroying everybody in it.

I found that routines helped me stay sane. Saner, maybe. Every morning, the same thing: shower, dress, coffee, meetings. Just run down the list, focus on doing items one, two, three, and try to hold it together through the long slog that was number four.

Relief happened at the end of my work day, when I stalked the night, ridding the city of the supernatural filth that came to my attention via the imps or the people I met during the day. But the days were long, and maintaining my sanity until that point was getting harder all the time.

I didn't know whether mornings were a blessing or a curse, now. On the one hand, I wasn't alone.

On the other, I wasn't alone.

This sucked.

I got up, showered. After I'd showered and dressed (my usual: black pants, black Chucks, black top) I started brushing my hair. I still startled myself sometimes at those rare moments when I happened to catch my reflection. My hair had grown longer in the past six months; it was now almost down to my butt. I couldn't make myself cut it. He'd enjoyed running his fingers through the strands, and it felt like losing more of him whenever I even considered it.

I knew it was stupid. It didn't matter.

More than my hair, though, was everything else. I'd gotten paler, my creamy complexion more of an almost alabaster, like someone who'd never seen the sun.

And then, there were my eyes.

They'd glowed orangey-red before, when I'd gotten angry. It was a typical demon thing. But since that night, the night I lost Nain and destroyed every group who'd allied with Astaroth, they'd changed, too. They glowed white, and they hadn't been normal since.

If I went out during the day, I had to wear dark sunglasses and hope nobody noticed. At night, I just had to be really careful to avoid the Normals. I made no effort to hide my eyes from other supernaturals, though. It seemed to intimidate them. I liked that.

I pulled my hair up into a messy bun. I glanced over at the tall dresser where his clothes were still folded neatly. I walked over to it, pulled the top drawer open, and breathed his scent in. Stupid. Compulsive, now, a habit I couldn't quit. It probably hurt me more than it helped. But any bit of him I could get, anything that helped me feel less alone, even if it was only for a second…I'd take it. I closed the drawer quickly.

His pillow had long since lost his scent.

I'd slept with it during the weeks after his death. I hadn't left the bedroom at all for the first two weeks. The team had finally pried me out. I'd become, for some reason, the de facto leader after Nain's death. They all looked to me, expected me to make the decisions and handle those parts of daily life that Nain had taken care of.

The way his widow would, I guess.

I hated that word.

I'd do this. I'd take care of this team. I'd keep the city safe. It was the only thing I had left, now. And doing his job made me feel closer to him.

I took a deep breath, opened the bedroom door and headed toward Nain's, my, office. Stone was sitting in the living room, and I called a good morning to him. Ada poured me a cup of coffee, shoved it into my hand, gave me a quick hug before I retreated into the office.

I sat down in the big leather chair, behind the mahogany desk that had been neat and painstakingly organized when Nain was alive. Now it was stacked with newspapers, books, notebooks. A photo of me and Nain that Ada had taken when I'd first joined the team. We were arguing, eyes glowing. I didn't even know he'd had it. It made me smile.

I settled in, had a few sips of coffee. The sunlight coming in through the windows proved to be too tempting to Stone's cat, Lola, who despised me but enjoyed basking in the sun. She sauntered in and stretched out on the wood floor next to my desk.

"Well, you look like you're going to be a big help today," I muttered to her, and she gave me one of those superior cat looks and turned away from me. Fine. She was not my biggest fan. The second my dogs had come to live with me at the loft, I'd been permanently added to her shit list.

After my little demonstration of power that night, so much had changed. One of them was that I'd become some kind of hero to many supernaturals who had been harassed and bullied by Astaroth and his minions for so long. I'd earned, thanks to my previous reputation as a finder of lost girls, plus what I'd done that night, a reputation for being the one who'd stand up to any foe.

They'd started coming to me, first, one or two per day, knocking timidly on the door downstairs, asking to see The Angel. And I saw them, because turning them away never even entered my mind. I took care of them, solved their problems, and more came, and now I was the one they all came to for help. And I was the one everyone feared the most. Those I helped always promised their help in return. The core of my team was small, without Nain, Veronica, and George. But our network of supernaturals allied with us was growing all the time. Nain had been more of an isolationist than I was, I guess.

After I'd taken a few sips of coffee, Brennan made his appearance.

"Your first appointment is here. Esmeralda. Leader of the coven over in the Brightmoor neighborhood."

I nodded. "What's her deal?"

"She claims that the weres in the neighborhood are harassing her women, especially the younger ones. She claims two of the weres tried to abduct her newest initiate, and she wants it dealt with."

I nodded. "Okay. Let her in."

I leaned back in the chair, folded my hands in my lap. I watched as Brennan led the witch into my office. She was stately, with snow white hair, skin like parchment. A simple black dress. A pentacle on a silver chain around her neck was her only adornment. She didn't need anything else.

"Angel," she said, bowing her head slightly, meeting my eyes. She was taken aback by them. Those meeting me for the first time usually were. It wasn't uncommon knowledge, but seeing them usually freaked people out a little. She was a little nervous, but not afraid. Calm. I appreciated that.

"Esmeralda," I said. "Have a seat."

"Thank you for agreeing to see me," she said, settling into the chair opposite me. "I know you are a busy woman."

"Brennan tells me you're having werewolf problems."

She filled me in on what had happened. Brennan stood by the door, ever watchful. My imps, Bashiok and Dahael, flanked me, arms crossed. Deadly little protectors. I'd seen them fight, really fight, during that final battle against Astaroth. I would not want to piss my imps off. If anything, they'd become even more devoted to me since.

She finished. "So it sounds like it is one or two young weres, not the whole pack that is causing the problem," I said.

"Yes, but their leader is allowing it to happen. You know how it is; as leader, you don't just let things like this happen. And if he doesn't know what his pack is doing, maybe he shouldn't be leader anymore."

"You're getting into two separate things, now," I said, leaning forward and meeting her eyes. "Do you want the young men who assaulted your initiate dealt with, or do you want the packmaster removed?"

"I would like the two problem weres dealt with. And maybe a discussion with the packmaster? If he hears from you, maybe he'll start to pay more attention to what his pack is doing."

I nodded. "Brennan, add a meeting with the Brightmoor packmaster to the list, please." He nodded, pulled out his iPhone, and started typing it in.

"It will be dealt with," I said.

I felt relief from Esmeralda. "Thank you so much,

Angel," she said.

I nodded.

She stood up. "I am sorry for your loss, by the way. I didn't know the Nain Rouge well, but he was well-respected in our community."

"Thank you."

She nodded, and Brennan showed her out, then came back in a minute later. "Who do you want on this?"

"Do you mind taking care of the two troublemakers? Take Stone later, if you want. Set up a meeting as soon as you can between me and the packmaster."

"Sure. You ready for your next one?"

I nodded.

"Vampire from midtown. Max Reynes. He's complaining that he feels threatened by his shifter neighbors."

"Is he?"

Brennan smirked. "He doesn't like that they won't let him eat all of the other people in the apartment building. I talked to two guys I know who live there, and they swear he is a slimeball. I have the feeling you'll agree with them."

"Okay. Let him in."

I folded my hands in my lap again, watched as the vampire entered my office. He was tall, good looking, as most vampires seemed to be. This one was obviously a daywalker, which was rare and made him more dangerous than his more common brethren.

I could sense him. Superior, annoyed. Active hate for Brennan. Disdain for me.

I didn't like him much, either.

"Reynes," I said in greeting.

"Angel. Thank you for making the time to see me," he said, though it sounded just as fake as he meant it.

"Pleasure," I said, just as genuinely. "What can I do for you?"

He spun a long yarn about how the shifters in his building were harassing him, how he felt unsafe in his home because he was outnumbered, and he knew they didn't like him. That all he was trying to do was live a quiet life, feed when he needed to, but he was constantly having to watch his back.

It was easy for me to pick up a lie. Emotions never lied. You had to be really clueless or really confident to come to me and try to bullshit. And this bloodsucker was giving Detroit's crooked politicians a run for their money. He didn't have much of a mental shield, either, likely never bothered to train properly. I could see girl after girl from his neighborhood, his building, drained to the point of death, and left to die. Too many.

I felt my rage rising the longer he talked. I would have loved to have ended him right then and there, but I didn't want the mess in my office. Later. When I could enjoy it.

I rested my elbow on the arm of my chair, rested my chin in my hand as he finished talking. I let the silence stretch out for a few minutes. Watched him. The longer we sat, the more nervous he became. He started talking again, complaints about the shifters.

I pictured how I would kill him. Fire would be fast and easy, but I would not use it. Knives were always fun. I did enjoy their fear the longer the fight went on and they felt themselves losing. Stake through the heart was the traditional way, if I could find him when he was sleeping. But not as fulfilling. So many options.

He stopped talking again, and I let the silence stretch out longer.

He was on the verge of panic. I had to keep myself from smirking at him. "Thank you for coming. Your complaints have been duly noted."

"Are you going to take care of this?"

"Oh, I definitely am," I said. "I will deal with it personally."

He stood up, nodded, and left without another word. Brennan escorted him out, and I heard Ada resetting the wards after he was gone.

Brennan came back in. "Who's on this?"

"I am."

"Molly…"

"I've got this one. That piece of shit was lying through his fangs."

He snorted. "Ready for the next one?"

CHAPTER TWO

I saw a steady stream of supernaturals. A few more
witches, a shifter, a sprite. Most of them were simple
enough. Someone treading on someone else's territory, an
insult given, a favor asked. I kept working throughout the
day. After the sprite left, Brennan came back into my
office with another cup of coffee.

"That was the last one. Shanti is here now."

He seemed uncomfortable.

"What?"

"I figured out what she is."

I raised my eyebrow, waiting.

"I had to pull her off of Stone. She was trying to eat
him."

"Vamp?"

He nodded.

"Oh, crap. Poor kid." I rubbed my face. "Is Stone all
right?"

"Of course. He was worried about hurting her."

I nodded. "Okay. Let her in, and then close the door,
all right?"

"Shouldn't I stay? I mean… she's hungry, Molly."

"Do you really think I'm incapable of handling myself against a vampire?"

"Of course not, but–"

"Just bring her in, Bren."

He gave a terse nod. Irritated. A few seconds later, Shanti was walking into my office, and the door closed behind her. Brennan was standing just outside the door, ready. I tried not to be annoyed with him. He was doing what shifter males do best: protecting the pack. And for better or worse, we were it.

I watched Shanti. The last time I'd seen her was over a year ago. The same night, I'd met Nain, I remembered, feeling a familiar stab somewhere in the vicinity of my heart. She'd been fifteen, a thin athletic girl who was able to smile despite the hell she'd just been through. She'd been kidnapped, and was nearly sold to one of the Puppeteer's puppets, destined to make somebody a whole lot of money. I'd rescued her before any major damage had taken place.

I inspected her now. Her coffee and cream complexion was paler. She looked stronger. She was gorgeous, her natural beauty only enhanced by becoming a vampire, and, now, frozen in time. I sensed for her. She was nervous, afraid, ashamed. She hated herself. She was desperate, and hungry.

Her thoughts were wide open, too. A constant stream, thinking about how she'd almost bitten that man, and how hot that guy is, and wow this is a nice house, holy shit what happened to her eyes?

I smiled. "Shanti. It's nice to see you again, kiddo."

I felt her relax a little. She gave me a small smile. "Thank you for seeing me, Angel. I wasn't sure you would remember me."

"Of course I do. Have a seat." She sat, and I thought of something. "Brennan?"

He opened the door. "Yeah?"

I waved him over and he bent so I could speak directly into his ear. "I remember Ada mentioning that Nain always kept bagged blood around for any vampires who happened to visit. Any left?"

"I'll check and warm it up if there's any. I forgot about that."

I nodded, and he left. I turned back to Shanti, who was gazing longingly after Brennan. I almost laughed. Poor kid.

"So. How did you get into this condition, young lady? Whose ass do I need to kick?" I leaned back in my chair.

"From what I hear, you already did. He lived in Indian Village. Tall, white, had an accent."

Another stab to the heart as my mind went back to that night. Memories that threatened to drown me.

"Angel?" Shanti said, concerned, after I was silent for a few minutes. I took a deep breath, forcing my mind away from the trail it was heading down.

"Yes. I know who you mean. I take it you didn't want to be turned?"

She shook her head. "He caught me in the alley behind my work when I was taking the garbage out. I thought he was going to kill me, but when I came to, I was this," she said, waving at herself in disgust. Then she became afraid, ashamed again. "I've killed people, Angel. Innocent people, because I can't control it. I attacked your friend…"

I held out my hand. "I know. It's okay. You'll learn to control it. I'll help you."

"I was kind of hoping you'd kill me."

We sat in silence. She looked anywhere but at me. Finally, I said, "Do you really want to die, Shanti?"

"Vampires are evil. I don't want to be evil," she said. Tears flooded her eyes, tinged pink. Vampire tears.

"Do you know what I am?" I asked softly.

"Rumor is, you're a demon, but I don't believe it," she said, shaking her head emphatically.

"Believe it. I'm a demon. I am many things. But I try not to be evil, if I can at all help it."

She stared at me.

I went on. "We decide who we are. Being a vampire, or a demon, or a witch…you can fall on either side. There are decent vampires in this city, just as there are shithead ones. And a vampire who's also a decent person can do a lot of good."

"I'm afraid of hurting people."

"We'll teach you to deal with it. You can live here if you want. We have room."

"You'd let me live here?" she said in disbelief.

"Sure. There are rules. Expectations. And if you ever put my friends in danger, I will definitely kill you, painfully. But I can't imagine that you'd do anything like that."

She swallowed. "I ran away from home. I was afraid of hurting my aunts. I almost drank from one of them."

"That kind of danger we can handle. Double crossing us or betraying us….that is the kind of thing that will bring my wrath down on you."

Brennan knocked on the door then, walked in holding a large cup. He glanced at me, and set it on the desk in front of Shanti. "Drink up," he said. Then he headed back toward the door.

"Oh my god. Thank you," she said, her voice lispy as her fangs lengthened in her mouth. She picked up the cup and slugged it back. I sensed relief, gratitude from her.

I sat and waited as she drained the cup. I could feel her becoming less tense, less on edge, as she drank. I remembered feeling that way, whenever I'd been starving and then been fed–

I had to stop this.

She put the cup down, wiped at her mouth.

"Better?" I asked.

"Much. Thank you so much," she said. I nodded. "So, I can really stay?"

"Yes. You'll have to allow Ada to put a spell on you that will prevent you from inviting anyone in here, as well as one that will let us know if you give secret information to anyone."

She nodded.

"And you'll have to learn how to shield your thoughts. Any telepath can pick up what you're thinking."

She stared at me. "Uh… you don't have any telepaths here, do you?"

I raised my hand, wiggling my fingers slightly, gave her a small smile. She paled. and I sensed total embarrassment flood her.

"Oh, god."

"Don't worry about it. I'm the only one, and I'm not all that easy to offend, really."

She shook her head. We were quiet for a minute. "I, um. I heard that you lost a friend a while back. I'm sorry," she said, fiddling with the edge of her skirt.

"He was my husband," I said softly.

Surprise filled her. "Oh, Jesus. I am so sorry."

"He was also a demon."

"Two good demons, eh? There is hope for me, then," she said.

"Of course."

"What was his name?"

"Nain," I said, his name still honey on my lips. I turned the frame around, and she picked the photo up, studied it.

She smiled. "He looks like as much of a badass as you are."

I nodded. "He was THE badass. I met him the night I rescued you, actually. Remember that truck that was following us?"

She nodded. "That was him? Really?"

"Yeah. My life changed that night." I bit my lip.

Do not cry in front of the confused teenage girl who is depending on you to be a badass, I told myself. Not now.

"Do you have anything you need to move in?" I asked, changing the subject.

She shook her head. "Just what's in this bag. Clothes and books."

"Okay. Want to get settled in, then?"

She nodded, and followed me out of the office, up the stairs to the room that had been Veronica's. Ada had gone through both this room and George's old one, donated clothing and other items to charity. All that remained was the furniture, a television and a radio.

"Here we go. There are bed linens in the closet, there. This room shares a small bathroom with the room on the other side, but that room's empty right now."

"This is amazing. I've been sleeping in parks and bus stops." She looked around, and I could feel the gratitude flowing from her.

"All right. No eating your housemates. We have some bagged blood in the fridge. I'll get a hold of more."

"I didn't even know something like that existed," she said.

"Neither did I. But, like I said, there are good vamps in the city, too. The bagged blood is synthetic. Was it close enough?"

She nodded. "I feel much better. It will work."

"Okay. So if you get hungry, it's in the fridge downstairs. You can heat it up for a minute or so in the microwave if you want to. I've heard it tastes better that way."

She nodded again.

"All right. I have some things I need to go do. Get settled, and when you're ready later we'll introduce you to everyone."

"Thanks so much, Angel," she said, grabbing me for a huge hug.

I hugged her back. "My friends call me Molly," I said, patting her on the back and stepping away. "Make yourself at home."

I made sure Shanti was settled, then I headed back downstairs. Brennan was waiting in the dining room for me, along with Ada and Stone.

"Well, we seem to have adopted a girl," I said, walking up to them. "Can you get a hold of more bagged blood? We'll need a steady supply."

Brennan nodded, pulled out his phone again.

"I can't just turn her out. Are you all okay with this?"

"Of course," Ada said. "That is just what Nain would have done."

"She's got little baby fangs. Fine with me," Stone said, winking at me. "Not even scary yet."

"It's fine with me. I'm glad you didn't turn her out," Brennan said, still looking at his phone.

"Thanks, guys. Ada, I'll need you to put the two protection spells on her, okay?" Ada nodded. "Before she leaves the loft again."

I sat down, and Brennan left, then came back and set a cup of coffee and a slice of cake in front of me. "Eat."

"You are so damn bossy," I muttered. Stone laughed, and Ada jokingly asked where hers was. Brennan sat next to me, making sure I ate.

"Whatever, Molly. Just eat the freaking cake."

"I don't need anyone to take care of me, you know," I said, digging into the chocolate cake.

"Yep. I know."

I finished the cake, slugged back the coffee. "She's going to be in her room for a while. Leave her alone. She'll come out and meet everyone officially when she's ready," I said. I stood up. "I have to—"

I didn't get to finish what I was saying. One of the Guardians, the beings who escort supernatural souls to the Nether upon death, swooped into the loft out of nowhere.

My team jumped up. Brennan knocked over his chair in his haste and surprise, leapt, of all places, *between* me and the Guardian. Ada and Stone stared. I could feel the fear coming from them. From Brennan, nothing but determination as he stood in front of me.

I crossed my arms and watched the Guardian. I'd

gotten used to this one. She'd followed me around all night the night Nain died, summoning her sisters every time I'd killed again. She'd sat by my bedside in the hours afterward, refused to sever my tie to the mortal world. I was still pretty pissed with her for that last one.

"Eunomia," I said in greeting. "I haven't killed anybody yet." I put my hands on Brennan's arms, gently pushed him aside.

"The night is still young, demon girl," she said cheerfully, landing on her feet next to me. I glanced at my team. I was used to seeing the Guardian, but they were not. The last time they'd seen her, she'd been there with her sisters, performing the ritual that would free Nain's soul of its Earthly ties.

I tilted my head toward her. "Please tell them no one is going to die."

She looked at the team, as if she'd just noticed them. "You're all safe. This is a social call."

They stood, still as statues, staring at her, then back at me, then at her again. She laughed. "Perceptive friends you have."

"Huh?"

She rolled her eyes at me, winked at the team. "Come talk to me." She fluttered into my office.

"I need to go beat someone up," I grumbled.

"Shocking. You never do that kind of thing," she said. I closed the office door behind us.

"What's up?"

"How are you holding up, devil girl?" she asked me, settling into one of the chairs.

I shrugged, plopping down into my chair. "I want to die. Same as before."

She watched me. Blinked. She reminded me again of a deadly bird. She cocked her head. "I lied out there. I'm here on business."

I stilled.

"Not that kind of business," she said, waving at me.

"They're not going to die. Don't worry."

I took a deep breath. "Okay."

"I'm here unofficially, of course. I am not supposed to interfere. I don't know why I keep doing so on your behalf."

"Because I'm so much fun," I said.

"Yes, that must be it." She paused. "Anyway. We've been having issues, as you would say, in the Nether."

"That sounds bad."

She nodded. "For some reason, the gate between here and the Pit is weakening."

"Um. You're going to have to explain that to me."

"Oh, right. Forsaken demons," she muttered.

"What's a forsaken demon?"

"You."

I gestured that she should continue. She sighed. "Forsaken demons are those demons who live here, among mortals. There are not many of you."

"Demons prefer the Nether," I said, repeating what Nain had told me a long time ago.

"Right. Forsaken are usually those that were born here, whose ancestors came here by choice or accident before the gateways were sealed. They are trapped here."

"Because traveling between here and the Nether is not possible, unless you're an immortal or whatever," I said, again repeating what Nain had told me.

She nodded. "That is usually true."

"Usually?"

"Forsaken demons have no way of getting back to the Nether, at least, not until they face their final judgment. Eternal punishment for leaving in the first place."

"Harsh," I murmured.

"The Lord of the Nether is a harsh being," Eunomia agreed. "And the gods decided, a very long time ago, that demons from the Nether should not be allowed to come here, either. They closed all of the gateways between here and the Nether, and now, as you say, only immortals like myself can come through."

"Okay. But you said that the gateway between here and the Pit, whatever that is, is weakening."

She nodded. "The Pit is the area of the Nether where the worst, most deranged gods and demons are exiled to. It is our version your mortal prisons. It is a terrifying place, guarded by the strongest and most trusted demons the Lord of the Nether can find. The Fury Tisiphone is in charge of keeping the gate secure."

"And when you say that the gateway between them and us is weakening...."

"I mean that they will make their way here, demon girl. We are working to repair whatever it is they've done to make the gate weaken, but it is not going well."

I took a deep breath. This could not be real. Couldn't be.

"It's real," Eunomia said.

"Okay. Well, so, what? There's one gateway weakening. Tell me it's in Siberia or something."

"There are gateways that end in other areas. A couple in Europe and Asia, one in Antarctica, and one that connects the Nether to Detroit," she said.

"Lemme guess which one is weakening," I muttered. "Why is there even a gateway to here at all?"

"It has less to do with Earthly locations than locations in the Nether. Each sector had a gateway. Detroit just happens to be where one of those sectors needed a gateway."

"Lucky us."

Eunomia watched me. "I do not think it is an accident that this particular gateway is the one being tampered with," she said.

I was silent.

"Whoever sent the demon Astaroth after you is becoming impatient," she continued. "Clearly, it was someone from my realm."

I nodded. "Can we find out who?"

"We will. I promise. But your foremost concern now should be that gateway."

"What am I supposed to do if it opens?" I asked, jumping up and pacing back and forth behind my desk. "You just said that the worst of demonkind is on the other side of that gate."

She gave me a steely look. "Do what you do best. Destroy them. You won't be alone."

I just looked at her, then continued pacing.

"Tisiphone has been working to guard the gate as well. With her and the demon guards watching on our end, and you on your end, we should be able to contain any problems before catastrophe."

"Oooookay. The Furies. I know I've heard of them. They're like the...what?"

"They are the next step in judgment of the dead. My sisters and I collect the dead. The Furies bring the dead before Lord Hades, and he makes his final judgment. Then the Furies take the soul for its punishment."

"Sounds like a fun group."

She just looked at me again, a kind of half-grin on her face. She was kind of creepy, really. "Yes. Fun. Too serious for their own good, always with the punishment and torture. Except Tisiphone, maybe. The other two are the punishers. Tisiphone is more of a warrior."

We were quiet for a bit as I tried to wrap my brain around all of it. "You really are just a ray of sunshine, E," I finally said, plopping back down into my chair and shaking my head.

She laughed then, a light, tinkling laugh that should have been completely out of character for what she was.

Here's the thing: she was the last thing the soul saw on this plane of existence. She escorted them to what was beyond. Some, the really, really good among us, went straight to whatever qualifies as heaven. The rest of us, the ones who have things to answer for, go to the Nether for our final punishment. Demons, like me, never leave.

We are the worst of the gods' creations. There is no happy ending for us. Once our mortal lives end, we are punished according to the Lord of the Nether's judgment. And then: nothing. Our existence will end in pain and punishment.

I had a hell of a punishment ahead of me someday.

But she wasn't scary. Creepy, yeah. Always. But there was a beauty, a purity, to Eunomia that made me feel safe with her, despite what she was. Maybe it was just a sign of how messed up I was that one of the beings I trusted most now was an agent of the Lord of the Dead.

"Well, think of it this way: it will occupy your time," she said.

"Sure. Hey! Do you suppose this means an early, you know," I gestured, drawing a line across my throat, "for me? Like maybe they'll come through soon and we'll battle and that will end me? Because that would be awesome."

She shook her head. "I have the feeling you have much more ahead of you, dear girl."

"It doesn't feel like it."

We sat in silence for a while. "I need to go take care of a vampire," I finally said.

"I'll come with you. The look in your eyes tells me an escort will be necessary."

I nodded. We stood, and walked through the loft. I waved to my friends, stalked with the Guardian out into the night.

I headed to my car. "Keep your crazy machine to yourself," Eunomia scoffed. "I'll meet you there." And with that, she winked out of sight. I got in the Barracuda, gunned the engine, cranked up the stereo. Bash and Dahael were already waiting in the back seat, along with three other imps. I still hadn't learned all of their names.

"Shall we go destroy a vampire?" I asked them as I squealed out of the parking spot.

"I love destroying vampires," Dahael said with a dreamy tone to her voice as she clung to the back of my seat.

Bashiok nodded. "Satisfying," he said in agreement.

I felt my rage surging through my body. Alive. I would enjoy removing this vampire.

I did the only thing I knew how to do anymore.

Destroy.

I didn't really give Reynes much of a chance. Once I cornered him in the alley where he was stalking a girl, it was just a matter of leaping onto him and going to work with my knives.

I felt a little thrill when he saw me, recognized that his death would come at my hands. "This is for all of those girls in your neighborhood," I growled.

He was dead before he even had a chance to fight.

Eunomia fluttered down, waited for her sisters, and they worked together to free the vampire of his Earthly bonds.

"Must you be so messy, demon girl?" Eunomia asked as she helped her sister cut the soul's tie to the mortal plane.

"Just be happy I left more than ashes this time," I muttered.

She rolled her eyes, shouted a "see you later" at me, and she and her sisters blinked out of sight.

The imps and I got back into the car and drove home. I checked in with Shanti, got her another cup of blood. She was settling in, but not yet ready to face anyone. I wanted to go up to the roof, hit the bag for a while, but I felt like I should keep an eye on her. We wouldn't want to leave her door unguarded. She might have a hankering for a midnight snack while everyone was sleeping.

I kicked my shoes off and sat in the leather armchair that had been Nain's. It didn't face the television like the rest of the furniture. It faced the wall of windows that looked out over the city. I sat, and looked out, and waited for another night to pass.

CHAPTER THREE

The next morning, I introduced Shanti to the team. I gave her more blood, and then left her in Ada and Stone's very capable hands. I spent a couple of hours in meetings, then begged off, and had Brennan cancel the rest of the day's appointments.

There was somewhere I had to be.

I headed out of the loft and walked toward Midtown. I found the parade route, and I leaned up against a tree in a mostly empty spot. I heard jazz music in the distance, the cheers and shouts of the revelers. It wasn't long before the parade started. First were the bands, and between them were people, in groups or singles, in costumes. They carried signs, each, in its own way, telling the Nain Rouge to get out of the city.

The annual Marche du Nain Rouge. Detroit tradition. The Nain Rouge was a harbinger of doom, the fairy tale went. This parade would keep him away for another year, banish his brand of evil from the city so we would be safe.

They could not have had it more mixed up if they tried.

I didn't even know why I was there. The last thing I wanted to see was a bunch of clueless Normals making a joke and a party of someone I'd known to be their biggest protector. He had his own motives for doing so, and I only understood some of them. It didn't change the fact that they had no idea how many times Nain had saved them from disaster, how many men and women had come home at night because he'd interceded at the right time. And the fools wanted to be rid of him.

They had their wish, clueless though they were.

It was just good for them that I was not the spiteful type. I wouldn't leave them to fend for themselves, no matter how badly I wanted to right at that moment.

And I wouldn't incinerate them, despite my inclination to do just that.

Idiots.

I watched for a while, still not even sure why I was there. Watched the bands, the costumed morons. Soon, I sensed Brennan not too far behind me. I took a deep breath, forced myself to try to be nice.

I just wanted to be alone.

He came and stood next to me, hands shoved deep into his pockets. The day was sunny, but cold, the kind of late winter day that just screams "Michigan." Winter holds on, even though it looks like spring.

We watched the parade in silence for several minutes. So many people dressed up like the infamous "red dwarf." None of them even close. I could feel sadness, irritation from Brennan.

"We used to come to this when I was a kid," Brennan finally said. "He got a kick out of it."

"Well, it was all about him, after all," I said, smiling despite the pain.

"Yeah. The costumes cracked him up. We even dressed up one year and marched in it."

I shook my head. I couldn't talk anymore around the lump in my throat. An image of Nain, Brennan as a gangly teenage boy, laughing and joking around watching these fools mock Nain... it was just too much.

"You probably shouldn't be here," Brennan said softly, watching me.

"I have to. I can't explain it," I said. I adjusted my dark sunglasses to make sure they covered my eyes.

He sighed. "Okay. I should probably get back and help Ada keep an eye on Shanti," he said. "Are you sure you don't just want to come back?"

I shook my head. "I'll stay a while."

"Don't hurt anybody," he said, starting to stroll away.

"You never let me have any fun," I muttered, and I heard him chuckle as he walked away.

The parade had passed me now, and I followed the sounds of merriment to the end of the parade route, where the attendees were hanging out. The music played on. Kids ran between groups of adults who were, at this early hour, in various stages of inebriation.

I leaned up against a tree and stared at one of the event signs. A grotesque little red dwarf decorated it.

I'd never known that form, of course. But I had a feeling that wasn't what the Nain Rouge had really looked like.

I could feel other people with power here besides me. I glance around, and I saw several familiar faces. Shifters, a few witches, two werewolves. Decent people. Each gave me a respectful nod as they felt my eyes on them. I nodded back at them, touched that they'd thought to come to this stupid event today.

I watched as another Normal stood up to make a speech about how great the city was, and how it was going to come back, stronger than ever, thanks to the community.

I had my doubts, actually.

"Molly Brooks?" A deep voice said behind my left shoulder.

I was getting out of practice. No one snuck up on me anymore. I turned, glanced at the stranger.

He stuck his hand out. "I'm Chief Jones, Detroit Police," he said.

I repressed a groan. This shit, I did not need right now.

"Chief," I said, shaking his hand very briefly.

"I'm surprised to see you here," he said, crossing his arms as he stood next to me and watched the revelers.

"Are you?"

"Not where I'd expect to find the Nain Rouge's widow," he said quietly.

I looked at him. Felt for him.

"Ah," I said, nodding. "Shifter."

I felt surprise from him. "What?"

I raised my eyebrow at him. "Please don't try to lie about it."

"I won't, but… how? This thing was supposed to be able to mask what I am," he said, showing me an amulet with a silvery gem. Irritation, worry washed over me like a wave.

"It was doing a good job. I didn't pick it up at first," I reassured him. "So, what do you want?"

He watched me for a minute, sizing me up. Shook his head. "You are scary."

"So I've heard. Good thing I'm one of the good guys. Relatively speaking," I said after a small pause.

The chief chuckled, and we stood there a while. I looked him over behind my glasses. He was supposed to be in his mid-40s, but, as with all shifters, he looked much younger than that. Tall, broad. Dark brown eyes, hair buzzed close to his scalp.

He glanced over at me again, tearing his gaze from the revelers. "You know the official word. I'm supposed to be investigating you for all of those deaths last October."

"And the unofficial word?" I asked, crossing my arms.

"I'm here to offer my condolences and thank you for cleaning a lot of the scum out of my city."

I looked at him.

"Do you realize that crime in the last six months is

down an insane 67% from what it was over the same period of time last year?"

I shook my head.

"Well, it is. Whoever all those beings were, and I have my suspicions, they were causing a lot of trouble. And you're still out there, doing your thing."

I didn't respond. We stood in silence for a while, sizing each other up. "My official word is going to be that the Angel is nothing more than a normal human woman, a vigilante who we are going to keep an eye on, but a woman who is clearly incapable of anything more than roughing up street thugs. My official word is that there are no supernatural beings here."

I smirked. "Lying, chief? I'm shocked. Shocked, I tell you."

He snorted. "I'm the last word, but not everyone is going to believe me. I have a couple of guys who are hell-bent on looking into this supernatural thing, and I don't doubt they're going to keep poking around. I don't think they'll be any real trouble for you, but you should know they're out there."

I nodded.

"So, unofficially, thank you. Could you maybe not leave so many bodies around next time you go on a killing spree?"

I stared at him. "Are you serious?"

"Dead serious. I appreciate what you're doing. But bodies lead to questions, and you know that those are the last things we need. When Nain was in charge, he always made sure things disappeared before questions were asked."

"I will try to clean up my messes when I'm done playing, Chief," I said, stuffing my hands into my coat pockets.

"Thank you." He paused. "I am sorry about your husband. I never met Nain, but I heard about him through my family, my pack. He was respected. If you ever need the assistance of the Northside shifters, you have it."

"Thank you."

He sighed. "My report won't make the general populace stop wondering about you. You're a legend. Please watch yourself. A Normal gets a photo or god help us, video, of you in action, and nothing I can say will make that disappear."

I nodded. "I am careful. I'll remain so."

"Excellent. I have to go. Take care, Angel. Don't let these fools get you down."

I shook his hand. "Chief, I don't think I can feel much lower anyway."

"I hear you. Nice meeting you."

I nodded, and watched him walk off. Well. At least I had one less thing to worry about now.

I left, wandered the city aimlessly for the rest of the day and into the evening. Thinking. Wondering how to do everything I'm supposed to do. How to keep Shanti, Brennan, Stone, and Ada safe and happy. How to stay on top of the never-ending influx of troublemakers into the city. The chief hadn't been wrong; I'd taken out most of the worst big bads in the city that night. The only trouble was that their deaths had left a gap, and there were plenty of beings out there who now vied for the power people like Astaroth and the Puppeteer used to have. The only difference now is that I didn't know these new enemies. They were more likely to take me by surprise.

And then there was the gateway. Demons, Furies, things you read about in mythology books and never even once think you'll ever come face to face with. A threat so much worse than the ones I already knew about.

Before I made my way home, I'd saved two women in the process of getting carjacked (by Normals, so it barely took any effort at all, really), taken out a warlock who'd been using local shifters in his sacrifices, and subdued a sprite who was wreaking havoc in one of the group homes on Grand Boulevard. Not a bad night's work.

It was near dawn when I finally arrived back at the loft. Tired enough that, for once, I actually went into Nain's room, fell into bed, and slept.

♦♦♦

The days all kind of melded into one long, endless cycle of meetings, destroying, and long mostly sleepless nights. The only distraction from the haze of pain, violence, and anger that was my existence was Shanti.

We were working at helping her control her bloodlust, at recognizing it and taking care of it before she lost control. Brennan was training her to fight, and she seemed to really enjoy it. She'd taken a few courses after I'd found her, so she was happy to learn more. Her training and guard duty was mainly falling to Brennan and I. He handled training and was ever-watchful to make sure she was fed regularly. She was getting much better at control. I'd started working on mental shielding with her, but, for the time being, I was mainly there for her to talk and vent to. Which was funny because when we "talked," she did all of the talking, and I mostly nodded. But, it seemed to work for her.

I watched as Brennan and Shanti finished with another late evening training in the loft. They sparred while I sat on the stairs and watched. She was getting stronger, more confident. Bren was a good teacher.

He knocked Shanti down, then helped her back up again as she grimaced. "I'm never going to beat you," she groaned.

Brennan laughed. "Why not? You're a vampire. You'll give me a run for my money someday."

She shook her head. "You're like, a foot taller than I am and about a hundred and fifty pounds heavier. No way."

Brennan glanced at me. "You've seen Molly fight."

"That wasn't even a fight. She had those guys down

before they even knew what was happening. And they were street thugs. Not like, uh, you." She said, and I felt her embarrassment.

Brennan met my eyes again, raised an eyebrow. I gave a tiny nod. Knew what he was going to do.

"Well. Should we see how Molly does against me, then?" Shanti looked between Brennan and I, nodded. I got up and strolled over to the training floor. Faced Brennan, remembering the first time we'd done this.

"Rules?" I asked, smiling a little.

He smiled back. "No punching in the face." I met his slate blue eyes, couldn't look away. He continued, slowly, and I knew he was remembering, too.

"None of that mind control bull shit. Other than that, use what ya got," he said, repeating words he'd said what felt like a lifetime ago. We looked at each other for a minute. We hadn't sparred since the incident with the Puppeteer, in which she'd used Brennan and nearly killed me. He hadn't let himself even come close to hurting me again. And I had my own issues with doing this.

I finally nodded, and we started. I got the first hit in, a punch to his gut. He grunted and swung, connecting with my side.

"You're holding back, Molly," he murmured.

"So are you." I pushed him away, swung at him again.

We kept fighting, eventually loosening up. Soon, our fight became a dizzying clash of punches, kicks, shoves, and feints. Before long, we were both sweaty, and breathless, and lost in the ebb and flow of battle. I could feel how much he was enjoying it, and, to be honest, I was, too.

"Come on, Molly. Don't make me a liar. Show her what a little woman can do to someone like me," he said, grinning. Then he feinted and stuck his leg out, tripping me. I fell, then jumped back up. He went for me again, overbalanced, and I took advantage of it. I kicked his legs out from under him, shoved him to the ground, pulled his arm roughly behind him. I held him down, straddling his back.

He groaned in annoyance, tried to flip me off of his back. I'm little, but I'm solid. I just pulled his arm back harder.

"Hey. All right. You win," he said, laughing. I let him go and stood up. Then I reached out and held out a hand, helped him up.

"That was good," he said, winking at me.

"It was. Thank you for not pulling my hair this time," I said.

"Thanks for not kicking me in the nuts. Much appreciated."

I laughed, really laughed, surprising myself. He grinned at me, still held my hand. I turned to see Shanti watching us.

"Uh, that was crazy. I am never going to be able to do that."

"Sure you will. You're in good shape. You're young. And vampires are fast and strong. You are going to be a force to be reckoned with, kiddo," I said. Brennan nodded.

She shook her head. "Remind me not to piss either of you off. That's all I'm gonna say."

Brennan laughed. Shanti strolled over to the fridge, grabbed some blood, and then went up to her room. I grabbed a bottle of water and leaned against the kitchen counter, drinking it. Brennan hunted through the fridge, muttering about grocery shopping. He ended up snagging a slice of cold pizza and devoured it, standing next to me.

I heard the door lock click, and glanced that way. Ada and Stone came in, laughing. They looked up, saw Brennan and I watching, then quieted down and went their separate ways to their rooms.

Once they were gone, I glanced at Brennan. "They were embarrassed. Something is up with those two."

His jaw dropped. "Holy crap. Do you think they're...."

I shook my head, "NO. No way. That's like catching your parents–"

Brennan laughed. "I bet they are. He's been flirting with her a lot lately."

"Seriously?"

He nodded. I glanced up toward their rooms. The rooms with a connecting bathroom. "Well, that arrangement is convenient, then," I said. He followed my gaze and nodded.

"It's nice that they have a chance to be happy," he murmured. I turned to him, found his eyes on me.

"Happiness is overrated," I said. "And temporary."

His gaze bored into mine. "Temporary happiness is better than endless misery."

"I disagree."

He shook his head. "You are still in mourning. Everything looks bleak to you, and that's normal."

"Who says it didn't look bleak before he died?" I asked.

He shook his head. "You know that's crap. You had hope, believed you could make things better. You did your zombie thing after he died, and then you threw yourself into being the badass, uncontested power in this city. You haven't let yourself just mourn. You haven't even had time to think about–"

"Do not," I began, aware that the building shook a little as I felt my power escalate in my irritation. "Do not suggest that I haven't thought about what happened. It is all I think about." I stared at him, hard.

"Did you think about this: Nain used you. He couldn't beat Astaroth himself, and that never sat well with him. The perfect weapon came into his hands, and he used it. Have you thought of that? Because I think about it a lot, and every time I do, I wish he was here so I could kick his demonic ass." Anger came off of him in waves, and I knew, the way I know anything, that it was not anger at me. It was for me, and it took me by surprise. Brennan is rarely angry. It freaked me out, more than anything.

"Do you think I'm a moron? Of course I've thought of that," I said, and I heard the snarl in my voice. He just watched me. "Do you think I don't know what he did? Do you seriously think that I am not spending every moment cursing myself for being so damned gullible?"

He watched me, muscle twitching in his jaw.

"Do you honestly think that I'm that clueless?" I said, more quietly. "He played me. He used me. I believe he thought it was the only way to keep me safe. Emotions do not lie. He loved me. But he lied to me and he used me to do the one thing I can't live with. He made me kill someone I love. I will never come back from that. Not entirely."

"I hate him nearly as much as I love him. I have never been hurt so badly in my life. This is not something you 'get over.' This is not something that you learn to deal with, put on a happy face so the people around you can move on. I can't do that."

Brennan bowed his head. "You deserve to be happy, Molly. You deserve someone worthy of someone as amazing as you."

I laughed. It was a bitter sound, and I hated myself a little more for it. "And is that someone you, Brennan?"

He just looked at me. "I wish it was. You know that. But I'm not enough and you deserve better."

I wanted to argue with him, tell him that the real issue was that he was far too good for someone like me, even if I could love again. "Well. Whether he's here or not, Nain was it for me. He was a bastard. He taught me very well why falling in love is a huge mistake. It is not one I'll make again. It clouded my judgment, and look what happened. The one person I could trust, *me*, became untrustworthy because I was distracted and stupid. That is not acceptable."

Brennan gave a small nod, ceded the point. We stood there, awkwardly, for a couple of minutes. I remembered my discussion with Eunomia. He deserved to know something was up.

"I'm going to be taking on some additional shit. If I ask you to keep things running around here…"

"You know I'll do it, Molly," he said. "I don't suppose you're going to tell me what's going on?"

"Not yet. Because I don't completely know. It might be nothing." I hope, I thought to myself. "Once I know, you will. I promise."

He nodded. Sometimes, I hated how clearly I could feel him. Nain had been tricky to read sometimes. Brennan's feelings were clear. Love, concern, sadness. Longing. It threatened to drown me, knock me over and pull me into its depths, and I didn't know if I would be strong enough to surface again.

"I care about you, you know," I said softly. "Just not the way you want me to."

He blushed a little. I knew he wished I couldn't feel him. It really did complicate everything. There was no place he could hide, not from me. "Like a brother," he said, irritation in his tone. Frustrated. Guilty.

"Like a friend. It is a compliment. I want you to be happy. And even if I could feel for you what you want me to, I would hurt you. Over and over and over again. You know it. I already do."

"It would be worth it. And you're not the monster you think you are," he said quietly.

"No. I'm much worse. Find some gorgeous shifter who will adore you. Make baby shifters with her. Be happy."

He shook his head. "That is not going to happen. You're asking me to replace you in my heart. I can't."

"Please stop saying shit like that," I said, felt tears slipping from the corners of my eyes. I hated that. I have this thing about crying. I don't do it, and those rare times I do, it makes me want to destroy things.

I'm a wreck, basically. I know. Emotionally stunted, or whatever you'd call it.

Brennan walked over to me. He gently cupped the sides of my face, wiped my tears away with his thumbs. "Okay," he said softly, soothing. "Okay. I'm sorry," he whispered.

I nodded, tried to force the tears back. He gently rested his forehead against mine.

We stood that way for a bit as I tried to get my emotions under control again. It took longer than I expected, and he waited it out with me. His presence, his calm, soothed me after a while. He took a breath, then murmured, "I am here for you, however you need me. I will be your friend, your receptionist, your butler. I'll be Alfred to your Batman, Jarvis to your Iron Man. I'm here. I'm not going anywhere, Molly."

I nodded again, took his hands in mine and removed them from my face, gently. "I'm broken," I whispered, releasing his hands.

"Not broken. Never. Not you. You've been twisted, ripped apart. But you are not broken," he said.

"Remind me of that when I start to fall apart, Alfred," I said, stepping back from him a little.

"I will," he answered, meeting my eyes one more time. Then he walked away, up to his room, and I went up to the roof to spend another night alone.

CHAPTER FOUR

Meetings and destroying, destroying and meetings. This was my existence. I hadn't been wrong about the fact that new adversaries would pop up in the void left by Astaroth and all of his people. I had, however, underestimated how damn many of them there would be.

They were power-hungry, impatient, and, usually, dumb as rocks. This was a really bad combination when it came to trying to protect the Normals from them, keep them out of the crossfire when two big bads decided to face off over territory. It was easy for me to catch and either destroy or gently convince the morons to go elsewhere. The hard part was trying to get to them before they hurt people. They were reckless in their desire for power.

In addition to frequent calls from Chief Jones (since when had I become a member of the Detroit P.D. anyway?), I also had my usual influx of supernaturals seeing me. Brennan had started convincing some of them to talk to him rather than see me, trying to take some of the load off of me, and he filled me in on these cases when we had a chance to breathe.

I hadn't slept in three days. And even with my freakish metabolism and endurance, it was starting to take its toll on me.

In addition to the craziness happening in the city, I still had the gateway Eunomia had warned me about on my mind. I hadn't heard back from her about it, and even if I wanted to be guarding it right now, I didn't know where it was or how to look for it.

I was sitting in my office after finishing up with a meeting with the Brightmoor packmaster, warning him to keep his werewolves away from innocents. He'd been afraid of me, and I had a feeling he would be more attentive to what his pack was doing from now on.

Brennan came in with a cup of coffee. "Last one will be here in a couple of minutes. I need to reduce the number of appointments I'm making for you. This is nuts," he said, setting the coffee down next to me.

"No, it's fine. You've already taken on a lot of this shit for me. These are things I need to know right away so I can take care of them." I picked up the coffee cup, took a long drink. "Thank you," I said.

"No problem." He leaned against the edge of my desk, next to me. "Hey, Molly."

"Yeah?"

"This next one...do you mind if I stay in the room with you for this?"

I looked up at him. "Why?"

"I just got a weird feeling when I was talking to this guy. Branford. Something seems off."

"Is anything ever *not* off about the people we deal with, Bren?" I asked.

He grinned. "Good point. But this guy seemed more off than usual."

"I don't need protection," I said.

"I know. I really am just being nosy. I want to hear what he says."

I shook my head, took another sip of coffee. "Fine."

"Good." He walked out of the office, and I enjoyed a few seconds of peace before Shanti came in.

"I cannot do this," she said, holding up the copy of *Wuthering Heights* I'd left in her room, along with instructions to read it and write a paper on it.

"Yes, you can."

"This is freaking impossible to read. These characters all seem like jerks, and I can't even understand what they're saying most of the time!"

"Give it a shot. You're smart. You will not regret reading it," I said.

She sighed. "Can't I just read, like, *Twilight* or something?"

I mock-glared at her. "Get your ass out of my office. When's the last time you sparkled, vampire?"

She walked away laughing. I heard Brennan mutter "Twilight?" as she passed him, and she laughed more. He glanced into my office. "He's here. Ready?"

I nodded, took another sip of coffee. Then I leaned back in my chair and waited. Brennan led my next appointment into the office, then closed the door behind both of them. Dahael and Bashiok, as always, flanked me. I felt them both stiffen in anger and hate as the man entered the room.

"Angel, this is Devin Branford," Brennan said, standing behind the chair Branford would be sitting in. Ready. On edge.

I could see why. Branford was a demon. A pretty powerful one, from what I could feel. Not as powerful as me, but he was powerful enough to cause trouble. He stood a little over six feet. Shorter than Bren. But he was solid muscle, biceps bulging under the black t-shirt he wore. He was not an attractive man. Shaved head. Eyes that were nearly black. A hooked nose, cruel-looking mouth.

"Angel. A pleasure to meet one of my kind," he said, bowing his head to me.

"Thank you. Please, have a seat," I said, gesturing to the chair. Branford nodded and sat, crossing one leg over his knee.

"Thank you. I would like to offer my condolences on the loss of the Nain Rouge. We did not always see eye to eye." He glanced back at Brennan. "I remember when you were a teenager. Probably the last time Nain and I faced off. You remember me?"

Brennan shrugged. "Not really. Nain didn't let me do much fighting back then."

Branford shrugged, turned back to me. I glanced up at Brennan, who was staring daggers at the demon. Whether Brennan remembered him or not, he clearly did not like him. I'd keep that in mind. Brennan's instincts about this stuff were usually dead on. And, my first impression of the demon didn't exactly endear him to me, either.

"So. What can I do for you, Branford?"

The demon looked at me. "Well. There are a few things I can think of off the top of my head." I felt it already of course. Lust. Ew.

Brennan was ready to rip the demon's throat out already, and he'd barely been in the room for two minutes. I caught Bren's eye, hoped he understood to calm the hell down. He seemed to, took a deep breath and shook his head.

"Well. Flattering as that is, Branford, that's not really what we're here for," I said, looking directly at him. Meeting his gaze. He met mine as well, and it was an unspoken challenge. Who would look away first? Stupid battles of wills, looking for signs of weakness.

"I have heard something I think you'd want to know," he said, still staring back at me. "There are people in danger, and that's the kind of bullshit you seem to care about."

"And why bring it to me? It's not like you care about Normals," I said, knowing it was true before the words even left my lips.

46

"No, I don't. But we've all seen the news. The P.D. is onto us. Supernaturals. We have them poking around, they're eventually going to figure it out. And while I really have no problems steamrolling any nosy cops, having to watch out for them puts a dent in my lifestyle. I figure, come to you with this, save us all some trouble."

I leaned back in my chair, still holding his gaze. We sat in silence for a few minutes. I let my power roar over him, felt the house tremble around us. He looked away. Victory.

"So, who's in danger?" I finally asked.

"There's this group. Coupla witches, warlocks. Couple shifters. They've been working the six and Gratiot area for a while now. They started taking women off the streets a week or so ago, keeping them locked in one of those big old houses over there. I don't know what they're doing with them, but I can guess, and I bet you can too."

"How many?"

"As far as I know? Fourteen women."

I could feel how anxious Brennan was. I caught his eye again, gave a small shake of my head. He nodded. The tension in him did not subside. His jaw was clenched, hands fisted as he crossed his arms over his chest. If looks could have killed, the demon sitting in front of me would have been dead about fifty times over.

"So. You're saying fourteen women. Held by a few witches and warlocks, shifters. Anything else I should know?"

Branford smiled like a cat who'd just cornered a mouse. Asshole. "I have the address if you want it."

"That would be great," I said. He pulled a piece of paper out of his pocket, set it on the desk in front of me.

"They're there. It looks deserted, but it has electricity and everything. Real overgrown in front."

"All right. I'll take care of it. Thanks for bringing it to my attention," I said.

"Well, I figured you'd want to know, considering the way you are about finding lost girls," he said. He was doing a good job of looking sincere.

"Absolutely. Thanks for coming," I said, dismissing him. Brennan walked him out, Ada reset the wards, and within seconds Brennan was back in my office.

"That bastard was setting you up. You know this," Brennan said, crossing his arms over his chest. Anger still radiated from him. Along with a strong desire to protect me.

"Of course I know it," I said. "He looked like he hit the jackpot or something when I said I'd go. I could feel it from him."

"Okay. So what do we do?"

I stood up, started loading up my pockets. "We?"

"Yeah. *We*. I know you're going to go because there are probably really women there to draw you out. And he's probably lying about how many bads are there. I'm not going to sit here while you walk into god knows what by yourself." Steely determination in his voice, in his eyes.

"Are you my sidekick now, too?" I asked, putting my sunglasses on.

"You start calling me Robin and you'll never get a good cup of coffee again, Molly."

I laughed, then headed out, Brennan close behind me. We got into the Barracuda, imps filling the back seat, and roared through the city toward the neighborhood the demon had specified. Night had fallen, moonless and cold.

We parked a few blocks away from where we needed to be. It's not like we really had the element of surprise on our side, since they'd feel us long before they saw us. I needed to ask the chief where he'd gotten his amulet. Too late now.

We got out and started walking toward the house.

"Leave the demon to me if he's there," I said quietly.

"Yes, ma'am," Brennan answered. Tension rolled off of his body, ready for a hunt, a fight.

"Do not do anything stupid trying to protect me. I have a healing ability. You don't," I continued.

"This is hardly the first time we've fought together, Molly."

"Just thought I'd remind you," I muttered.

"You're sure I can't go after the demon? I'd really like to put the hurt on him," Brennan said, a bit of a growl in his voice.

I shook my head. "You can hurt him vicariously through me, how about that?"

"You are no fun at all."

We reached the house. Exactly as the demon had described it. I sensed for whatever was in the house. The asshole had totally lied to us. There were at least ten supernaturals there, plus him. And they felt me. Fear, anger, worry.

"They know we're here. Eleven of them, plus several Normals," I said softly.

He nodded. I glanced at him, met his eyes for a second. He nodded, and we moved.

We charged in and the house exploded in gunshots, roars, howls, and growls. Brennan had already shifted into his cat form, and he was a blur, racing around the room, tearing out throats. My imps used their little teeth, tiny daggers on anyone who got close enough. I found the asshole with the gun, a Normal who was trying to be badass.

"You're in over your head, son," I said, grabbing the gun as he shot me in the stomach with it. Healing ability or no, it hurt like hell. I bashed his head back into the wall behind him and he slumped over, unconscious. I pocketed the gun, headed toward where I felt Branford. Basement. Always the fucking basement with these people.

I headed down as Brennan finished dispatching the last of the warlocks in the main floor. I found the bottom step, and saw Branford standing in the middle of the unfinished basement. Women, chained to the concrete walls. Most terrified, crying, but, thankfully, still dressed and alive. Bait.

"You really are a freak son of a bitch, you know that?" I said, strolling casually into the basement, taking in the details as I kept his attention on me.

"I'd love to have you join them," he said.

"So. What's the game here? Get me here, down in the basement with you? To... what?"

He held up a remote, grinned. Then he pointed to the corner of the basement.

"Brennan get out!" I screamed. "GO!"

"Oh, he's got a minute, I think." He hit the button.

"Have fun trying to get them out, Angel." He said, laughing as he walked up the stairs.

The women were wailing now, screaming.

I looked around. There were more than he'd said. Seventeen. Their chains were cemented into the walls. The good news was that he'd underestimated how strong I was. That wouldn't slow me down much.

The bad news was that the fucker had also cemented the women's feet into the concrete floor.

I looked around for something to break it with. Sledgehammer, hammer, anything.

I heard roars from upstairs, figured Brennan and Branford had met up.

The women were screaming now, most of them either staring at me or the bomb, counting its way down.

I walked to the first one, yanked the chain out of the wall, freeing her hands. I did that with the rest of them. They pulled uselessly at their feet. I tried punching at the floor, resulted in breaking my hand, barely cracking the concrete around one of their feet. They were crying now. Their fear rolled over me, and, just this once, I let it feed me. I'd need whatever strength I could get.

So. Damn. Tired.

Thirty-two seconds.

31...

30....

I picked up a chair, started bashing it against the floor. The chair broke long before the floor did.

"Goddamnmotherfucker," I shouted, looking around for any other way to free them. Innocent, here because of me.

24...

23...

I had one more chance. I let my power rise over me. Let it roar. It was hungry. I'd let it sit, unused for too long. I let it have free rein now. It thundered, and the house creaked and shook around me. I gave in, let my power reach its max level.

Cracks appeared in the walls, and, thank god, the floor.

I continued to let it roar, and bits of the wall started falling in. The floor was a series of cracks, crumbling now around me and the women.

"Try pulling your feet out. The second you get free, run for the stairs as fast as you can!" I shouted.

The first got free, stumbled toward the stairs. Then another. And another. I felt like I was about to split apart, like if I didn't let my power free, it would burn me from the inside out. More women freed themselves and ran out.

There were two more, still struggling to free their feet, weeping. Brennan was on the stairs, pulling women up. Damn him for not listening to me.

12...

11...

I ran over to the last two, bashed my fists into the concrete around their feet. It shattered, and shards of concrete went flying. My hands were both limp now, dangling uselessly from my shattered wrists.

"Run!" I screeched.

8...

7...

I shoved the last one up the stairs. She ran fast enough to get up and out. I stumbled on the stairs, the pain in my hands, wrists, and forearms causing my vision to swim.

Dizzy. I got up and tripped again, hit my chin on the step above me.

And that was when the air exploded around me, fire washed over me, disintegrating my clothing and turning the world into an inferno. I screamed in agony and heard Brennan screaming my name before everything went black and silent.

CHAPTER FIVE

The blackness was inviting. I was aware that I was not dead, and the pain had mostly stopped. It felt more like I was floating in nothingness, suspended somewhere between life and death.

It was peaceful, but I was not yet ready for peace.

Shapes, sounds began to appear, like a movie on an old film-reel projector, flickering, ethereal. Lives I'd never lived, things I'd never seen, yet I knew them just the same. Battles, men in armor, men in loincloths, gods. Lightning cracked the sky, and waves pounded cities to nothingness. Always, amid the chaos, winged women.

Eunomia and her sisters, fluttering around bloody battlegrounds like vultures over roadkill. Winged, terrifying, gnashing teeth and sharp claws.

And then, there were the other winged women. Those of flaming swords, snake-headed whips. Those who avenged the innocent. Merciless. They filled me with pride, with a feral, wild fire that nearly consumed me. They brought evil to its knees, made it beg for mercy.

And they gave none.

They were me, and I was them. My stance, my coldness, my anger. They were unstoppable, ceaseless in deliverance of vengeance. Righteousness, personified. Frightening, intense. Millenia of vengeance, delivered, always the same, tireless.

Responsibility. The weight of the promise, that wrongs would be punished. A sacred oath, given freely and undertaken with the gravity necessary. Protectiveness for those who relied on them/us to do what needed to be done.

I watched it all, removed, yet part of it. It called to me, pulled at my soul, changed the last something in me that had been human.

I'd never been human.

A lie.

My humanity was a farce. Part of me had always known this.

I watched my own evolution.

Nain bringing my more demonic traits to the forefront.

His death, stripping away more of the humanity I wore like a mask.

This death and rebirth by fire, another phase of becoming what I was meant to be.

What I was born to be.

I am a warrior.

I am forever.

I am vengeance.

And I still have work to do.

I floated in nothingness for a while longer, felt life calling me back, slowly but surely. I embraced it, completely.

CHAPTER SIX

"I wish you would leave."

"I told you. It is not her time. I'm not here to take her from you, shifter." A pause. "And if I tried, she'd probably punch me."

A laugh. "How do you know it's not her time?"

"Because her light has not yet faded. You know her better than anyone. Do you really think something like a little fire can kill her?"

"Yeah, a little fire. An explosion that took out an entire house. I've seen fires smaller than that kill demons."

"You know as well as I do that she is more than a demon."

A long pause. "What is she?"

"I am not sure. I have my suspicions."

Silence. "She's waking up."

Another pause. "How do you know she's waking up?"

"I can feel her."

"Interesting."

"Jesus Christ would you two shut up?" I groaned, my throat barely working past the dryness in it. My body was one massive pain. A different kind of burning. Healing.

Damn, it hurt to come back from the brink of death.

"Welcome back, my friend," Eunomia said, brushing a cold hand over my forehead. It felt good against my burning skin.

I struggled to open my eyes. I was in my room, back at the loft. Brennan was sitting in the chair next to the bed, so close his knees were touching the edge of the mattress. His head was bowed, resting in his hands. I sensed for him. Immense relief, fear. Eunomia stood at the other side of the bed, smiling down at me, as she ran her hand through my hair.

Hair?

"Uh. How do I still have hair? Or, anything?" I asked. She poured me a glass of water, put a straw to my mouth. I took a few sips, and it felt like heaven.

"You regenerated all of your skin, a few fingers, and an entire leg. I'm pretty sure hair was not much of a problem," she said, smiling.

I stared at her. "You're kidding."

"No. I am not."

I looked over at Brennan. "Bren?" I whispered. More freaked out by whatever the hell I was now than ever, the echoes of my visions during my regeneration stirring at the back of my mind.

He looked up at me. He was pale. Dark circles under his eyes. He looked thinner. His hair was wild from running his hands through it, which he always did when he was tense.

"Add explosions to the list of shit that can't kill you," he murmured. "You scared the hell out of me, Molly."

"How long was I out?"

"Four days. Eunomia came and helped me pull what was left of you out of the house. She flew you here."

Everything came back to me. "The women?"

"All safe. You saved them all." He dropped his face down into his hand again, rubbed his face. Still terrified.

"Brennan," I whispered. "You're afraid of me."

"No. Not even close. I'm still reliving the explosion, seeing what you looked like when Eunomia pulled you out of there…" He shook his head again. "I was sure you were gone."

"Me and cockroaches. We'll be here forever."

He shook his head.

"Branford?"

Brennan growled. "I was killing him. Your imps pulled me off of him. They said you'd want him."

"My imps are smart little bastards. Where is he?"

"We've been holding him here. He's chained up in the garage. Your imps and Stone have been guarding him."

I was about to sit up, then thought better of it. I looked under the sheet. I wasn't wearing anything. My body was whole, unmarked. The new skin was sensitive to everything. Even the cotton sheets against me set my teeth on edge.

"I am going to get up now," I said.

"Molly, relax a while," Brennan said, meeting my eyes.

"I've been out for four days, Bren. Who knows what the hell has happened since. Oh…the gateway. E?"

She shook her head. "We're still working on it, but they have not yet broken through. It's fine."

Brennan looked between us, confused. I met his eyes. "We'll talk later."

He nodded. "You should still relax. It hurts you when you heal. Rest."

"And how do you know that?"

A pause. "You told me."

I studied him. "I have the feeling there are things you haven't told me."

"Join the club," he said softly, smiling a little.

"We are going to have a long talk."

He nodded. "But not today."

"Not today," I agreed. I tossed the covers back, gathered the sheet around me as I stood up.

"Molly…" Brennan started. I glanced at him, and he was doing his best not to stare at me.

I shook my head. "I regenerated half my body. I am starving," I said to him. He looked up at me, and I met his eyes. "And you have lots of power and you're sitting here tempting me." I could feel my hunger, burning my throat, an internal ache, distracting and overpowering. "I have a demon to deal with. And I'll feed."

He nodded, finally. "Fine. Call me if you need anything. I'll be right outside the door." He and Eunomia walked out, and Brennan closed the door behind them. True to his word, I could feel him standing on the other side of the door.

I hadn't lied. I was starving, and I was weak with it for the first time in forever. I walked slowly into the bathroom, brushed my teeth and splashed water on my face. I looked at myself in the mirror. The impossibility of what had happened was too much to wrap my brain around.

What was even more shocking was that, rather than feeling cheated that I'd been saved by myself once again, I was actually happy to be alive. I thought I was ready to leave. Nain's death had undone me, taken the will to live from me. I thought I would greet death happily when Eunomia and her sisters finally came for me. Instead, I was thrilled to have another day. It was as if the fire, and whatever had happened between there and here, had cleansed me. Changed me.

So much to do, still.

People to take care of.

Figure out who or what I was.

I dressed. My uniform: jeans, black top, black Chucks. I braided my long hair over one shoulder. Finished, and leaned against the counter, looking at my reflection. I looked nothing like the girl I'd once been, but, somehow, this being with the white glowing eyes and alabaster skin was more me than I'd ever been. I didn't know what it meant, but I was at home in my body for the first time ever.

My body that fire and explosions, along with gunshots, stab wounds, and vampires could not kill. I remembered my dreams about women with swords of fire and smiled a little to myself. I had a demon to deal with.

◆◆◆

I finished up and left the bathroom, walked through my room into the loft, where Brennan still stood right outside my door. He held a cup of coffee out to me.

I met his eyes and smiled a little. Sipped the coffee and sighed with contentment as a shiver went up my spine. Brennan laughed.

"Shut up, Bren," I said, laughing a little.

Shanti walked up to me. Her eyes were red, and she looked exhausted. She wrapped her arms around me, sobbing, and I handed my coffee back to Brennan so I could hug her back.

"It's okay," I murmured against her hair as she sobbed. "You really think something like a little explosion is going to kill me?"

She laughed a little, took a deep breath. "I thought you were gone. Don't do that again!" she said, hugging me harder. I grimaced at the sensation against my skin. Brennan gently pulled Shanti off of me.

"I'll try not to," I said, holding her hand. "I'm here. It's okay."

She wiped her eyes and nodded. "You. You are so badass it's not even funny."

"Yeah? Watch *My Girl* with me sometime and see how badass I am," I said, smiling.

She laughed then. "*Wuthering Heights* still sucks, by the way," she said. She started walking toward her room. Relief, happiness from her, embarrassment over crying in front of me.

I smiled again. "Read it anyway, you little brat."

She stuck her tongue out at me, then headed up the stairs to her room.

I looked at Brennan. Damn, his power was tempting. I tried to force the thought away. "I need to see Branford, now."

He nodded, and took my hand. I let him. He needed it and, just this once, maybe, I needed it too. We walked to the elevator together, took it down to the underground parking garage.

"You guys have been feeding him, right?"

He nodded. "I was against it. Your imps said you'd want him strong."

"I love my imps."

He shook his head. His eyes were on me the entire time, a combination of puzzlement and love coming from him. I met his eyes. "Trying to figure me out?" I asked.

"Every second of my life," he said, giving me a small smile. I shook my head and opened the grate into the parking garage.

Stone was standing with a shotgun in his hand, eyes on the demon. Branford had dropped his human skin, and stood there in his demon form. Just as ugly as he'd been as a human. Still tall and muscular, skin the dark gray of dirty water. My imps were ringed around him. He was chained to one of the concrete pillars, arms behind his back. He slumped against the pillar. Dozing.

I stalked toward him. "Good evening, Branford," I said loudly. His head jerked back, and he looked at me.

And I felt it. Fear. So good. I felt it feeding my demon immediately. His fear only grew as I stalked closer. He actually whimpered. And pissed himself.

"Demon's about to hurt," Bash said in his gravelly little voice, red eyes glowing in the dim garage.

"About to bleed," Dahael agreed.

"Branford. I was sure you were potty trained by now," I murmured. I walked up to him and gripped his jaw, forced him to look at me. He tried to pull away, but there was nowhere for him to go. His terror continued to feed me.

"What's wrong? Don't you like being chained?" I asked, tightening my grip on his jaw as he tried to pull away. My fingernails cut into his skin.

"How?" he finally stammered.

I smiled at him. "Do you really think something as insignificant as you can kill me?" I squeezed his throat, just a little, and he panicked.

Damn, it was delectable. I let it wash over me, felt it feed me.

I glanced back at Brennan and Stone. "Unchain him."

Stone came, took out a key and unlocked the three locks securing the chains. Branford massaged his wrists when the chains dropped.

"I don't want you to see this," I said.

Stone nodded. "Welcome back, kiddo," he said, grinning at me before he walked away. Brennan stayed put.

"You too, Bren."

"Nope."

"This is not going to be pretty. I'd prefer you didn't see me like this." These words only made the demon more afraid, and I nearly smiled at the taste of his fear.

"Gut him," Bashiok said.

"Burn him," Dahael cooed. I felt Branford's fear spike again, and I could have laughed. Creepy little fuckers, my imps were.

"It better not be pretty. I need this just as much as you do," he said, meeting my eyes.

"Fine. Just stay back."

I shook my head and turned back to the demon, who was trying to fight his way out of my grip. I ran my fingers along his neck, then hauled my fist back and punched him in the gut. "Why did you do it?" I asked him.

He lunged for me then, which was exactly what I wanted. I punched him in the stomach again, kneed him in the groin, and he whimpered and bent over in anguish. His pain fed me now, as much as his fear. I felt myself strengthening with it.

"Tell me." I grabbed his throat again, made him look at me. Looking at me scared him even more. "You lured me there. Tried to make damn sure I died. Why?" I accented the question by bashing his head back into the concrete pillar behind him.

Demonic fear, anger, pain. I felt my power singing through me, exalting in being fed.

We circled each other, and I knew he was looking for a weakness. Good luck with that. "Tell me, and I will end this quickly. I try not to be cruel, but I am more than happy to be, in your case. Please. Make me drag this out," I said, and I heard the feral snarl in my voice.

He spat at me, tried to grab my arm, and I punched him in the face. His nose shattered under my fist, and his pain washed over me. He lunged for me again, grabbed my hair. I wrenched it free, lunged back, and kicked him hard in the stomach. He fell, clutching his gut.

I stalked back over to him, hauled him up by his throat as if he weighed nothing. "I can do this all night," I growled up into his face, then I tossed him back into a pillar and hauled him up again. "I can make you feel what I felt. Wanna know what it feels like to have all the bones in your hands break at once?" I broke into his mind, manipulated his thoughts, made him feel what I'd felt in the basement, and he screamed. I shoved him away from me and he fell at my feet, cowering.

"Too easy. I don't even need to touch you to hurt you," I snarled. "Any answers yet?" I stalked back and forth, and he watched me warily, but clamped his mouth shut. "All right. How about having your skin burned off your body?"

I forced the thought into his mind, and his screams echoed throughout the garage. Damn, it was good. I let my head fall back as I fed off his terror, let it fill me. After a few minutes, I let up, pulled the thoughts back.

He was terrified now, sweating, trying to get away from me. I picked up a length of extra chain Stone had left on the floor, wrapped it around his neck, pulled it tight, forced him to stand up and look at me.

"Or. I can end this now, quickly." I felt Eunomia land behind me, near Brennan. Knew he would give in, then.

"Bitch," he muttered, trembling in fear and rage.

"You tried to blow me up. I'm pretty sure I have the moral high ground here, asshole."

"What are you?"

I just smiled, pulled the chain again. "Answer me. Why?"

"I've been trying to get things going for myself here. Have what Astaroth had. And every goddamn time I grow my organization, you come barging in and destroying it. I figured, the Nain Rouge is gone. Get rid of you, and everything else was easy. It would have been mine."

"So, greed? You seriously blew me up, kidnapped almost twenty women, set all this shit up, because I was messing up your Don Corleone fantasies?"

"No one can do anything in this dump of a city without you ending up on their ass," he said.

I leaned in, close enough to kiss him, smiled. "Exactly." I broke into his mind, saw the hundreds of murders, tortures he'd caused in his long existence, and knew it was my duty to end him, completely. I found his power, tore into it like a wild animal, devoured it as he screamed. Then everything went silent as his life force left him along with the power I'd taken. He fell to my feet, an empty husk.

I turned to Brennan and Eunomia. They were both watching me. Eunomia smiled one of her knowing little smiles, walked over to Branford's body as she waited for her sisters.

"Better now?" Brennan asked, his voice low and hoarse. I sensed for him. Contentment. Love. Roaring need, desire that made me blush.

"Why aren't you disgusted? I hurt him, and I liked it. That's sick."

"Like you said. You had the moral high ground. And you were still nicer about it than I would have been."

I studied him. He shook his head and laughed a little.. "I'm not going to be disgusted by you. You have this idea in your head that you're a monster and I'm an angel or something. Neither is true. We're all monsters here, Molly. We just also happen to be the good guys."

I watched him. He must have seen disbelief in my gaze. "If you would have seen me when I caught Branford, you would have no doubt how much of a monster I can be. It took several of your imps, plus Eunomia to pull me off of him. And the only reason I stopped was because I figured that pissing off a Guardian was probably bad luck."

I had an idea, of course. I knew what it felt like when Brennan used his power in anger. And I'd seen the teeth and claw marks on Branford's throat and arms.

I nodded, ceded the point. "Well. You can worry about me less now, I think," I said, watching as Eunomia and her sisters escorted Branford's soul away. "I'm pretty sure there's not much that can kill me."

"Yeah. Pretty sure. Crazy thing is, I'll still worry about you. It's what I do." He shrugged.

I walked past him back toward the elevator, and Brennan reached out and snagged my back pocket with his fingers, pulled me back to him. He stepped closer to me, meeting me halfway. I tensed as he folded me into his arms, gently, mindful of my sensitive skin. My stomach fluttered, and I was uncomfortable, unsure of myself near Brennan. After a moment, I relaxed, put my hands on his hips, leaned into him and rested my forehead against his chest. I breathed him in, and it smelled like home. We stood there for a long time, and I tried to tell myself that it didn't mean anything.

CHAPTER SEVEN

After my Lazarus thing following the fire, Ada and Stone seemed weird around me. Not mean, or unkind. Just nervous.

"They think you're a god," Brennan finally explained to me one day a couple of weeks later, when we had a minute between meetings.

"Uh. What?"

"A god. They think you're a god and they want to show you the proper amount of respect," he said, plopping down into one of the other chairs in my office.

"Oh, for fuck's sake," I muttered.

Brennan laughed. "Language, Molly," he murmured, smiling and shaking his head. I had decided to try curbing it, mostly for Shanti's benefit. I wasn't doing a very good job. Old habits die hard.

"You don't think I'm a god, do you? Please tell me you don't," I said.

He grinned. "Well, I've always thought of you as a goddess, but that's probably not what they're thinking."

I flung a pen at him. He ducked it and laughed again.

"You haven't told me about the gateway Eunomia mentioned," he said after a while.

"Speaking of gods," I muttered.

"Yeah."

I took a breath. "So, there's a gateway between here and the Pit, which is a Nether prison, basically. Baddest of the bad, worst of the worst. All that. And it's weakening. Something or someone, or several somethings, are trying to get through. Eunomia thinks it's related to the whole Astaroth mess last year."

He sat in silence for a few minutes, thinking it over. "No ideas who?"

I shook my head. "She says they're looking into it, but they're mostly concerned with keeping the gateway strong. She said some of the Nether's strongest demons are helping guard it, as well as a Fury, Tisiphone. But she thinks it's just a matter of time before they break through."

"Where is it?"

I shrugged. "I haven't been able to grab E for more than a second or two. I guess when she gets worried enough, she'll tell me."

"And you're just going to…"

"Yeah. Kill anything that comes through."

He sighed, leaned back and closed his eyes. "Like you don't have enough going on."

I shrugged--. "If they get through, anything else I'm doing will seem kind of pointless."

He was silent for a few seconds. "Demons, right?"

"She said some exiled gods, too."

"Christ."

"Probably not that one."

He snorted, shook his head. He was about to say something when the buzzer went off. "Probably your next appointment. Representative from the Grosse Pointe shifters, coming to pay respects, offer their loyalty. The usual. Word got around about what you did to Branford. Expect the ass-kissing to increase."

I nodded. He got up and answered the door. I took a deep breath, tried to put my calm, polite mask back on. I'd played cool with Brennan. I was terrified of what would happen when the gate opened, and I was tired of dealing with the turf wars happening among the supernaturals. I felt like I was failing in every possible way. God, my ass.

I could feel when the shifter entered the loft. Powerful, as far as shifters went. Not as powerful as Brennan, but he was easily the most powerful one I'd ever met, and no one else was even close.

I looked up, slightly surprised to see a woman entering my office. Shifter packs, while generally pretty egalitarian, usually sent males to do things like this. I'd just gotten used to it. I studied her as she walked in. Tall, blond, and leggy. Gorgeous. And she was clearly torn between paying attention to me as Brennan introduced us, and staring at Brennan. I took a breath.

Brennan looked at me. "Angel, this is Anastasia Ryan, of the Grosse Pointe shifters. Miss Ryan, the Angel." With that, he left and closed the door behind him. Anastasia walked over and shook my hand.

"It's so nice to finally meet you. Thank you for seeing me," she said, and it was clear that she actually respected me. A bit of awe, nervousness.

"Nice to meet you, too. Please, have a seat," I said. She did, crossed her legs and sat there patiently. I felt like a toad sitting in the same room as her.

"I am here at the behest of my father, who is the leader of our pack," she began. "He would have come himself, but my mother has been ill, and he thought it better to send me than to delay visiting you."

"I am sorry to hear about your mother. Is there anything I can do to help?"

She stared at me. "Um. Actually..." she looked away, and I sensed nervousness in her.

"What is it?"

"She has not yet seen a doctor, because Normal

doctors are useless with our physiology. There is a doctor who specializes in shifters, but he's out of Toronto, but his schedule is insane. I think we'll lose her before she even made it to her appointment with him." She paused. "My father does not know I told you about this. I was not supposed to. I was supposed to come here to pledge our loyalty. Which I am!" she said, looking up at me. "You can call on us, any time, and we will be honored to assist you, no matter what. But I'm asking this as a daughter. Is there any way you can help my mother?" she finished.

Damn it. I'd wanted to dislike the shifter when I'd seen her look at Brennan that way (something I didn't want to think about too deeply, actually.) But she was sincere, and honest.

"Do you have the doctor's name and contact information?"

She nodded, pulled her phone out of her bag. She scrolled for a couple of seconds, then handed the phone over to me. "That's him."

I nodded, picked up my phone, dialed. A receptionist answered first, and I asked to speak to the doctor. Got the usual, "he's not available right now" that I knew I would.

"I really do need to speak with him. Can you tell him the Angel, from Detroit, is on the line, please?"

"I really don't—"

"Just tell him. I'll hold."

A sigh at the other end of the line. "One moment, please."

I sat, holding the phone against my ear. Anastasia watched me, nervous, hopeful. "Don't get your hopes up," I said. "This might not help at all."

"It's better than we've done so far," she said. "We couldn't even get him on the phone."

"Doctor Hylar," a deep voice said on the line.

"Doctor Hylar, this is the Angel," I said.

"Yes. How may I help you, Angel?"

I explained about Anastasia's mother. There was silence at the other end.

"I know you are a busy man, doctor. I would see it as a personal favor to me, if you made the time to come here and see the woman."

"It would be an honor to assist you in this. My schedule is fairly light on Friday. I'll have my secretary re-schedule my appointments, and I'll be there early in the morning."

I thanked the doctor, handed the phone to Anastasia so she could hammer out the details with him. She hung up, beaming.

"I... thank you so much for that. I can't believe he's coming here!" she was smiling, and crying, and the emotions coming from her were overwhelming.

I shook my head. "I'm glad I could help. I hope he's able to help with your mother."

"Like I said... if you need ANYTHING from my pack, EVER, you have it," she said.

I smiled. "Thank you. Please let me know how it all goes."

She nodded. I got up, and so did she. We shook hands again, and I saw her out into the loft. Brennan was sitting at the kitchen counter, and I felt her desire spike a little when she saw him.

Shit.

Brennan stood up and walked her to the door. She chit-chatted with him. Part of me wanted to stay and be nosy. Part of me wanted no part of watching this gorgeous, charming woman work her magic on Brennan. Even if she was perfect for him.

That part won out. I grabbed a muffin, headed to my office, and closed the door behind me. I could still feel her in the loft.

She was taking her sweet-ass time about leaving.

I tried to shrug off the annoyance, the sense of ownership that I didn't realize I'd had toward Brennan.

Wasn't this what I told him I wanted for him? A gorgeous shifter who adored him? There she was.

I kind of despised her.

And that was so messed up I didn't even want to think about it.

After what felt like an eternity, I felt her leave. I shoved the rest of the muffin into my mouth and started flipping through that day's newspaper. I could just read it online, but Stone preferred paper, so we always got it that way. It also gave me something to look at for when Brennan made his way back into my office. He sat in one of the chairs opposite me and I kept my eyes on the paper.

"She told me what you did for her mom. That was amazing, Molly," he said.

"I didn't do anything. I made a phone call. Besides, the Grosse Pointe shifters are one of the most powerful packs in the area. They're good allies to have."

I could feel his eyes on me. "She asked me if I wanted to go to this dinner thing they're having tonight."

I tried not to have any visible reaction. I was good at that, at least. I could feel rage bubbling under the surface, a weight pressing on my chest making it hard to breathe. What the ever-loving hell was wrong with me?

"That's nice," I finally managed, as noncommittally as I could.

"So, do you think I should go?" he asked. I sensed for him then. The usual. Warmth, longing. I wondered now, though, if that longing was for me, this time. Better for him, if it wasn't.

"You don't need to ask me for permission to go out, Brennan," I said.

"I'm not asking permission. I'm asking if it's all right with you," he answered.

I shrugged. "Why wouldn't it be?"

I felt some irritation from him.

"What? Do you want to go? Then go! What are you asking me for?"

I got up and walked out of the office. He followed me out and I could tell he was annoyed, too.

"I don't really especially want to go, no. She said it would be a big deal to her pack if I showed up at this dinner thing they're having for her brother. Why are you getting pissed off at me about it?"

"I'm not pissed off at you," I said. "Do what you want." I pulled my shoes on and headed for the door.

"Where are you going?"

"To do things. It's what I do. I sit here all day and talk and talk and talk, and then I go do things. Are you new here?"

And with that, I slammed the door behind me and headed down to the parking garage. Dahael and Bash trailed me as I headed toward the Barracuda. I started it up and roared away, looking for something to hit.

As I drove, I gripped the steering wheel. Christ, that was childish and stupid. The worst thing about it was how surprised I was at my reaction. Where did all of that come from? Was I just so used to the idea of having Brennan there for me that I got freaked out when someone else recognized how amazing he was?

And she had totally recognized it. She was attracted to him physically, and, as a powerful shifter, he brought plenty of other attributes in addition to being nice to look at. As a shifter without a pack, she would be more than happy to give him a pack, a family. Which was something Brennan wanted. I knew this about him the way I knew all of the other things he didn't say. It really was probably the best thing for him if he decided that she was better for him than I was.

Why did she have to look like a damn supermodel while I looked like some freaky-ass alien?

This was all so goddamned confusing.

I worked my way across the city, taking out a few troublemakers. I broke up a fight between two warring werewolf packs, eliminated a small shifter cell that had been causing trouble on the west side, grabbed a dumbass who was beating up his girlfriend and abandoned him at a local police precinct after ordering him to turn himself in, which he did. I got into a fight with a demon who'd been skulking around Wayne State's campus, causing problems. I was probably, maybe, a little more aggressive than I needed to be.

I was still full of pent-up anger, confusion. Other feelings that, until now, had been completely foreign to me. Feelings I didn't want to investigate too closely.

Without thinking really about where I was going, I headed to Belle Isle. I'd come here a lot as a teenager, as soon as I could drive. I'd walked the woods, sat on the beaches. There usually weren't a ton of people around, and I could have a break from hearing everyone's thoughts, feeling emotions. It was the one place I could truly be alone with my own thoughts. How pathetic was it that I still found myself coming back here, years later when I needed to figure myself out?

I pulled up alongside the beach and got out of the car. Bash and Dahael trailed me, keeping their distance. I wandered over to a bench and sat down.

It wasn't an accident, of course. I'd sat on this same bench what felt like a lifetime ago, with Nain, and he'd told me what I was. Not just a demon, but a mindflayer, a parasite who fed on the powers of others. And I'd sat here with him, and he'd told me I could feed off of him to keep everyone else safe from me. He'd flirted with me, wanted me.

I'd never felt any of these screwed-up, crazy feelings with Nain. We were uncomplicated. Passion, anger, lust. He wanted me, took what he wanted, and I gave it because I needed him, too. He molded me, maneuvered me, made me become the destructive force he knew I would be.

I was so much younger then. At least, it felt like I was younger. Immature. Naive. I'd never wanted a man in my life, and Nain had forced his way in exactly when I needed one.

Exactly when I'd needed a demon, I guess.

I remembered. Kisses that felt like battles, lovemaking that was as much about power as pleasure. He coaxed my demonic traits out of me, with each touch, each kiss, each time we fought. He made me, and he broke me.

You'd think that after going through all that, whatever was going on with Brennan would be no big deal.

So why was it that in light of everything else going on in my crazy life, the fact that one pretty woman was paying attention to my best friend suddenly had me questioning everything I'd ever been, ever wanted?

I sighed, stood up and started walking down the beach, watching the water lick at the sand.

I didn't even have the time or energy to think about this, whatever *this* was, right now. I had supernatural turf wars and other fuckery happening all over the city. A gateway between here and the Nether that could collapse at any moment. A teenage girl who wasn't getting the attention she needed right now, because I barely had time to pee, let alone be anyone's friend or mentor. I was still dealing with my guilt and anger over Nain's death, and driving myself nuts trying to figure out what was a lie and what was real.

Did having these screwed up feelings or whatever they were for Brennan make me a really shitty wife to Nain? Shouldn't I have to mourn longer before getting stupid about another man?

Maybe I really was the garbage I'd always believed I'd been. The kid nobody wanted, the teenager nobody cared about. The woman who creeped everyone out so much they avoided making eye contact, even before I'd really come into my powers. Maybe they'd all seen something I hadn't. There was clearly something wrong with me. In so many ways.

I sat down on the sand for a while, and breathed.

And then a howl, and a scream, cut the night, and I was up and running toward it before I even knew what I was doing. Instinct.

I burst into a copse of trees to find two twisted, idiotic warlocks torturing a woman they'd caught, getting ready to use her for one of their bullshit sacrifice rituals. I ended them before they'd fully realized what was happening, manipulated the woman's memory so she wouldn't remember them or me, took her home.

This was what I did. If I knew nothing else, it was that at least I managed to do some good every now and then. I dropped the woman off, stood and watched her walk into her house. Dahael and Bash stood next to me on the sidewalk. After the woman had gone inside and closed the door behind her, Dahael pulled at my pant leg.

"Time to go home, Mistress," she said. "Can't run forever."

I sighed. "All right. Let's go home, then." And the imps and I piled into my car, and we made our way home again.

CHAPTER EIGHT

It was nearly four a.m. when I made my way home. I was a mess. Gore and other grossness on my jeans, who knows what on my top. Blood that was not mine crusting on my arms and face. I took the elevator up, crept into the loft.

The living room lamps were on, and Brennan was sitting in one of the recliners, wearing dark pants, a gray shirt, and a tie. Head back, sleeping. I watched him for a minute, knowing how dumb it was to watch someone sleeping, yet, stupidly, unable to look away. I shook my head and headed toward my room.

"Hey," he said, and I jumped about a foot.

I tried to still my pounding heart. "Shit. I thought you were asleep."

"I was. Sorry I startled you," he said. I waved it off. "I was waiting for you."

"Why?"

He stood up and walked toward me. "Because you left the house pissed off at me, and I hate it when that happens."

I shrugged. "How was dinner?" I asked, not really wanting to know.

He shrugged. "Fine. The pack is nice. Mr. Ryan was happy I was there, and he sends his regards. He sees me as a good connection to have, a tie between their pack and our team."

"Right. Especially if you start dating his daughter," I said, trying to keep any emotion out of the words.

He raised his eyebrow. "Yeah. I guess. Except that I don't want to date his daughter."

"She wants you," I said. " A lot. And she's gorgeous, and powerful. Well-connected." I looked away.

"Okay. Whatever. But I don't want her." He paused. Confusion, anxiety, irritation. "Wait. You don't expect me to date her to make the pack happy, do you? Or are you trying to push me off on somebody else?"

I looked up at him, dumbfounded. "Hell, no. I don't want you dating…" I clamped my mouth shut before I could do anymore damage. Stupid.

"Did you think I was interested?"

I didn't answer and he watched me. Irritated, again.

"Is that why you were pissed?"

I just looked at him.

He let out a small growl of irritation. "You can sense emotions, Molly. You never, ever read mine wrong. You know me inside and out."

"I thought I knew Nain, too. Look how that worked out."

He was silent for a minute, eyes searching mine. "I am not Nain. Did you get any sense, at all, that I was interested in her?"

I looked away. Wished for a hole I could fall into. He came up to me and took my chin in his hand, gently, and made me look at him. "You thought I wanted her?" His voice was a low growl, and it made my stomach flutter, my spine tingle. His eyes bored into mine, and love, longing, rolled off of him like a wave.

"She's perfect for you," I finally managed.

"Uh, no. She's really not."

"Yes, she is."

He watched me for a few seconds, took a breath. Nervousness. "We were going to have a long talk after the explosion. Remember?"

I just looked at him. He still held my chin in his fingers, and his eyes mesmerized me.

"You wanted to know how I knew it hurt when you healed. Eunomia asked how I knew you were waking up. I know other things too, Molly. I know when you're hungry. I know when you're in pain, and I know when you're tired. Not emotions, not like you. I feel, physically, what you're feeling. Do you know how?"

I forgot how to breathe. I just stared at him.

"It's because I love you," he said, slowly, deliberately, watching me, still holding my chin gently in his fingers. "I gave myself to you a long time ago. Because, no matter whether you can love me back or not, you're mine in a way no one else ever has been or ever will be. Your essence, *you*, are so much a part of me that when you're in pain, it hurts me. When you're hungry, I want to feed you. When you're cold, I want to make you warm again."

I finally came to my senses, pushed his hand away. "What? For how long?" I hated the way my voice trembled, the way my stomach flip-flopped.

"Since the first time I laid eyes on you."

"In the loft, when Nain introduced me to everyone?" I asked, dread settling into my stomach.

He shook his head. "Before that. Remember, Nain was following you around the city for a long time before he finally talked to you, trying to figure you out? I was with him a lot of the time. The first time I saw you, you were beating the hell out of two guys who were about four times your size. It hit me like goddamned lightning, the second I laid eyes on you. I bonded to you, immediately, as my mate. There is no one else for me. Ever."

I was trembling now. "All that time...with Nain..."

He reddened, gave a terse nod.

I charged at him, tried to hit him, and he caught my hand easily, and held my wrist in his hand. "How could you not tell me?" I tried to hit him with the other hand, and he grabbed it as well, held it in an iron grip.

"What difference would it have made?" he said back, still holding my wrists against his chest. "At first, I thought I had a chance with you. Remember that? I wanted to tell you then. Then things changed, and suddenly you were with Nain. I couldn't make myself say it, not when you were in a relationship with my best friend."

"With the Puppeteer..."

He nodded. "I felt how much pain you were in, even as I caused it and couldn't fight against her to stop it."

"I..." I shook my head.

"I'm sorry. I should have told you before. Or I should have just kept my mouth shut. I don't even know what the right thing is anymore." His grip on my wrists was starting to hurt. The second I felt it, so did he. He let go of my wrists and stepped back, raking his fingers through his hair.

I stared at him, a thousand little moments, memories hitting me all at once. Realization that, despite what I wanted to believe, he wasn't messing with me about this. "You lied to me," I said. It was the first thing I could think of, the thing that hurt the most. He knew how much Nain's lies had hurt me, and here he was, telling me he'd done the same thing.

He nodded.

"You're not going to make excuses for it?" I could feel my power rising as my temper flared, and the building gave a shudder around us as it did. "Aren't you going to tell me it was for my own good, or because you loved me so much it totally made lying to me okay?" I asked, and I could hear the venom in my voice.

"No. I was an idiot."

"Is there anything else I should know?"

He shook his head. "It's all there. I love you. You're

mine. I can feel you. And me telling you this is just going to make things more screwed up between us, and I know it. I'm not going to lie to you anymore."

I shook my head, tried to remember to breathe. "I can't believe this." On one hand, part of me could admit that this was everything I wanted to hear from him. He loved me. He wanted me. On the other, I'd been jerked around, lied to, left behind. And this man standing there before me, pleading with his eyes, was supposed to be my best friend, the one I could trust completely. And he'd lied to me. Not just a fib, not an "oh, yeah, you look great in that dress" type of lie. This wasn't a crush he had. This wasn't just attraction. He'd imprinted on me as his mate. That is a huge freaking deal for a shifter. They mate for life, and do so only once they've found their true mate. My best friend, and he'd chosen not to share something that huge with me. Especially since it kind of involved me.

He watched me. "It bothered you that I was going to this thing with her tonight. Why didn't you just tell me not to go?"

"Because I don't own you. I have no right to tell you where to go or who to go out with or who to talk to or anything else." I closed my eyes, shook my head. Why did everything always have to be so goddamn hard? Even my best friend couldn't be straight with me. I felt like I'd been punched in the gut and the heart at the same time, and it confused me as much as it enraged me.

"Except that you do own me. Completely," he said. "Remember that next time you think it's even possible for me to want someone else." He watched me, started loosening his tie. "And then maybe think about why it is that the idea of me wanting someone other than you bothers you so much." He met my eyes one more time, then headed upstairs, leaving me to try to figure out how to deal with the turmoil of my warring emotions.

♦♦♦

After my little conversation with Brennan, I'd been doing my best to avoid him. I wasn't mad that he could feel me. Shit like that, I knew from my own powers, was beyond our control. The fact that he hadn't told me was what pissed me off. The fact that, for basically our entire friendship, there had been this lie between us.

I hurt for him, too. If my own little jealous (yeah, I could admit it) freak-out over the shifter was any indication, I could only imagine what he'd gone through all that time. Knowing that he loved me, and that he'd not only stood by and watched me choose someone else, but that he'd had to endure feeling my pleasure when some other man loved me...it was just too much.

And I was confused over just about everything with him. I don't handle this type of thing well.

So I avoided him, and he let me do it. We said as few words as possible to each other throughout the days that followed. It was starting to put me in a bad mood, frankly.

We did our best to keep things running smoothly, but after a little over a week of avoiding each other, things were starting to fall apart, just a little bit, fraying at the edges. We'd been bickering with each other all day over stupid things. Shanti was sitting in the dining room working on the algebra problems I'd assigned her. Brennan was cleaning up after dinner and I was sitting at the counter in the kitchen reading through the reports Chief Jones had sent over for me.

"What's going on tonight?" he asked me.

I shrugged. "Normal crap."

"Want me to come with you?"

"I can handle it."

He took a breath. "I know you can. Never said you couldn't."

"Then stop trying to help me."

Shanti groaned. "Oh, shit. Here we go again," she said, gathering up her books. "Y'all can do this by yourselves.

It's all reruns with you two lately." And with that, she headed up to her room and shut the door.

"Watch the language," I called after her.

Brennan shook his head and went back to washing dishes, irritated. "I know you don't need me *or* my help. I just thought we'd get out of here and do something else for a while."

"Why?"

"Because I'm tired of the pissiness lately. Maybe if we beat someone up together you'll get over it," he said, giving me a look and turning away.

"Aw, I'm not fun anymore, huh? Maybe you can find company elsewhere. Lemme think," I said.

"Don't even, Molly," he warned.

"Or what?" I asked.

He turned around, crossed his arms. "What, do you want me to threaten you? Should I rough you up the way Nain used to when you disagreed with him? Maybe you'd want me if I acted like an asshole all the time." I stared at him, and my jaw dropped. He took a deep breath, and I felt him trying to draw back his anger. "Shit. I'm sorry. That was stupid." Silence as we both tried to handle our own anger. "I shouldn't have told you," he said, turning away again.

"Yeah. You totally should have just kept lying to me."

"Apparently."

"It doesn't change anything."

"Yeah. Because you clearly couldn't stand me before," he said, and the growl in his voice was unmistakable.

"What, did you expect me to be charmed? Was I supposed to be all 'oh, Bren! I'm yours! Let's live happily ever after, baby!' Please." I got up and tossed the police reports in the garbage.

"No. I know you too well for that."

"You don't know me. One person in this whole world knew me, and he's dead," I said.

He went absolutely still. Glared at me. "If you really

believe that, then you haven't been paying attention. At all." His anger, pain, love, need roared over me. He was overwhelming, in every way, and being around him was driving me completely insane, ready to snap at any second.

We glared at each other for several long seconds, and I felt like I was either going to cry or scream. So I did what I always seemed to do with Brennan lately.

"I do not need this," I muttered. Then I walked out, slamming the door behind me.

I took it out on big bads, of course. I was just finishing fighting a sprite who'd tried stalking a girl as she walked home from work. As I sent his ass home afraid of me, I felt Eunomia flutter down behind me. I turned to look at her.

"You really need a new hobby," she said, shaking her head.

"Yeah, I'll take up crochet sometime," I muttered.

She laughed. "You're in a mood. Even more than usual," she said, landing and sitting on the ground nearby. I plopped down next to her. The imps moved away from us, seeming to know when I wanted privacy. They went to the street and perched on the hood of my car, keeping an eye out for trouble while I talked to Eunomia.

I shook my head. "I got into another fight with Brennan and said something stupid," I said, plucking a clover blossom from the patch of lawn we were sitting on.

"From what you tell me, you've been saying many stupid things to him lately," she said, watching me.

I shrugged.

"Does he deserve it?" She asked after a while.

"He lied to me."

"Yes. And he admitted it. Does he deserve for you to continue acting like this?"

"No," I said. "Every time I start feeling something for him, I panic. And then I throw Nain's memory in his face. I know it's cruel, and I do it anyway."

We sat in silence for a few minutes. "You know.

You've told me all about all of this. I sat with you afterward, remember?" I nodded. "Consider something, from someone who knows something about eternity and vows and all of that. You loved your demon husband. I know you did. And you bound yourself to him and you meant it. *He* broke that bond, by choice, by not telling you what would happen when you destroyed his enemy. Not you. You do not have to spend the rest of your life in some kind of self-assigned purgatory."

"I'm afraid," I said, my voice barely above a whisper.

"Of what?"

"Doing this again. Letting someone in. Losing them." I sighed. "He's my best friend. He's my right hand. I'm able to do everything I do because he has my back in every possible way."

She raised her eyebrows. "And, so, you treat him like garbage, because....?" Eunomia said.

I didn't answer. Shook my head. "Stupid Guardians and their stupid logic," I muttered.

"All I'm saying is, maybe stop being so wrapped up in your own fears that you overlook the good things in your life. Look at what the man has been through for you." She ticked the points off on her fingers as she talked. "He helped train you to fight. He's had to cope with hating himself since the Puppeteer took control of him. He watched you love someone else. Stayed by your side for months when you mourned the man he lost you to. Became your partner, your confidante, even though it must have hurt him a lot of the time."

She stopped for a second, then went on. "And, just to top it off, he pulled your burnt, broken body out of a fire, and he sat by your bedside day and night, watching, praying that you'd come back, and he's been calm and strong through every insane situation you've put him through." She paused. "You know what? Forget you. The shifter is enough to make me reconsider my maiden status."

I smacked her lightly on the arm. "Not funny, E."

"You see what I'm saying, don't you? Please tell me you are not that clueless."

I sighed. "I do. He's too good for me."

She rolled her eyes. "And, that's where we end the discussion because we've veered into Stupidville. Clearly, you need a distraction. How about guarding the gate?"

I stared at her. "Are they through?"

"Not yet. It's weak, though, and we haven't been able to stop it. We've tried everything. We're at that point. We need you to protect your end."

"Why didn't you just say that? We don't have time to chit-chat."

She tilted her head, studied me. "Because you needed to talk. You're not a robot, demon girl. Admitting you have emotions is not a weakness."

"I don't have time for emotions. I don't have time to think, let alone try to figure out any of this shit with Brennan," I said.

"You need to make time. What are you fighting for, really, unless it's to protect those you love?" She let me think that over for a bit. "All right. Should we go now?"

I nodded. "Where?"

"Let's fly."

I stared at her again. "Hell, no."

"You've flown with me before."

"I was mostly dead at the time," I pointed out.

"Want me to knock you out?" she asked sweetly. She straightened her robes, flexed her wings, and grinned at me with her sharp little teeth.

"Try it, Big Bird," I muttered, and she laughed.

She grabbed me under my arms, and we soared through the air, the city below us a blur. I closed my eyes and tried not to puke. When she finally set me down, I felt like kissing the ground.

She laughed. "Who would have guessed that the big bad Angel was such a baby?"

I gave her the finger. And then I looked around, froze. A thousand bad memories hit me. Screams, the smell of burning flesh. Anguish, emptiness. I could still hear my own screams reverberating off of concrete.

She watched me. "I'm sorry, my friend. This was another reason I put off showing you where the gateway was," Eunomia said softly.

"What are the odds?" I whispered as I looked around the abandoned Packard plant. Crumbling walls, garbage.

Where Nain had died.

I felt myself nearing the edge. A few months ago, I would have gone over.

I was different now. I would not be destroyed by this. Not again. I let myself feel my grief. Let myself mourn again, for just a moment, remembering. Remembering everything. The good, the bad. The passion and the pain. Honoring him for what he'd given to me.

I also, insanely enough, felt myself letting go. Letting go of the anger, the hatred. The guilt. Letting go of him, even as I wept for him again.

I settled myself down, wiped my eyes, and I took a deep breath. Shook my head. "It's fine. We have things to do."

She watched me.

"Really."

Then she smiled. "Good." She fluttered to an end of the factory, almost exactly where we'd fought that night. "Come here. See if you can sense it."

"Should I be able to?"

She shrugged. "I'm curious. Humor me."

I walked that way, making a point of not looking at the spot where Nain had died. I could pinpoint it, seared into my mind. I reached Eunomia, looked around. Nothing but concrete and trash. Then I closed my eyes, felt an unpleasant sensation, like a pull, almost physical. I opened my eyes, pointed to my left. "It's there."

She nodded. "Yes."

"I can feel it because of the demon thing, right?"

She shook her head. "I do not think so. Anyway, this is the gateway. If something comes through, kill it."

I laughed. "Right. Because it will be that easy."

She raised her eyebrow. "I think you can handle it."

"If they get through, it's because they fought their way past a bunch of demons and a Fury to get here. If they get through, I'm pretty sure we're fucked."

"Deal with it. It's what you do."

I felt it then. Something was bashing the barrier between the gateway and us. "Feel that?" I asked Eunomia.

She nodded. "Something is coming."

CHAPTER NINE

The words were barely out of her mouth when the first of the demons barreled through the gateway, seeming to appear out of nowhere. Six of them, huge, hulking, eyes glowing. Skin the color of old bruises. I readied myself, dove into them, punching, cutting.

"You have to use your powers, devil girl," Eunomia yelled, before winking out of sight, back to the Nether to find out what was happening.

I tried to ignore the sick feeling in my stomach as I unleashed fire on the two nearest me. One was grabbing my hair, and I sent mental knives behind me, at him, and I glanced back to see his eyes bleeding. He still held onto me, though, and another came at me, black, cruel-looking sword gleaming. He slashed, and I felt it rip across my stomach.

I gritted my teeth against the pain. I hated feeling my blood streaming out of my body. "Big mistake, asshole," I growled. I launched forward at him, leapt onto him and coursed fire into his body as he screamed. Soon, he was still, and I turned to take on the one that was already bleeding as the first two lay in smoking lumps.

Two more. The first charged toward me, knocked me down, put his gigantic hands around my throat and started squeezing. I fought him, but it was like fighting steel, and I was already weakening a little from healing myself. He looked down at me, grinned a slimy, sharp-toothed grin, and reached for my pants.

"Sorry, buddy. There's only one demon I've ever let into my pants, and it's definitely not you," I said. Then I smiled up at him, shot mental knives at his stomach, and he fell off of me, screaming. I rubbed my bruised throat, looking around for the other one while his teammate laid blubbering at my feet.

I saw him running for the exit. I ran after him, determined that he not leave the factory. If he got out, it would be easier for me to lose track of him. He looked over his shoulder, and I could feel his fear.

Damn, demonic fear was good. It strengthened me, and I put on a burst of speed, leapt onto his back as he tried to get away.

"Who sent you?" I asked him, standing up and throwing him back into the factory. He roared in pain as he struck the concrete wall. He sprung up and tried running at me, but I tossed a small fireball at him. It struck, and he panicked and started rolling around on the floor, extinguishing the flames. I waited patiently as he got himself together again.

"I'll ask again. Who sent you?"

My imps were surrounding the two of us now, watching, waiting. The demon rose to his knees.

"Nobody."

I conjured a fireball, bobbled it in my hand, and felt his fear spike. "Are you sure?"

"I swear. Nobody sent me." His voice was a little high-pitched for a demon. He seemed young, compared to the ones I had come across.

"Then how did you and your buddies get here?" I still held the fire, and he stayed on his knees.

"There was a fight. A bunch of us were bashing at the gateway, trying to get through. The Fury and her guard demons got distracted when the mob attacked them, and a few of us were able to come through before they realized what was happening."

"Is the gateway really that weak?"

He nodded. "If they are not working to keep it intact, it opens."

"Why did you come here?"

He looked at me as if I was stupid, which really annoyed me. "Freedom."

"What was your crime?" I asked, genuinely curious.

"I murdered my parents."

"The Furies tend to look down on that," I said. I remembered the things Nain had told me about his own parents, though, and had a feeling this demon's parents probably weren't worth mourning.

"Yeah." He watched me. "You're like them. You're going to send me back."

I studied him. "I don't know how to send you back," I finally admitted.

We sat in silence. "So I have a choice to make here. Do I kill you, the way I did your buddies, there?"

"They're not my buddies. I didn't even know them."

I sensed for him. Nervousness, fear.

"Or do I let you go? The problem with that is that unleashing a murderous demon on my city is not something I feel comfortable doing."

"I'm not murderous. I have killed."

I almost smiled. Ridiculous that I could totally relate.

"No murdering. No raping. No causing pain to innocents. If I hear of you doing any of these things, and I will," I added, gesturing at my imps, thirty or so of which had gathered around us now, "then I will hunt you down, and I will kill you slowly and painfully, and there will be nothing left for the Guardians to escort to the Nether."

He gulped, and he watched me, and he looked at my imps. "Then I'll be weak, and something else will just kill me anyway."

"Use your strength for something good. There are more than enough evil bastards out there to keep you satisfied without ever preying on an innocent."

He was watching me. "So you want me to play the hero?"

I smiled. "I do it, every day of my life. Why not?" I waited as he sorted through it all in his mind. "What is your name?"

"Levitt." Not his demon name, that, he was keeping to himself. I understood. Names have power and all that.

"So, what do you say, Levitt?"

"You're giving me a chance to redeem myself," he said quietly. "Why?"

I extinguished my flame, looked around. I shook my head, remembering. "Because someone showed me, once upon a time, how much good a demon could do. I'm doing this in memory of him. If you make me regret it, there will be no place dark or far enough for you to hide from me."

He looked around at my imps again, who took that moment to bend knee to me, as one, and thump their fists to their chests.

The demon, Levitt, watched them do it. And then he went to one knee, bowed his head to me, and thumped his chest, in the same way. "I swear I will honor you," he said and when I sensed for him, there was almost the same sense of adoration and obedience I got from my imps.

"Go on. Do good," I said. Levitt stood up, thumped his chest one more time, and made to leave.

"Oh, Levitt," I said, smiling.

He turned. "Yes?"

"You might want to put on a human skin."

He looked down at himself, looked at me. "Oh. Right."

He focused for a moment, and the air shimmered around him. The skin he wore perfectly matched the demon he'd been. Average height, solidly built. Brown hair, brown eyes, a light beard. A black t-shirt and cargo pants. "Good?" he asked.

I nodded. "Good."

"Thank you," he said, thumping his chest again.

I nodded, and he turned and walked out of the factory. I watched him go, and took a deep breath. Bash and Dahael came to my side, and Dahael took my hand.

"Mistress is so good," she said, smiling up at me.

"Right thing to do. Good in him," Bash agreed.

"Demon skin would have been proud," Dahael said, giving my hand a squeeze. We stood there for a bit.

"I'm going to stay here tonight. I can still feel them bashing the gateway," I said.

"We will stay, too," Bash said.

I pulled out my phone and called the loft, got Ada. I told her to tell Brennan that I was on guard duty, and that he would know what that meant. I did not tell her where I was. I didn't want any of them anywhere near here. For many reasons.

I hung up and looked around. Without thinking, I headed toward the last spot I'd seen Nain alive. The concrete was blackened, burned, from when he'd combusted when I'd attacked Astaroth. I sat down, right next to the spot, ran my fingers over the blackened concrete. The imps gave me space.

"I miss you," I whispered, feeling stupid for talking to an empty factory. It didn't matter. "You destroyed me. I should hate you so much for that." I sat, fighting back tears, and failing. "But I can't. Not as much as I should." I closed my eyes, felt his blood still running through my veins, remembered things I'd let myself forget in my anger and grief.

"You were starving. One night with me, and you're fully fed. I'll take that as a compliment, Molls."

"All I know is I can't stop thinking about you. I try, but it's pointless. You're addictive."

"I think I might be in love with you, you bastard."

"It's about fucking time, woman. I've been in love with you since the moment I laid eyes on you."

"Now, you're officially mine."

"Already was."

"What am I supposed to do now, you bastard?" I whispered into the empty factory.

Part of me still belonged to him, whether he was here or not. And I knew that it had nothing to do with blood, and everything to do with the fact that, for a little while, at least, we had been two halves of one person. How did I move forward from that? Maybe it was pointless to even try. I thought of Brennan, the things he'd said to me. I wished I could give him what he wanted, but I was not whole. Maybe I never would be.

I stretched out on the concrete, kept my hand on the last spot he'd been alive. I sensed for the gateway, which had finally gone quiet. And I closed my eyes and slept, and dreamed that Nain was with me and I felt whole again, if only for a little while.

◆◆◆

I spent the next two days guarding the gateway. Four times, a demon or two got lucky and managed to get through. None seemed to have the humanity in them that Levitt had, and I finished them off before they could go out and cause any pain. I slept, fitfully. The imps brought me food and stuff to drink when I needed it, sneaking into restaurants and stores, invisible to the Normals.

It was my third night in the abandoned factory. I sat, leaned up against the wall. This was like one of my own personal hells, just me, alone in this crumbling factory with all of its ghosts. When I wasn't remembering Nain, I was thinking about Brennan.

I felt alone. More than just physically. I hadn't gone more than a day without talking to Brennan since we'd met. I'd gone longer without talking to Nain, actually, than I ever had with Brennan. This was three days of not talking, using Ada or Stone as intermediaries, after over a week of arguing. I wondered how strong our friendship actually was; whether I could get over this and, more importantly, whether he could forgive me for acting like a complete jerk.

Night was falling again. It usually didn't bother me; night was my time. But tonight, it did. I wanted lamplight, and noise, and warmth. I hated this. Every second of it. It was necessary, and I'd do it, but I hated it.

My phone vibrated in my pocket, and my stomach fluttered stupidly when I saw the number. Bren. I took a breath, and answered.

"Molly," he said, and I could hear the tension, the worry, in that one word. "How is everything?"

"Everything is a mess," I said, and hated the lump that rose in my throat.

"Yeah," he said, an edge of emotion in his voice as well. "Stone said you said earlier that a few had come through. Anymore?"

"Three came through today. So far I'm doing okay with getting rid of them as soon as they come through. E says they're working hard to shore up their side of the gateway. These are just random lucky ones getting through right now," I said.

He was quiet on his end.

"How are things there?" I asked.

"Okay. I've been handling the meetings we had scheduled. You've had lots of 'call me,' messages from the people I've met with, which I just know you'll love dealing with when you get back."

"Right."

We both went silent again. "Do you want some company? I mean, I can send Stone or Ada if you want."

"Are you worried about me?"

"Yeah. Do you want them to come or not?"

"No. I don't want them to come," I said, and I heard him sigh at the other end.

"Molly..."

"But if you feel like hanging out in a dark, depressing place with me for a while, I wouldn't mind that," I said.

"Honestly, that sounds better than anything else has in a long time. Where are you?"

"Packard plant," I said.

Silence.

"Oh, shit. Molly," he said.

"I'm okay."

"I know. I'll be there in a few minutes. Do you want clean clothes?"

I wished I could have hugged him through the phone. "That would be great. Thank you."

"Okay. I'll be there soon." We hung up, and I waited.

True to his word, within fifteen minutes, I heard footsteps at the far end of the plant. Dahael gestured that she'd go guide him to where I was, and I nodded. I stood up, and soon, I saw his flashlight beam. He reached me, and looked me over.

"Hey," Brennan said, setting down his flashlight and a big duffel. His eyes roamed me, looking, I knew, for signs of injury, even though he knew better than just about anyone how well I could heal. He set the flashlight and duffel bag down without taking his eyes off of me. Love, relief, came from him, strong and warm, and I was on the verge of tears. He walked up to me and only hesitated a second before pulling me into his arms, and I leaned against him and felt like for the first time in a long time, something was right for once. I pressed my face into his chest and breathed him in. He held me tighter, and we didn't say a word for several long minutes.

"I missed you, Molly," he said after a while.

"I missed you too," I whispered. "I'm sorry about how I acted. I said some shitty, awful things to you, and I didn't mean them."

I felt surprise from him. How terrible was I that he was surprised I'd apologized? He took a breath. "I'm sorry too. I know this isn't easy for you. You've got the weight of the world on you, and then you have me here and I can't hide what I feel from you and I just made things weirder the other night. It has to be crazy for you."

"You don't deserve the way I treat you," I said, looking up at him. I don't want to hurt you anymore," I whispered.

"I'm here, no matter what. You know that," he said.

I nodded. "I'm glad you're here, Bren. I couldn't do this without you."

He let me go, looked down at me. I met his eyes and he smiled at me. "You don't have to do anything without me."

"I've heard that before," I said softly.

He looked around, then he studied me. "I've been overstepping lately."

"Meaning?"

He took a breath. "I was thinking while you were gone."

"Dangerous."

He laughed. "Shut up, Molly."

I laughed, and waited for him to continue.

"I was thinking that no matter how much I would like it to be otherwise, you'll probably never be mine. I can see it every time you look at me. You'd like to be able to take a chance. The idea of being loved again is attractive. And maybe you do love me, at least a little bit. But you're still in love with someone else. And when he died, it knocked you on your ass and you're not sure you'll ever be right again. And I can't even begin to understand what you had with him." He paused, looked at me. "Right?"

"I'm sorry, Bren."

"Don't be. It's who you are. When you say something, when you make a promise, you mean it. And I know you've been going through the grieving process, and anger is part of it. I mistook your anger at Nain as a possibility for something between us. I have no interest in being a second-class replacement."

"There is nothing second-class about you," I said.

"Okay. Well. Nice to see we're on the same page. I love you Molly. You're the person I'm closest to in this world. That's not changing. But if I need some distance sometimes, I hope it doesn't hurt you. I have to figure out a way to handle the way I feel about you. I think we both needed these few days apart to get some breathing room."

Tears pricked my eyes, and I nodded. "Okay."

He nodded. "Okay." Then he bent down and started rifling through the duffel bag. He pulled out a pile of my clothes and set them down. Then he pulled out two sleeping bags and I stared.

"You're a damn genius," I said, and he laughed.

"I haven't even gotten to the good part yet." He pulled out a large metal thermos and two coffee cups.

"Oh god thank you," I said, sitting next to him.

He laughed and poured me some coffee. We sat and he filled me in on what was going on at the loft. He stopped partway through, coughing harshly.

"Are you okay?" I asked. He nodded and took another gulp of coffee.

"I feel like I'm coming down with a little something," he said, waving me off.

"Bren, you should be at home. It's damp and cold here, and you never get sick…"

"Molly. It's a cold. It's fine." I watched him, and we went back to finishing off the thermos of coffee. The peace was only interrupted when I started feeling something bashing the gate.

"Ready to fight some demons?" I asked, standing up.

He grinned at me. "I thought you'd never ask." We

stood ready, in front of the gate, and within moments, a group of demons was hurtling through. I saw ax blades, and glowing eyes, and way, way too many of them.

I started blasting them with flames, but one of them just laughed and ignited. "Fire demon?" I asked him, and he nodded, still laughing.

"Fine," I said, and I hurled mental knives at him, shredding his throat, and he fell, clutching his neck fruitlessly. I glanced around and saw Brennan fighting two more, while five surrounded me.

"Hey. This is her," one said.

"How convenient," the other, taller one said, grinning, exposing a row of sharp teeth. The first tried to grab me, and I fought him back, started hurling flames and knives.

These were not the amateurs that had been coming through. These demons were organized. They were focused. On me.

I heard Brennan howl, and I looked over to see him bleeding. I hurled fire at one of the demons attacking him, and it gave him enough of a distraction to be able to jump and rip the other demon's throat out with his teeth. Once that was finished, he leapt into the group of demons surrounding me.

All were fire demons. My fire was worthless. These demons knew me. They were not as prepared for the mental knives, but they were determined, even bleeding and in pain, to get what they came for.

Brennan and I fought on, and soon my arms were aching from punching, and my sides and stomach were bleeding. I limped after one sliced through the back of my knee with his sword. I finally managed to get one down, slicing roughly across his throat with the knife I always carried in my pocket.

I glanced toward Brennan. He had gashes along his side, and his right front leg bled.

"Brennan, you should go," I shouted.

Panther-Brennan gave me a very Brennan look, one of

his "are you insane?" looks, and continued fighting. We were so screwed.

I managed to get one more down, and we were down to three. One of them slashed out with his sword, cutting me deep across the abdomen, and I fell to my knees in agony. I heard Brennan roar, saw the same demon ready his blade for another strike. If Brennan hadn't been there with me, I would have, maybe, been okay with letting him end me. I figured beheading would do it.

But Brennan was there, and I wasn't going to let them kill him, too. I jabbed my knife up into the demon's stomach, sliced hard upward, gutting him, and he fell on top of me, roaring in pain, his blood soaking through my clothing. Good thing Brennan brought extras, I thought numbly.

My imps were helping Brennan with the last two, but it was not going well, and the freaking fire demon who'd landed on top of me weighed at least four hundred pounds. I shoved at him uselessly, watched as one of the demons fighting Brennan moved to hit Bren with his ax.

And then I felt something powerful come through the gateway. Like, easily as powerful as me. And my breath caught in my throat and my heart raced as I saw the being that came through the gateway, flying with great, bat-like wings. She carried a flaming sword in her hand, and beheaded the final two demons within seconds.

Brennan shifted back, helped pull the fallen demon off of me, and then he pulled me up. We were both bleeding, exhausted, and we looked at the being who had saved us, who now stood there, staring at me.

Eunomia and her sisters had arrived to claim the souls of the dead, and Eunomia landed next to me. "Demon girl," she said. Then she looked at the being that had saved our asses, and gave her a respectful nod. "Tisiphone," she murmured.

I couldn't take my eyes off of the Fury. Tisiphone. I looked into my own white glowing eyes. Dark hair, alabaster skin.

She stared, and I stared back. Except for her black, bat-like wings, she looked almost exactly like me. Taller, thinner, but the similarities were remarkable.

"Oh, no," she whispered, and her voice soothed me in a way I couldn't understand. "They found you."

"Who?" I asked, chills going up my spine.

"Oh, my dearest daughter. My love. I thought I had hidden you so well."

CHAPTER TEN

The factory was deathly silent around us. Eunomia, Brennan, the Fury and I stood like statues. I stared at the Fury, the Fury looked at me, and Eunomia looked back and forth between us, one of those little half-smiles on her face. Brennan took my hand, squeezed it reassuringly.

Daughter.

That one word was enough to knock me on my ass, make me wonder if I hadn't finally just lost my damn mind.

"Excuse me?" I finally said. I could hear the tremor in my voice.

"You are my daughter. And I would like to know how in the Nether you managed to break the enchantments I put on you to keep you hidden," the Fury said, watching me. Her power thundered over me, around me, and I recognized my own strength in it. I felt for her. Worry. Warmth. Pride. Mostly worry, though.

"Uh…" was all I could manage. Then I shook my head and looked at Eunomia. "Did you know about this?"

"I suspected. But since there was never any talk of

Tisiphone having a child, I thought there must be another explanation."

"You didn't think to say something to me?" I said, exasperated.

She looked at me, cocked her head to the side. "What would I have said?"

I sighed, shook my head. I didn't doubt what Tisiphone had said. I could feel that she spoke the truth the way I could feel the ground beneath my feet and the cool night air around us.

"I will leave you now. Duty calls," Eunomia said, and she blinked out of sight.

The Fury and I stood there for a while. "Come sit with me," she said after a while, and I did, pulling Brennan along with me and plopping down on the ground next to her.

We watched each other for several long moments. "So I'm not human. I knew that already. But I'm not a demon, either," I said.

She looked thoughtful. "I think 'demon' is too small a word. Demons are of the Nether. We, Furies, are of the Nether, as are the Guardians and several other supernatural beings. So there are definite similarities to the way our power feels, the way it reacts to other beings of the Nether. We are very alike in many ways. You thought you were a demon?"

"Well, I sure the hell didn't think I was the child of a goddess," I muttered. Then something came to me. "Am I immortal?"

She smiled a little. "No. Me leaving you here was basically the same as banishing you from our realm. When that happens, we lose our immortality. You will be very hard to kill, and you'll have an exceptionally long life compared to humans and even demons, but, eventually, you will die."

"So, what? You didn't want me?" I looked down, hating how much the answer meant to me. Brennan squeezed my hand again.

Tisiphone took my other hand in hers. Her skin was cool, like Eunomia's, like demons', and, I realized for the first time, like mine.

"Beautiful girl. I wanted you. I have missed you every day since I gave you up. You were loved. You always have been."

I kept my eyes on the floor, unable to look at this magical being who claimed to be my mother. "Then, why?"

"You know what Furies do, yes?"

"Deliver justice."

"Yes. To mortals *and* immortals. We are the only ones with the power and authority to punish a god." She paused, and I sensed worry from her. She seemed to be thinking, coming to a decision about something. "The Furies have always been maidens. We do not take lovers. We do not have children. It is just the way of things, and with good reason. The unthinkable happened, though. I have been in love with a god for eons, and he with me. When I finally gave myself to him, finally surrendered myself, you were the result."

I looked up at her. "My father is?"

She hesitated, then smiled, the small, shy smile of a woman in love. Universal. "Cithaeron. A mountain god."

I thought for a minute, trying to remember the mythology I'd picked up since meeting Eunomia. I narrowed my eyes. "Uh. Isn't the story that you killed him?"

She nodded. "That is the story. Your father is very much alive and well. My sisters and I spread that story, kind of a cautionary tale."

"And the point of the tale is?" I asked.

She looked at me, and her eyes blazed. "That no one, not even those beloved to us, escapes the wrath of a Fury."

My heart pounded in response to her words. Pride; feral, wild pride coursed through me, and we looked at each other, and she smiled. She knew exactly what I was feeling.

I tried to get myself focused again. Shook my head. "Okay. So why leave me here?"

"As I said. The Furies are the only beings with the power to punish a god. Sometimes, they need correction, and that is our job, when the rest of the gods deem it necessary." I nodded, urging her to go on. She took a breath, looked at me intently. "The unthinkable, an abomination, the child of a Fury and a god, is the only being truly capable of deicide," she said softly, her voice barely a whisper. I sensed something from her, a mix of guilt, fear. Her face was calm, but I had a feeling there was more to the story.

Not that I needed any more surprises, mind you.

I sat, stunned. I stared at her, felt concern, sadness from Brennan beside me. "So, what? I was too dangerous to keep around?" I asked, angry, irritated for myself, mourning for the helpless little girl I'd been. Unloved, turned away.

She felt it, and she held my hand tighter, pulled me into her arms and hugged me, and I let go of Brennan and awkwardly put my arms around her. She was strong, solid, under the tailored black pants and shirt she wore. "No! Never that. I would have kept you, raised you among the gods. Never that." She hugged me tightly. "It was what other gods would have done to you," she said.

"They would have feared you. And they would have used you, a weapon against their rivals, a way to gain power. You never would have been at peace. I could not let that happen to you. They would have either wanted you banished and then killed, or controlled. The might of my sisters and I is nothing against the rest of the pantheon. We would have had nothing but never-ending war and strife. I wanted something better for you," she whispered in my ear.

She released me, and I sat back, still watching her. She glanced back at the gate. "I have to leave soon," she said, and I could sense the disappointment in her.

"You'll come back soon?" I asked her.

She smiled. "I will do my best. I don't get to this realm much. If I start coming often, it will raise suspicions."

"Someone already knows I'm here," I said. "Eunomia suspected this already."

She nodded, and her expression hardened. "Yes, she mentioned her theory to me, but her theory was about a female demon, and I wrote it off as nonsense. This explains why they're so focused on breaking through. Not to get out. This has always been too organized than to have just been an uprising. Someone there knows about you, and wants to use you."

"I won't be used," I said.

She smiled. "That's my girl. For now, we will keep our knowledge of each other to ourselves, at least until we have an idea of who it is that is so focused on getting to you." Then she paused. "When I left you here, I put enchantments on you so no one would know what you were. You would be human, and everyone, including yourself, would have no reason to suspect otherwise. By hiding your true nature, I hoped to keep you safe. How is it that the enchantments have been broken?"

I shook my head. "How much time do you have?"

"Give me the abbreviated version," she said, smiling.

So I did. I told her about my powers manifesting. About Nain. About Nain's death. About explosions and fires and gunshots and every other way I hadn't been killed. I told her about my dream after the explosion. By the end, tears ran down her cheeks, and she pulled me into another fierce hug.

"I am so sorry, my love," she whispered, kissing the top of my head, the way I'd always imagined a mom would. I cried, too, in my mother's arms, knowing things would only get crazier from here on out.

She backed up, held my face in her hands. "We will find a way to end this before anyone else is lost to you. We will make those who have harmed you pay, and dearly. I promise you."

I nodded. "I will enjoy making them pay."

She grinned, and it was deadly. "As will I. I really do have to go now. We will talk again soon. I love you, Mollis."

"Mollis, huh? Here, they call me Molly," I said, holding her hand.

She shook her head. "The mortals are often more perceptive than we give them credit for." We hugged, and she took another long look at me, and smiled, and she spread her wings and flew back through the gateway.

I stood there, wondering if it was real, and then I turned to Brennan and the look on his face told me all I needed to know.

"So...I'm a fucking god?" I said.

He shrugged. "I always told you you didn't really feel like a demon."

"Know-it-all," I muttered, and he took my hand, and we stood there, guarding the gate, protecting the world against the monsters trying to break through because of me.

◆◆◆

Finally, after another night in the factory (thankfully, with Brennan by my side, which made a world of difference) Eunomia came through and told us they'd beaten back the raging horde and they had not only Tisiphone, but also a couple of other gods using their powers to keep the gateway closed.

So we were able to go back to our normal life, except

COLLEEN VANDERLINDEN

that there was nothing normal about it, and even if there
was, nothing was the same anymore. At least, not for me. I
made Brennan promise not to tell Ada and Stone about
the Fury thing. They already acted a little funny around me
since that whole regenerate-half-my-body-after-an-
explosion thing, and I just didn't want any more weirdness.

Brennan's cold, or whatever it was, was getting worse,
and I'd ordered him to bed. He kept trying to play it off,
but I had a bad feeling it was more than a cold. The doctor
I'd called in on behalf of the Grosse Pointe shifters was
still in town, because whatever the matron of the pack had
was spreading through the pack now, and we had them
under quarantine. Over half of them, and now the doctor
himself, were sick. Whatever it was, it was only affecting
the shifters, and everyone I asked, including Ada who had
some skill in healing, said they'd never seen anything quite
like it before.

I couldn't stop thinking.

My parents were gods. I was an abomination, even
among gods. People were dead because of me, because
some god, or gods, had a stick up their ass about my
existence. Veronica. George. Nain. Who knew how many
innocents. All dead because of me.

I spent the first day back home trying to catch up on
everything. Phone calls. Emergency meetings. And there
were three turf war situations (shifters and weres) that I
refused to let my team handle, and I went out that first
night and handled all three situations, and I came home
bloody and angry and feeling wrong in my own skin.

And when I got home, I found Shanti in the kitchen,
scrubbing at her eyes, trying to pretend she hadn't just
been crying. I could feel the sadness, frustration, anger
coming from her. I walked up to her, forgetting about my
bloody clothing.

"Hey," I said. "What's wrong?"

She shook her head, waved it off.

"Shanti," I said, and was immediately over-run by more

106

guilt. I'd brought her in, and pretty much ignored her. "I'm here. Do you need to talk?"

She shook her head again. "It's stupid."

"The things that upset us are rarely stupid," I said. "Tell me."

She sighed. "It's my birthday. I'm eighteen."

I watched her. "Happy birthday, kiddo. I'm sorry I didn't know it was today."

"It's okay. It's not even that, really. It's knowing that I'm eighteen, and birthdays really don't mean a thing anymore because I'll always look like this," she said in disgust, looking down at herself. "I'll always look sixteen. I'll never have so many of the things I thought I would. I'll never have a big white wedding out in the sunshine. I'll never have a child growing inside of me. I'll never be any goddamn thing other than what I am right now," she said, and tears started rolling down her face again. I pulled her into my arms, and she cried against my shoulder, great, wracking sobs that tore my heart in two. I felt tears sting my eyes, too. She started talking again. "I am going crazy here. I appreciate you giving me a home, but I'm going nuts. I haven't left the loft since you took me in."

"I know. I'm sorry. First we were focused on getting the bloodlust under control, and then things just got..."

"Crazy," she said.

"Crazy," I agreed, letting her go and stepping back. Then I smiled at her. "Well. It's your birthday, right? We should go out."

She stared at me. "Are you serious?"

"Yeah. It's night time. It's your birthday. I just need to get cleaned up and then we can go out to eat if you want."

"Oh, hell yes," she said, laughing. "Can we hit Slows?"

I nodded. "Sure. Just give me a few minutes."

I went to my room. Showered and dressed, found my darkest sunglasses, and shoved my car keys and money into my pockets. Then I went up to Brennan's room, knocked gently. He didn't answer, and I let myself in.

He was sleeping deeply, and I didn't like the way his breath wheezed. I put my hand on his forehead. He was hot, and clammy, and it made me even more worried. He stirred, and looked up at me.

"Molly? What's going on?" he asked, starting to sit up.

"Nothing. It's okay," I said, gently pushing him back down. "I was just checking on you. How are you feeling?"

"Like crap. Chest hurts," he said, settling back down. "It's okay," he said when he saw my face. "I'll be fine. Stop worrying."

"I can't."

"I know," he said, smiling a little.

"It's Shanti's birthday," I said, pulling his covers back up and straightening them.

"Oh, shit," he groaned. "I forgot."

"It's okay. Things have been nuts. I'm going to take her out to dinner. She needs to get out of here for a while."

"Be careful," he said.

"You know me," I joked.

"Exactly."

"We're going to Slows. Want me to bring you back anything?"

He shook his head.

"You love Slows," I said, worry knotting my stomach.

"I can't eat it, Molly. It'll just go to waste." Then he looked up at me. "Stop worrying," he repeated.

"Right." I smoothed his blankets, feeling more helpless than I'd felt in forever. I hadn't told him about the Grosse Pointe shifters. The quarantine. The doctor. "We'll be back soon."

"Have fun," he said, closing his eyes again. I left his room, closed the door behind me, tried to keep the worry off of my face so I could at least give Shanti a nice birthday dinner out.

Shanti and I left and drove to the restaurant. She looked out the car windows like a tourist, like someone seeing the city for the very first time. Dahael and Bashiok sat in the back seat, and we had AC/DC on the radio. We passed a tattoo parlor, and I noticed Shanti staring at it with interest.

"Can vampires get tattoos?" she asked.

I shrugged. "Sure. I've met a few that have them. I think the key is making sure there's no one else getting tattooed at the time. Blood, you know," I said, and she nodded.

"Yeah, that could be tempting." She paused. "You have one, right?"

I nodded.

"How does a chick with a healing ability have a tattoo? Wouldn't it just disappear?"

"The trick was keeping myself from healing while the tattooist was working. Once the ink was in, it was in," I said.

"Hm."

"Why? Do you want one?" I asked.

"Maybe," she said, looking out the window again. We arrived at the restaurant, and ordered, and stuffed ourselves like absolute pigs on ribs and macaroni and cheese and cobbler. I watched her as she studied the people around us. She tried not to watch a young couple snuggling in the booth across from us, but her eyes kept darting that way, and I could feel longing, sadness coming from her.

"Hey," I said, nudging her leg with my foot under the table. "That's not impossible for you, you know."

"Right. Because people are just lining up to date someone who can kill them."

"Vampires are hot," I said quietly, smiling. "And you're an amazing, smart, beautiful young woman. I don't think you'll have any trouble finding someone to love you."

"And if I do? And he doesn't stay? If he realizes it's just too crazy being with someone like me?" she asked.

"You cry. And you mourn a little. And you are grateful for the memories you made," I said softly. "You realize that what you had was worth the pain."

She was watching me. "I'm sorry, Molly."

I shook my head. "It's okay. There's no reason to be. There's one thing I can give advice about," I said, laughing a little. "Don't be afraid to love, on the off chance that there might be pain."

"You mean, don't do what you're doing with Brennan?" she asked, quirking her eyebrow at me.

"That's different. I am still messed up over Nain. I can't give Brennan what he deserves. And he understands that."

"Right. Except that you actually very obviously love Brennan, even if you still love and miss your husband, and anyone who spends more than five seconds with the two of you knows how disgustingly perfect you are together."

I frowned, couldn't quite look her in the eye. "It's complicated."

"You two are complete idiots," she said. "If this is what love does, maybe I'm not in such a hurry after all," she said, shaking her head. I handed the waitress the money for our meal, and Shanti stood up and stretched. "I think I want a tattoo. Can we go?"

I sighed. "Sure. Happy birthday, you insufferable little brat." She laughed, and we headed back to the tattoo parlor we'd seen on the way over. I handed her a flask of blood I'd brought with me, and she guzzled it in the car before we went in.

I used a tiny bit of mental persuasion, and the two waiting customers decided to leave. We watched as the tattooist finished with his current customer.

"What are you getting?" I asked as she watched the process.

"A cross. On my wrist, I think," she said.

"Nice." I remembered the way she'd prayed when I found her what seemed like a lifetime ago, the way she'd said she believed that God sent me to her.

"You should get one too," she said.

"Not this time," I said.

I held Shanti's hand as the artist created an ornate cross on her left wrist. She hissed at first in pain, but she was all right after a while.

We drove home, and I was relieved that she seemed much more content than when we'd left. We went into the loft, and Shanti hugged me before heading up to her room.

"Happy birthday, kiddo," I murmured, hugging her back. She grinned, and once she was gone, I headed into Brennan's room to check on him. His breath was shallow, his forehead almost searingly hot. I got a cool cloth and pressed it to his forehead. He didn't even react to my touch.

I watched him. And I sat by his bedside. Just after dawn, my phone rang. The doctor from Toronto who was quarantined along with the Grosse Pointe shifters.

"Angel," he said, his voice hoarse, his breathing ragged across the connection.

"Doctor. How are the shifters holding up? Any progress?"

"I'm afraid, the opposite. We lost two last night. Everyone's condition, including mine, is worsening. I don't know how to fix this."

I closed my eyes, fought back the panic rising inside me. "I am sorry, doctor," I said, feeling the weight of two more deaths on my conscience, the impending doom of more. Almost paralyzing fear for Brennan.

"This seems very localized. I have been in contact with other doctors across the globe. No one else is seeing anything like this." He broke off in a coughing fit, and hung up with a strangled, "I am sorry."

I hung up and watched Brennan. "I will not lose you," I said to him. And I laid on the edge of the bed next to him, and put my arm around him, over his chest, and watched him sleep.

CHAPTER ELEVEN

I felt helpless. I stayed by Brennan as much as I could, and he eventually told me to go beat someone up, and I left him. I wasn't happy about it, though. I ended up making my way toward Grosse Pointe. Bash and Dahael were in the back seat, and Ada rode along with me. As we drove, she joked, and told me about things that had happened at different sites throughout the city as we passed them. Her cheerful, warm nature was a soothing balm, and I was glad she'd offered to come with me.

I glanced over at her. "Thanks for coming, Ada," I said.

She grinned at me. "Of course. I keep thinking I'm missing something with Brennan's illness. I've never seen anything like it, but there's a feeling to it....I can't describe it." She shook her head in frustration. "Anyway. Maybe by checking over a few more of the shifters, I'll get an idea of what's happening."

I nodded. Then I gave her a sly look. "Distract me. Tell me about what's going on between you and Stone."

She laughed, and it was girlish and embarrassed, and I

laughed a little, too. "Oh. You know…" she said, laughing again. Happiness washed over me, from her. Contentment. Love.

I couldn't help smiling. "You are so cute," I said.

She laughed again. "I ignored my feelings for him for so long," she said shaking her head.

"How long?"

"Oh, at least fifteen years."

I glanced at her, and she shrugged. "I wasn't ready. He and my husband had been friends, and it just felt wrong."

I looked back at the road in front of me. "Yeah."

"I regret that now. I could have had years of this happiness. I could have been loved, had a warm man in my bed at night instead of feeling so alone." I could feel her eyes on me.

"I don't need a lecture, Ades," I said, studiously keeping my eyes on the road.

"I'm not planning on giving you one. Hear me out on this: I knew Nain for over fifty years. Yes, he loved you. Adored you. Died trying to make sure you lived on. Do you really think he did all of that so you would be miserable and alone forever?"

"It's like disrespecting his memory to even think of loving someone else," I said quietly.

"Honey, I adore you, but that is just crazy. And you even saying that reminds me that you loved him, and he loved you, but the two of you really didn't know each other that well."

"He was jealous of Brennan when he was alive. We got into it at least once over him," I said, confiding something in Ada that I'd never said to anyone else.

"Yes. He was a demon. From what I understand, demons tend to be pretty territorial, yes?"

I nodded.

"Okay. But he was also, at his core, a good man. And you know that. Would he have wanted you to be miserable to satisfy some territorial bullshit on his behalf? Especially now that he's gone? He was the main one who told me I should give Stone a chance. And my late husband was one of his best friends when he was alive."

"I feel like I have no idea what I'm doing, or what I'm supposed to do, or anything," I said, jamming the car into park after I'd pulled into the driveway at the shifters' main residence. We sat there for several seconds.

"You're a good woman, Molly. You're the strongest, most caring, responsible person I've ever met. Stop thinking so damn much. And stop talking yourself out of what you know is right." She stopped, sighed. "You know, as well as anyone, that life is crazy. We only have right now. You have a good man by your side, one who would try to move heaven and earth if he thought it would make you happy. Life is fleeting, even for us supernatural freaks. You know this."

We were quiet for a bit. I took a breath. "We should go in."

"All right," she said, reaching over and patting my hand. We got out of the car and headed up to the porch. I rang the bell, and a young male shifter opened the door. When he recognized me, his eyes got huge, and he bowed, thumped a hand over his chest. I said hello, tried not to grimace. For some reason, the other supernaturals in the city had started adopting my imps' show of respect as their own. It freaked me out, more than a little. I did not deserve the respect or trust they had in me.

"We were hoping to see a few of the ill shifters," I said softly to him. "I understand you've had losses. I am so sorry," I said.

He looked up at me and nodded. "We lost two of our younger shifters last night. Children. We thought this thing would take the elders first, but the young seem to be succumbing more quickly. We lost another just a little before you arrived. He was in his thirties," he finished, walking up the stairs, leading us to the second floor. I asked him to describe the symptoms, and he did, recounting the same symptoms Brennan was showing. My gut twisted with worry. Shifters bowed, thumped their chests in deference as we passed, and I tried to make a point of saying hello, shaking hands.

"Anastasia's mother? How is she?" I asked, remembering the first shifter who'd contracted the illness.

Our guide shook his head. "She seems worse the last day or two. Her breathing is worse, and she's mostly delirious." He stopped, looked at me. "Based on what we saw with the ones we've lost, once they hit the delirious phase, it seems to progress rapidly. It's as if their innate strength as shifters gives out at that point, and it overtakes them." I could feel the helplessness, sadness from him. "When the doctor first arrived, we were hopeful. A few more of us had started showing symptoms. She seemed better at first, when the doctor gave her the first dose of antibiotics. But then it was all downhill."

"Have any of you tried shifting to stall the symptoms? I know Brennan is more resilient when he's in his animal form," I said, feeling stupid not to have thought of it before.

He nodded. "We thought the same thing. If anything, it makes it worse when we shift. It seems to speed up the process."

He showed us into a long room that seemed to be being used as a sick room. Six small cots lined the walls, nothing else in the room. "We have four rooms like this. We're trying to keep the sick shifters together, away from the rest. The healthy shifters are all living in the other house, and the sick have been moved here."

I looked at him. "So, you... ?"

He smiled grimly. "I started showing symptoms yesterday morning."

I nodded. I watched as Ada checked over the ill, talked to them in low tones. After a while, she turned to me, eyes bright with tears. She shook her head. She walked over to me. "This is beyond anything I know. Whatever this is, it is like nothing I've seen before. And I've seen a lot. I've healed a lot. I thought maybe getting an idea of how other shifters were responding would help me, but they all have symptoms identical to what I'm seeing in Brennan."

The young shifter nodded. "It's kind of creepy how exact the symptoms are. With the flu or something, you might see similar symptoms, but some will be worse in some people and not so bad in others. Two people can have the flu, but be experiencing varying levels of discomfort. This? You can almost set your watch by it: cough, fever, loss of appetite, sweating, chills, increased sleep, festering sores on the chest, delirium, infection of sores, death."

I looked around, and felt my fear about to drown me. Beating up monsters? I could do that. Living through massive explosions? Fine. There was not a damn thing I could do for this. There was no one I could rough up to make this better, and there was no one I could kill to end it. I wanted to tear my hair out in frustration and fear. All I could think about was Brennan.

We stayed a while longer, and I asked the shifter to call me if they needed anything at all. He thanked me for coming, and I felt like shit. I had done nothing for them. Nothing. These were my people, in my city, suffering, and I couldn't do a damn thing for them.

Ada and I drove home in silence. When we got there, she went to her room, saying she needed to meditate.

I want up to Brennan's room, stayed by his side through the rest of that day, into the night. The following day, I canceled appointments, sent Ada and Stone out on patrol, called in favors from those who owed me for help I'd given them. The city could survive without me for a little while. I was not leaving him.

He was mostly delirious. Fear gripped me, wouldn't let go. The fever just rose, and I constantly put cold cloths on his forehead, behind his neck. I made him drink when he did manage to wake up. I cursed the fact that here I was, a god, basically, and there was nothing I could do for him.

I stretched out on the bed, held him whenever I wasn't fruitlessly applying cold cloths to his head. He woke up, briefly, around midnight, slate blue eyes opening and finding me next to him.

"Molly," he said hoarsely.

"Hey," I said, running my hand over his forehead, through his hair. "I'm here."

"You're here," he murmured. "I love you."

I rested my forehead against his shoulder. I bit my lip against the sobs that wanted to escape. "You too," I whispered. He was already out again, and I stayed, holding him. After a while, I got up, wetted another cloth, pressed it to his burning forehead. I went to pull the sheets up to his throat again, and realized they were damp.

He'd soaked through them with his sweat. I pulled the old ones off to replace them with new, dry ones, and glanced at his bare chest. It rose and fell shallowly. I could hear each rattling breath he took. The long scar he'd gotten as a teenager stood, stark and painful looking on his now-pale skin. I stared when I noticed a tattoo. He hadn't had that before, but it had been months since I'd seen him without a shirt. On his chest, over his heart, an "M" in black; sharp thorns poking from the curves in the letter. "Brennan," I whispered, as I wiped my stupid, teary eyes.

I also noticed that he was starting to break out in oozing sores. I fought against the panic rising inside me. I washed them, rubbed them with antibiotic cream, and covered them with gauze, knowing it was pointless.

I covered him up after glancing at the tattoo again. I wondered when he'd gotten it. Wondered if he regretted it. I laid down next to him again, and held him, and willed him to be better. Heat just radiated from him, almost too hot for me to be comfortable near him. I stayed anyway.

I dozed off, until I felt power in the room, and saw Eunomia swoop in, black wings extended, and land at the foot of Brennan's bed.

CHAPTER TWELVE

I lost my mind.

"You are not taking him!" I screeched, launching myself at her and knocking her to the floor. I barely registered the look of shock on her face as we tumbled to the ground.

She struggled against me as I wrestled her down, held her there.

"Would you get a grip demon girl? What the Nether has gotten into you?" she asked.

"You can't take him. I won't let you," I said, and I felt my face crumple and sobs wracked my body. "You can't."

"I am not here to take him from you," Eunomia whispered. "My friend. I swear it. I am not taking him."

"Promise me. I can't lose him," I whispered.

"I promise. I promise," she said, soothing me even as I pinned her to the floor.

"I'm sorry," I said, climbing off of her and wiping at my tears. I helped her up, and she stood next to me, watching Brennan.

"Three shifters died yesterday," I said, trying to explain my reaction.

"And four more last night. We just collected the last. That was why I came to check on you." She continued to look at Brennan. "May I?" she asked. "I just want to feel him. I am not taking him," she reassured me again. "It is not his time. Not just yet, anyway."

I nodded, watching her like a hawk. She went to Brennan's bedside, put her hand on his forehead, his chest. She closed her eyes, and grimaced.

"Come. See if you can feel what I feel," she said. "Put your hand on his chest, and focus."

I closed my eyes, splayed my fingers over Brennan's chest. At first, I felt nothing. And then, I felt something familiar, something dark, something otherworldly. Blackness, vileness.

"What the hell is that?" I asked her, opening my eyes, keeping my hand on Brennan's chest.

"You feel it then? This is something that should not be," Eunomia said, watching Brennan with concern.

"What is it, E?"

"This is from my realm. Our realm."

"Something from the Nether caused this? Oh, god," I said, staring. "Did I cause this, somehow?"

"Not you. No. But something from our realm targeted your local shifters." She watched me. "I felt the same with the others."

"It's not a coincidence," I muttered.

"Especially considering that your beloved and closest confidant is a shifter, I'd say no," Eunomia said.

I grimaced a little at the "beloved" comment. Was I really so obvious? "Who could have done this?"

"There are beings. The Nosoi. Gods of sickness and pestilence. They do this type of thing, if the price is right."

"They are of the Nether?"

She nodded.

"You are going to take me to them," I said.

She shook her head. "It is unwise. We will tell your mother, and she will–"

"E. One of them probably knows who is targeting me. You are going to take me to them."

"And what about him?" Eunomia said, pointing at him. "Going to the Nosoi is not going to help him!"

"Damn it," I growled. I needed to hit something so badly I was about to burst.

Eunomia sighed. "I am not supposed to do this." Then, "have you tried your blood?"

"What?"

"Your blood, demon girl. It heals."

"My blood heals?"

"You are a god. Of course your blood heals," she said. "So much you do not know about yourself," she murmured, walking over to Brennan and pulling the gauze off of his sores. "There. Open wounds. Apply your blood to them."

I stared at her, and she gestured impatiently for me to do it. I took the small knife out of my pocket, sliced my wrist, and rubbed my blood over his wounds. I watched, and hoped, and within seconds, the sores started to close. I tried not to cry.

"It worked."

"Of course."

"He's still sick, though," I said.

"Yes. Your blood won't heal this thing inside of him. It will heal the surface wounds, which seem to eventually lead to further infection, and then the shifters die from that even if whatever is inside doesn't kill them first. You can keep him alive longer."

"But we need to get rid of this."

"Yes. This was caused by gods. It will take another god to fix it."

"Who? Can you bring someone?"

"I cannot. But you should be able to summon some help."

"How?"

She watched me. "It's time to start listening to yourself, Fury. Be still. Instinct will take over. Trust yourself, and do what needs to be done." And with that, she blinked out of sight.

"Thanks. That was a huge fucking help, E," I muttered.

I sat on the bed next to Brennan's sleeping form, and I took his hand in mine (suddenly finding it impossible to stop touching him) and I closed my eyes. I tried to clear my mind, tried to listen, as Eunomia had said, even though I had no idea what I was listening for.

I don't know how long I sat there, but eventually, a name came to me: Asclepias.

I thought his name, over and over, a litany that I hoped would save Brennan and the other shifters affected.

After a while, words came to me, ancient and previously unknown to me. They felt right, and I murmured them:

Hear me, Asclepias,

God of healing,

he who protects the ill

and blesses the healers.

Hear me, Asclepias,

Heed my call,

Heal my loved ones,

Right the wrongs,

Help me turn the tides.

Hear me, Asclepias…

I whispered it until my mouth was dry, until I felt like I'd used every bit of energy within me, until my soul was raw, and I had no idea if it did a damn thing.

I stayed at Brennan's side. Watched him breathe, more and more raggedly. Watched him sweat, heard him moan in pain. I checked his body for sores, healed them as they appeared. The entire time, I thought Asclepias' name.

I settled myself next to him, wrapped my arm around him, watched Brennan as if watching was enough to keep anything else from harming him. He thrashed a bit as he dreamed and the pain and delirium only made it worse.

"I am not letting you go, Brennan," I whispered. "I will chase you through the fucking Nether if I have to, and I will drag your ass back here and we will figure out what this is between us. But I am not letting you go."

I continued to hold him, and heal his sores when they appeared. I was arranging his blankets around him again, when it suddenly felt as if all of the air had been sucked out of the room. Power roared over me, so strong it made my stomach turn, made me shiver uncontrollably.

I turned, keeping my body between Brennan and whatever this was now.

The being before me stood around seven feet tall. Skin that absorbed the meager light in the room. His eyes glowed white, like mine, and huge, black feathered wings sprouted from his muscular back. He wore a long black robe. His face was both frightening, due to the intensity of his gaze, and achingly beautiful. He watched me.

"Hello, little Fury," he said in a voice older than time itself. I could barely breathe.

I bowed. "You are not Asclepias," I said softly, feeling my power respond to him, welcome him.

"Rise, Fury. You bow to no one."

I rose, and I watched him.

"I am not Asclepias. I am known by many names. I am Hel, and Lucifer, and Osiris. I am Pluto, Mictlantecuhtli, San La Muerte. Some simply refer to me as the Devil Himself. I prefer Hades."

I stared. "Oh, shit." It left my lips before I even thought, and I clamped my hands, horrified, over my mouth.

Hades laughed, and the building shook. He stopped, looked around. "Your mortal dwellings are not made for me," he said.

I just stared some more, hands still clamped over my mouth. He watched me. "So, little Fury. Mollis. Your mother has told me about you. It is a pleasure to meet one of my own."

I nodded, still unable to speak, though I did drop my hands back down to my sides.

"I heard your call. Asceplias is unlikely to hear your summons in time. Those of the Aether don't live with the immediacy those of us from the Nether do." He looked around me toward Brennan. "The Furies are in pursuit of the Nosoi now. This will be avenged."

I watched him. "Can you fix him?"

He studied me. "You know that the dead are my domain. The Nether. Healing is of no interest to me." My stomach sank. "However, you are a Fury, and valuable, and I am the Devil Himself, after all."

"So," he said, smiling at me, "shall we make a deal?"

I nodded.

"You will work for me, as your mother and aunts do, as a Fury. You will be present when I meet with other gods. In exchange, I will have Asclepias come here and heal him, as well as any others affected by the Nosoi and their nonsense."

I studied him. "May I ask a question?"

He nodded.

"Did you do all of this? Did you send the demon after me last year? Are they breaking through because of you? Did you put the Nosoi up to this?"

He smiled. "My dear, do you think I'd have to play games if I decided I wanted you?"

I dropped my gaze. "But making a deal is not beneath you?"

He laughed. "I enjoy making deals."

"Do you know who has been after me?"

I felt irritation, frustration from him. "I do not, little Fury. Your mother has filled me in, and it angers me greatly that someone in my realm is involved. We will find out who is playing these dangerous games."

I nodded, looked back up at him. "You could have just

forced me to come and work for you, couldn't you?"

"Yes. I could have tried." He sat in the chair next to Brennan's bed, looked at him for a moment. "I have watched gods, humans, and other creatures for eons. Do you know what I love best about them?"

I shook my head.

"Their ability to choose. When you see which choices, which decisions, a being makes, you see what is truly meaningful to them. They may say many things, but the choices they make let you see their souls."

"And what do you see in me?"

He was quiet for a moment. "I see that you will go to any means to protect those you care about. And that you care about many. I see that there is nothing you would not sacrifice to keep those you love, especially this shifter, safe."

"So you want me to take my official role as a Fury. And you want me to be present when you meet with other gods," I said, looking up at him. "Are we making a point?"

A smile quirked the corners of his mouth. "Possibly. What point do you think we make?"

"That you're the one who has the godkiller," I said softly. "Hades, as he is, is fearfully powerful. Hades, with a godkiller in his service…"

"Is even more terrifying, yes," he said mildly. "You may not believe me, but I want you in my service more to protect everyone than anything else."

I looked up at him, and I knew he could see the skepticism in my gaze. He smiled again. "Think, little Fury. At least a few gods know what you are. Likely, we deal with minor gods, otherwise we wouldn't be here speaking to each other right now. My guess? Gods who are tied to either the Nether or the Aether, or they would have come after you more directly here in the mortal realm. Those gods crave power. They would use you as a weapon, to gain that power. We would have war, death." He paused. "But, if it is clear that you belong to me, they would have to be stupid to try to take you or use you."

"So. I would be spending a lot of time in the Nether."

"Likely. Yes."

"I have responsibilities here, Hades. People who need me."

"So you do not want our deal?" he asked, watching me.

"I would like an addendum," I said. He grinned.

"We shall see. What is it you want?"

"I ask that he and the other shifters be healed. And I ask for protection for him. Someone knows how important he is to me. He will be targeted again. You claim no one will come at me directly once you make it known that I serve you. I'm willing to risk myself. But they will still target those close to me, as they have been for over two years now. That... I'm not willing to risk it anymore."

"That is something I cannot give you. I have already tampered with Fate by agreeing to save those destined for death, including this shifter. If he is destined to die at the hands of your enemies, I will not stop it from happening."

I nearly growled in frustration.

"However, there is something *you* can do to protect him," Hades said.

I looked at him, waiting.

"Claim him."

"Meaning?"

"Claim him as yours. You forget that you are a powerful god in your own right. You would have the right to severely punish anyone who tried to take or harm what is yours. You would know if he was in danger, or injured. You would be able to find him, no matter how far apart you are."

"How would others know he was claimed?"

"We'd be able to sense it. Even Earth-bound beings, would feel your claim on him. It's almost a visible thing. It's not common, because we gods are so far removed from the lives of mortals."

"Will it hurt him?"

"No. It will make him stronger. Less susceptible to magic, illness. Harder to kill."

"Will he know I've claimed him?" I asked, realizing it was something Brennan would never agree to, if it required any type of sacrifice on my behalf.

"No."

"How do I do it?"

"You are a god. Listen to yourself, little Fury."

"Why does everyone keep telling me that today?" I said in frustration.

Hades smiled. "Because it is the truth. And because you need to learn to believe in yourself."

"You make it sound so simple," I murmured, looking at Brennan again.

"Because it is. Do we have a deal, Mollis Cithaerus?" Hades asked, and I noted a bit of a sneer as he said the name. He reached his hand toward me. "I have him and the other shapeshifters healed, and you take your place among the Furies and attend me when I request it. When not attending to those duties, you shall dwell here in the mortal realm."

I nodded, put my hand in his huge, strong grip. "We have a deal, Lord Hades," I whispered.

He smiled. "Excellent. I will send Asclepias to you immediately. And I will inform your mother of your decision." He nodded, then disappeared, as if he'd never been there at all.

I went back to Brennan, brushed his hair back from his face. I'd just made a deal with the Devil Himself. I was about to lose a good portion of any freedom I'd had to run my life the way I wanted to. I'd have to find a way to keep everyone safe here, while fulfilling my duties in the Nether. I didn't know how I would manage it, already overwhelmed at the prospect.

I ran my hand over Brennan's cheek, the coarse hair of his beard.

Totally worth it.

♦♦♦

I was healing Brennan's sores again when I felt a presence enter the room, looked up to see my prayers answered. A god. Clearly. He was kindly looking, with a long white beard and a shock of curly white hair that trailed down the back of his light blue robes. He carried a cracked, ancient-looking leather bag in his hands. In every way that Hades had been terrifying, this being was comforting.

I stood up, bowed to the being. He was insanely powerful. His power was different from mine. Warmer, brighter.

"Mollis. It is a pleasure, my dear. I wish we could have met under different circumstances. I am Asclepias, and I have come at Hades' request."

"Likewise," I said, taking his hand in mine and shaking it. "There are no words to express my gratitude." His skin was warm, almost hot, against mine. "You're not of the Nether," I said.

He smiled. "No. I am from the Aether. I am a friend to you, Fury."

I nodded. "Can you fix him?" I asked, and I hated how childish, how vulnerable I sounded.

"Let's have a look, shall we?" he said, and I stood aside and he approached the bed. He uncovered Brennan, started running his hands over Brennan's body, specifically his chest, and I heard a low hum coming from the god.

As he did it, I felt Eunomia enter the room again. "Well done, demon girl," she murmured. She stood next to me and took my hand. "Your aunts are tracking down the Nosoi," she said quietly as we watched Asclepias check Brennan over. "Your mother is at the gateway. There is another disturbance there. A group got through and slayed the guards we had there. The other guards managed to fight them back, but there are at least three demons roaming your city."

I shook my head. Knew I should go hunt them down before they could hurt anyone. Eunomia seemed to read what I was thinking. "Stay. That demon you showed mercy to? Levitt. He is hunting them. He's been keeping an eye on the area as well."

I breathed a sigh of relief, nodded. I really should check in and see if Levitt needed anything. I made a mental note of it. Later.

Brennan woke after Asclepias had been working at him for a few minutes, and I could hear him softly conversing with the god. After a while, Asclepias nodded. Then he turned to me. "You'll want to get a basin of some kind, my dear. This is going to be messy."

I went down to the kitchen and grabbed the small garbage can we used for recyclables, and brought it back into the room. Asclepias was running his hands over Brennan's back. Bren was sitting upright in bed, legs over the side of the mattress, eyes closed. I could feel the power emanating from Asclepias, and I bowed my head in wonder and gratitude.

"Give him the basin," Asclepias murmured, still focusing.

I handed Brennan the garbage pail, and he took it, eyes still closed. I watched as Asclepias continued to run his hands over Brennan's back, rubbing some kind of spicy, herbal salve over his skin. The healer god's power only increased, and the room thrummed with it. After a few minutes, Brennan heaved, and retched, and threw up reddish-black grossness into the trash can. It seemed to go on forever, and though he was in pain, I could feel him getting stronger again as it left his body.

After a few minutes of retching, Brennan slumped forward. I grabbed the can, and Asclepias caught Brennan and settled him back against the pillows. I took the can into the bathroom.

"If I flush this, is it going to hurt anyone?" I asked Asclepias.

"No, my dear. It's quite all right. Now that it has been expelled from his body, it has lost all of its more dangerous qualities."

I nodded, flushed it, and came back into the bedroom. Asclepias was running his hands over Bren's chest again, and then he nodded, satisfied. Brennan was lying in bed now. His breathing was steady, and he already had some color to him again. I put my hand on his forehead, and he was not feverish or clammy.

I turned to Asclepias. "I cannot thank you enough," I said, bowing to him.

"It was my pleasure, my dear. I will see to the rest of your shifters while I am here."

"There are a few dozen of them."

He smiled. "I am a god. I have all the time in the world."

I smiled at him. "That seemed really nasty," I said, leading him out of Brennan's room, glancing back at Brennan's sleeping form.

He nodded. "It was, as you say, nasty. As you saw, there was quite a lot of it in your friend. That much would have killed a weaker man days ago. Astonishing he fought it this long, really. It starts as nothing, and grows, and makes it impossible to breathe, essentially suffocating the shifter from the inside. Very bad," he said, shaking his head. "I am ashamed that one of our kind caused this. I hope whichever of the Nosoi did it is punished, severely."

"Oh, they will be," I said, as mildly as possible, even as my need for vengeance roared through me.

We reached the main floor of the loft, and I called Anastasia over at the Grosse Pointe shifters headquarters to alert her to Asclepias' imminent arrival and to tell her that he'd cured Brennan. She was happy, and promised me she wouldn't let anyone freak out when Ascelpias appeared.

I thanked Asceplias over and over again before he left, and then went up to Brennan's room. I ran my hand through his hair, down his cheek, and he nuzzled his face into my touch in his sleep. I stretched out next to him on the bed.

I watched him. And one word came to me: mine.

As terrified as I was of loving anyone again, as sure as I was that we would be a mistake, I couldn't ignore my feelings for him anymore. Everything, including Nain's blood still flowing through my veins, told me it was wrong. Why did my crazy, foolish heart keep insisting it was right, even when I tried to talk myself out of loving him?

Mine.

I moved my hand from his face, and placed it over his heart, felt it beat, strong and steady, under my palm. He rested easily now. It would take some time to regain the strength he'd lost. But he was safe. And I would make sure he stayed that way.

I decided to do what Hades said: I let instinct, whatever inner knowledge had prompted me to ask for Asclepias, take over. I would claim him. I would keep him safe.

I closed my eyes again, keeping my hand over his heart. I rid my mind of everything else, thought only of him. I don't know how long I stayed that way. Memories flooded over me, a million moments of warmth and love between us, the many ways he'd saved me, protected my heart over the time we'd known each other.

I felt warmth inside of me. Bright, beautiful, like the sun.

Mine. Mine. Mine, pulsed in my mind, in my soul, in time with the beat of his heart under my hand.

Mine. Mine. Mine.

The warmth grew, and I felt the moment I'd fully claimed him. A warmth entered my soul, brightened all the dark corners of me, the places I tried to hide. Brennan, in his purest form. I felt tears leak from under my closed eyelids. I felt him, so clearly, as if there was a delicate, yet unbreakable chain linking his soul to mine. I couldn't hear his thoughts. I still felt his emotions. But now, more than anything else....now I felt Brennan.

And he was more beautiful, more magical than I'd ever imagined.

I sat there, reveling in the sensation of having his soul linked to mine. I knew I should have felt guilty for doing this without asking him first. If this saved him from pain or danger even once between now and then, it was worth it.

Mine.

Yeah. Ada had been right. Demons were territorial. If what I was feeling at that moment was any indication, though, demons had nothing on Furies.

Mine.

I opened my eyes, and watched him as he slept, and eventually felt my eyes drooping. I laid down next to him, dozed, feeling his heart beat in perfect time with mine.

Eunomia appeared not long after, breaking the peace.

"Mollis, they're fighting to get through again. We need you now, girl."

I cursed, and Eunomia grabbed me. "This will be unpleasant," she warned, and we were not flying. Instead, we seemed to fall apart and pull ourselves back together seconds later in the Packard plant.

"So that's how you get everywhere so quickly," I muttered. "Handy."

She grinned and disappeared again, going back to the Nether, and I started fighting. The stress over Brennan, my anger over being pulled away from him when by his side was where I really wanted to be, my desire to find and punish whoever had hurt him, all of it combined, and I felt my body nearly splitting at the seams with righteous, white hot rage. I exploded, much as I had on the night Nain died, unleashing my powers and reducing the dozen or so demons around me to dust.

I was not finished yet.

I stared, felt the gateway pulling for me. And this time I gave in. I leaped through. I wouldn't wait anymore to see who else they would hurt, which of my loved ones they would target next. They wanted me so badly? Fine.

Time to take the fight to them.

CHAPTER THIRTEEN

When I arrived in the Nether, there was no time to think. I came out into a mob of angry, fighting demons and gods. I slashed out at demons, set more than a few ablaze, turned others to ash. It was easy for me to distinguish between the troublesome demons and those who worked to fight them. The problem demons all wore collars, chokers of heavy chain; the guards wore black uniforms, not unlike what I'd seen on my mother.

The fighting went on, only more furiously once the demons realized who and what I was. I stabbed one, gutting it. Here, I felt my power soar, as if the Nether welcomed me home with open arms. A demon rushed me, and I smiled, and felt power travel down my arm. I looked at my hand and saw a flaming sword, much like the one my mother wielded. But mine had a flame of blue, and it was long, thin, and deadly. I smiled wider, and slashed.

The sword was part of me, and I used it as naturally as breathing. The first few unsuspecting demons were cut down before they realized what was happening. The others, seeing what was happening, tried to run back to the prison they had been trying to escape.

They did not get far. I chased them, cut them down without remorse or hesitation. When the last one was gone, I stood amid dozens of fallen demons, sword in hand, blue flames casting everything around me in an eerie, ghoulish light.

The Nether was silent around me. The demon guards watched me with respect, fisted their hands and thumped their chests, much as my imps did. There were gods, and they watched me with a mixture of awe, fear, and anger. My mother landed directly in front of me.

She smiled at me, and pride coursed through her.

"My brothers and sisters of the Nether, may I present my daughter, servant of Lord Hades himself, the Fury Mollis Cithaerus."

The assembled gods also bowed in respect to me, some, more grudgingly than others, and I bowed back to them, keeping my eyes on my mother and the two goddesses who flanked her. My mother smiled, and so did they.

"Welcome home, daughter. I have a gift for you."

I raised my eyebrow, and she smiled again.

"Shall we go interrogate a Nosoi?" She asked, and my aunts, the other Furies beside her, both grinned at me, feral, frightening grins that I knew mirrored my own.

"Mother, it would be an absolute pleasure," I said, and I walked with my mother and my aunts, the Furies, through the throngs of demons and gods, and all I could think about was vengeance.

I didn't spare much attention for my surroundings. I registered that the sky was amethyst, that the trees were blackish-gray shapes that rose into that alien sky. Demons were everywhere, in all shapes, sizes and colors, going about their daily life as if this was any other city.

My mother and aunts led me to a large building made of shiny black stone. My mother took a moment to introduce me to my aunts, Megaera and Alecto. They both looked like my mother, except that Alecto was shorter, curvier, and Megaera had a seriousness to her that even my mother lacked.

"This is our home, our workplace," my mother said, leading me and my aunts down a hallway. She unlocked a door, and we were in a dark room, empty except for an angry little being sitting on a stool in a corner. I sensed for her, and knew her instinctively to be a god. I looked at my mother.

"Nosoi," she murmured, affirming my thoughts. "We questioned several of them. This is the one who transferred the shifter plague to those in your realm." I looked back at the Nosoi, who was about my height, but very thin and delicate looking, almost elfish. She had a short cap of black hair, eyes that glowed yellow, skin the color of putty. She glared at me, made some kind of gesture which I could guess was meant to insult me. "She's all yours, darling," my mother told me.

Just don't kill her, she said in my mind.

Does she know I'm not allowed to kill her?

My mother smiled, just a little. *No, she does not.*

I got to work. It wasn't pretty. I found myself doing something very similar to what I'd done to the demon, Branford, after he'd tried to kill me. I manipulated her thoughts, put her in extreme pain without ever having to touch her. I hadn't realized, back when I'd destroyed Branford, that this was something only Furies could do. Handy.

Before long, she was broken, and revealed all she knew: she was the weakest of the Nosoi. The god, a minor god who had disguised his or her true nature from her, promised her respect and power if she did this favor. Brennan was the target, because taking him from me would weaken me beyond repair. I dug hard at her regarding that point. All she knew was that it was more than simply that I cared for him. From her understanding,

I needed him in order to succeed. She didn't know why, but that was what the god had told her. They became frustrated when they couldn't get to him because he was always with me. So the Nosoi had bided her time, and planted the illness in the most prominent local shifter family, figuring Brennan would come into contact with them eventually, and she'd succeed that way.

Well, she nearly did.

Remembering how close I'd come to losing him, how he'd looked as he drifted in and out of consciousness nearly made me lose any control I had. I came very close to killing her, despite my mother's warnings. I was on the brink, between causing her pain and ending her completely. My aunts and mother had to pull me away, break my connection to her to prevent me from doing it. My mother hugged me, sent me home, telling me we'd talk soon.

I left, still tasting the Nosoi's soul. It would have been good to destroy her. Maybe another day.

◆◆◆

I walked out of the gateway, through the factory, nodding at the demon guards as they bowed to me, thumped their fists to their chests. Back in my own realm, I trembled with the aftershocks of the adrenaline that had run through me with the Nosoi, and I was sickened at how easily it would have been for me to lose control. I took deep breaths, tried to get myself straight again before going home.

I got into my car and sped toward the loft. I glanced at my watch. Just after midnight. It had been at least an entire day since I'd left. I hadn't meant to be gone that long, but time passed differently in the Nether. There, I didn't notice the hours passing.

Mostly because I was in full vengeance-lust mode during my time there.

I hoped Brennan was okay. I had thought of him almost constantly, still reveling at the feeling of his soul linked to mine. Part of me hoped he was awake so I could talk to him. Part of me was nervous about seeing him again now that I'd admitted to myself how much I needed him. How much I (yes) loved him.

I parked, took the elevator up to the loft. I looked down at myself. Bloody and gross, as usual. Freaking demons. I sighed. When I unlocked the door, I could hear the television in the living room, saw that the lamps were still on. Brennan was sitting in one of the recliners, dressed in his usual jeans and white t-shirt.

He looked good.

Not just healthy, which he was. He looked…like the best thing I'd ever seen.

He stood up and walked toward me, blue gaze taking in every detail as he approached me.

I ran a hand through my hair. "Hey," I said. "You look so much better." I saw the grossness on my arm, dropped it back down to my side. "I'm a mess," I muttered, suddenly unsure what to do with my hands or where to look, or how to breathe past the way my heart pounded. He stopped in front of me, watched me, silent, his gaze warm, a hint of a smile quirking at the corner of his mouth.

"I'm glad you're home," he said softly.

"Me too."

"E came to check on me while you were gone. She told me you were all right and not to worry. As if that's even possible."

I nodded.

"She told me other things, too."

I just watched him.

"She told me that you tried to kill her when you thought she was coming for me." His gaze bored into mine. "She told me that you summoned a powerful god to heal me. She told me that you used your own blood to keep me strong, that you didn't leave my side until you knew I was all right."

"E has a big mouth," I muttered.

He smiled a little. "I remember waking up next to you. In your arms."

I nodded, and we stood in awkward silence for several long moments.

He looked at me, his gaze raking over my face, as if he was taking in every detail. "Do you have any idea how completely beautiful you are?" he asked softly.

I shook my head, let out a short, nervous laugh. "Yeah, I'm a real dreamgirl," I said, looking down.

"You have no idea," he said. He closed the last small gap between us, put his fingertips under my chin.

"I think we should talk. I..." I met his eyes again, and I was lost.

"I think I'm done talking, Molly," he murmured, and I shivered. I stopped breathing as he closed in.

Oh gods he's going to kiss me.

I shouldn't let him. This is dumb. Bad idea. I am only going to mess this up.

But the second his warm, soft lips met mine, all the arguments were washed away. His kiss was sweet, and slow, and tender, and it brought something to life inside of me. His hands were on either side of my neck, thumbs tracing my jawline. He kissed me in a way that made me feel precious, beautiful, as if I was the only thing in the world.

I kissed him back, meeting lips, tongue; focusing on kissing him with just as much care as he was kissing me. He moaned, deep in his throat, and it sent a shiver through my body.

He feathered a few more kisses across my lips, the corners of my mouth, and then stepped back, running his fingertips down my arms as he released me.

I was dizzy. Actually physically dizzy. I looked down, felt my face burning. My heart was racing. I could feel his racing, too, through the connection I'd made with him.

"Molly," he murmured, putting his hand under my chin and gently forcing my gaze back up to his.

"I..."

"What?"

"I don't think I can do this," I whispered.

"I know." And then he lowered his lips to mine again, kissed me in the same achingly tender, slow, deep way as his thumbs trailed up and down my throat. I put my arms around his waist, leaned into him.

I'd always thought the whole "knee-weakening kiss" phenomenon was a joke, until Brennan stood there and showed me otherwise.

He devoured my mouth like I was the most delicious thing on Earth, and he was planning to savor every last taste. He sucked and nibbled my lower lip and had me clinging to him, sighing, pulse racing. When he finally pulled away my whole body was weak, and I felt like I was on fire.

I felt it down to my toes.

We stood there and for just a while, I stopped thinking about anything but the two of us. I had my arms around his waist, leaning into him. His hands were at my hips, and his thumbs rubbed gentle circles at my hipbones. I rested my forehead against his chest, and he rested his chin on the top of my head. I was at peace and on fire, all at the same time, and it scared the hell out of me, but right then, there was nowhere I'd rather have been.

"So. What have you been up to?" he asked me.

I laughed a little, and he did too. I stood there in his arms and told him all about the gateway and Furies, about Hades and his deal, about the Nosoi, about the way I'd punished her, the way I'd barely held myself together. I poured my soul out to him the way I always had, I realized. Being in his arms was comforting and distracting all at the same time. His fingers traced up and down my hips the entire time as he listened to me.

Being Brennan, the fact he focused on was that I was in danger now that everyone knew what I was. And the fact that I'd given up freedom.

"You shouldn't have done that," he said softly.

"You would have done the same for me," I said, breathing him in. "And I would have ended up doing a lot of this anyway. I want to. Even if I didn't, it would have been worth it."

"Now everyone knows what you are."

I nodded against him. "Tisiphone and Hades both think the best thing was to just put it out there," I said against his chest. "Kind of a big 'fuck you' to whoever is trying to get to me. It seems like the best plan. If they want to come at me, they'll have to do it with everyone knowing what I am and who I serve."

He was quiet for a minute, thinking. "It makes sense. Now anyone who moves against you, even knowing what you are, risks pissing off any gods allied with the Furies and Hades. Which, I'd imagine, would be a lot."

I hugged him a little tighter. I'd just told him a whole bunch of new, crazy shit, and he'd barely batted an eyelid. My rock. "I think so. I don't know though. Maybe everyone hates Hades and the Furies," I finally said. "I feel so clueless. It's like having to converse in a language I've never spoken."

"You're a Fury," he said, after a few seconds, as if it was just now fully hitting him.

I looked up at him. "Do not sound like that."

"Like what?"

"All in awe of me and shit. I'm me, and that's all."

He bent his head down and kissed me again, sending shockwaves through my body. He pulled me closer to him, pressed my body to his and I could feel his heart pounding in his chest, felt his love, need roar over me. Then he pulled away, kissed my jawline, just under my ear. "I was already in awe of you," he whispered, and his breath tickled my earlobe and I felt warm all the way to my core.

I couldn't even come up with a response before he kissed me again, and I surrendered to it, completely.

◆◆◆

It took every bit of strength I had to pull myself out of Brennan's arms and go to my own room. He was intoxicating, and his kisses were already proving to be addictive. But I did, and I slept.

And I dreamt of Nain.

Over and over again. Flashes, partial memories of what we had been, nightmares about him angry with me. A particularly heartbreaking dream in which he was drowning, and I was the only one who could save him, and I left him there, hearing him roaring my name as I walked away.

I sat up, breathing hard, sweating. I took deep breaths, tried to calm myself down. I put my face in my hands and tried to stop picturing the dream I'd just had.

Of course, I knew logically that the nightmares were because I was feeling guilty over not only the kisses I'd shared with Brennan the night before, but more, the effect they'd had on me. Kissing Nain had been passionate, hot, almost violent. His kisses had turned me on, without a doubt.

I thought that was it. I expected the same reaction when Brennan kissed me. But his kisses had been soul-shattering, toe-curling, mind-numbing. Like a slow fire that spread from my lips to the rest of my body, until I was consumed. Immediate connection, at the deepest level.

I put my fingers to my lips, closed my eyes, remembering. My heart pounded at the idea of seeing him again. I looked at the ceiling, as if I could see up into his room above mine.

I wondered, if I felt all of this from a kiss, what he could do to the rest of my body. I blushed and tried to shove the thought away. I flopped onto my stomach, pulled my pillow over my head. My stupid body was still thrumming from just the memory of being in his arms.

I tried to go back to sleep. Tried thinking of nothing. Tried counting sheep. I ended up reliving either Brennan's kisses or my dreams about Nain, no matter what else I tried to force my mind to focus on.

I gave up after a while, got up and showered and dressed. Told myself I wasn't paying more attention to my appearance than usual. I was only wearing lip gloss because my lips were dry.

Right.

I started to leave my room, figuring I'd check my messages and figure out what immediate disasters I'd need to deal with that day before heading into the Nether to meet with my mother and aunts. I was about to open my bedroom door when I felt him out in the loft. I felt a flush rise to my skin, closed my eyes and tried to settle myself down.

"Stop acting like a pre-teen girl with a crush. You're the daughter of gods, for Christ sake," I muttered to myself. I took a breath and opened the door, walked out into the loft. Brennan was in the kitchen, making coffee. Jeans, t-shirt that fit him better than seemed fair. I couldn't take my eyes off of him, though I did try. And when he turned and looked at me, and grinned, I felt a ridiculous blush rise to my cheeks.

"Good morning," he said, smiling at me.

I stopped a couple of feet away from him. "Hey." I glanced up at him. He was still smiling at me, and he winked when I looked at him. I looked away. "You're up early."

"So are you," he said.

"Did I wake you up?"

"Maybe."

"You should go back to sleep. We were up late last night."

"Only if you come with me," he said, and I could hear

the smile in his voice, even though I was still doing my best to avoid looking at him. Damn blushing.

I gave a little laugh, and he stepped closer to me.

"Look at me, Molly," he murmured. And I did.

His eyes met mine. God, he was mesmerizing.

"That's better," he said. "Did you sleep all right?"

"Not really."

"Me neither," he said.

"Brennan?"

"Yeah?"

"Can you kiss me again?"

He lowered his lips to mine, and it was just as soul-shattering as it had been the night before. Hot, sweet, sensual, soft, and insistent all at the same time. He put his arms around me, and I clung to him. His hands ran up and down my spine as he kissed me, over my backside, and when he cupped my behind in his big hands and pulled me closer to his body, I whimpered.

"Oh, I like that sound," he murmured.

I clenched my thighs together against the heat pooling there. After a while, he pulled back, slowly. The desire, white-hot need pouring off of him only added to everything else I was feeling.

He kissed my cheek, my jawline, then kissed his way down to where my pulse raced at the base of my throat, and a small moan escaped my lips. After laving that spot with attention for a bit, he finally stepped back. His eyes met mine again.

"This is going to be an adjustment," he said, and his voice was hoarse and husky.

"Yeah?" I could barely breathe.

"Now that I've kissed you, it's all I want to do. Even more so than before," he said, and he smiled down at me.

I smiled, felt a bit of a blush rise to my face. "I don't think you're going to get much of an argument from me," I said.

He leaned down and kissed me one more time, briefly,

just a brushing of his lips over mine. "Guess there's a first time for everything, huh?" he murmured against my mouth before he pulled away again.

I laughed and shoved him. He laughed, too, then went to get me a cup of coffee. We sat in the living room, on the couch. He pulled my legs onto his lap, and I turned toward him, unable, now, to get enough of the sight of him. We sat, and went over the day ahead, the meetings I had scheduled. His hand ran up and down my leg, from my knee to my toes, then back up. Light pressure, a massage, and when he massaged the back of my calves, touched the area behind my knee, I gasped and the sensation went straight between my legs. He laughed a little, kept talking about meetings as if nothing was happening.

When he did it again, I bit my lip against the sensation, and he laughed again.

"You're doing that on purpose," I said, smacking his hand away.

"Doing what?" he asked innocently.

"You know damn well what you're doing," I said, laughing and taking my legs off of his lap.

He grinned. "There's a certain advantage to being involved with a shifter who's bonded himself to you, Ms. Brooks."

"Oh?" I asked, knowing my face was burning.

"I know when you're tired, or hungry, or in pain," he said, running his hand through my hair, resting it at the back of my neck. Then he leaned in. "The other side applies, too. I know when you're feeling good. I know when something I'm doing drives you crazy with need. My body is completely attuned to yours."

I just stared at him, involuntarily clenched my thighs together. He noticed (of course) and laughed. "Why do you think divorce is so rare among bonded shifters?" he asked, grinning.

He stood up, leaned down to kiss me. "Better focus,

Molly. Your first appointment will be here in a few minutes."

I grabbed his shirt, held him close to me. "I love you, Brennan," I whispered.

He grinned, and I felt pure happiness from him. "I know you do. I was just waiting for you to admit how crazy you are about me," he said, laughing when I smacked him. "I love you too." Then he kissed me again and walked away, and I tried not to stare at him as he did. I failed.

I managed to get through my first several meetings with the appropriate amount of seriousness and acting like a badass. In between, increasingly toe-curling kisses from Brennan that left me breathless and needy.

The man was going to kill me. But I had a feeling I'd go out smiling.

Once I'd taken care of the few things I had to deal with, I got ready to head to the Nether for my meeting. Brennan kissed me, told me to be careful, like he always did, and I could feel how much it bothered him that I was going back. He wasn't the only one.

♦♦♦

When I arrived in the Nether, via the gateway, it was much calmer than it had been the day before. Demon guards in their black uniforms lined the walls around the Pit, guarded the tunnel between the Pit and the gateway. They bowed and thumped their chests in respect as I passed, and I greeted them. Or, I tried to. I was mesmerized by my surroundings. I'd taken in only the barest of details during my last visit. This time, I studied everything. The amethyst sky, those blackish, grayish trees. The buildings were a jumble of architectural styles, mostly I guess what we'd call Gothic style architecture in the mortal realm, but with a good mix of classical Greek and Roman architecture mixed in. Statues of the various gods of the Nether were a regular sight as I walked the road between the Pit and the residence of the Furies. I guessed even the gods enjoyed having their egos stroked.

Maybe even more than mortals did.

I arrived at the large black building I'd been in the previous day. It was simple, very stark and plain in appearance. I knocked on the heavy door, which was some kind of ebony wood. I waited.

After a few moments, Alecto answered, greeting me with a small smile. She took my hand and led me in.

"Lovely to see you again, my dear," she said in a soft voice.

"Thank you. Likewise," I said. I let her lead me through the house, down the long hallway we'd gone down the last time. This time, however, she led me through a door on the right.

I almost laughed when I took in the room she'd led me into. This was clearly the Furies' living area. We were in a living room that instantly made me think of a 1980s music video. Pink and purple everything, including low, modern-looking sofas covered in what looked like bright pink velvet. Pillows were everywhere. The carpet was dark purple. There were posters on the walls: Michael Jackson, Cyndi Lauper, Joan Jett. I stared, and I didn't even realize my jaw had dropped until Alecto laughed. I tore my gaze away from the 80s vomit that was my family's living room, and looked at her.

"We enjoyed the 1980s," she said with a shrug. "Especially Megaera. Don't get her started on Richard Marx."

"Are you speaking of my love, the only man I'd ever give my virginity to?" a voice said behind us, and Megaera entered the room, followed by my mother.

I couldn't help it. I burst out laughing, and I couldn't stop. I bent double, and tears started streaming down my cheeks. It was like a crazy, alcohol or drug-induced dream. I was standing in this room with probably the three most terrifying beings I'd ever met, and they were fangirling over Richard Marx and their house looked like three teenage girls lived there. I heard them laughing, too, mostly over my reaction.

I tried to get myself under control, and only succeeded in erupting in another fit of giggles. My mother came over to me, laughing, and led me over to one of the pink sofas. I took deep breaths, wiped my eyes, and looked around again as my aunts settled themselves, smiling and shaking their heads.

"I'm sorry," I finally said. "This was so not what I was expecting to see here."

"And you haven't even seen Alecto's bedroom yet," my mother said. "Elvis, everywhere."

"If only you'd let me punish him when he came through," Alecto said dreamily. "I would have made his time here something…"

"Al…" my mother said, laughing.

"I thought you all, well, except for you," I said to my mother, "had the maiden goddess thing going."

They nodded. "Oh, we do. Doesn't mean that certain men don't send our lady parts all a-tingle," Alecto said. "Every age has its particularly spectacular examples of manhood."

I shook my head. "Does anyone else know about this?" I asked, waving around the room.

"No. And who would believe it? We are the terror, we are vengeance. We do a great job of maintaining our image, don't you think?" Megaera asked, smiling at me.

"That, you do," I agreed. "It's so weird. You guys, Eunomia… you all feel so warm, so alive to me. I would not have expected that."

My mother nodded. "We and the Guardians have a lot in common. And if you think this is something, you should see the home of the Guardians," she said, shaking her head.

"I think we all appreciate beauty and life a lot more

than the other gods," Alecto said, gaze intent upon my face, as if she was studying me.

Megaera nodded. "Yes. We deal in death. It makes beauty so much more precious to us."

"And we are better at carrying out our duties because of it. We are not so far removed from the daily lives of mortals that we believe ourselves separate from them, the way many gods do," my mother said.

"Which brings us to why you're here," Alecto said, getting serious. "You agreed to serve as a Fury, at Hades request."

I nodded.

"We have been discussing it. We are happy to have the help, and you proved yourself to be more than capable of punishment with the Nosoi," Megaera said. I waited for a reprimand for my behavior, but none came.

"Based on your history, we have decided that we have the perfect assignment for you," Alecto said. I waited.

My mother watched me. "You will be responsible for punishing those who have caused harm to girls and women. You shall avenge the world's lost girls, daughter."

I bowed. "It will be so. And I will be ruthless in my duties."

"We would expect nothing less," my mother said, and I felt this new part of my reality sink in, absorbed this truth as I had so many others. Something changed in me, just a little, as I fully felt the role of Fury take hold. I only hoped that I was up to the job.

CHAPTER FOURTEEN

My mother led me, eventually, out of the 80s living room, across the hall, to the room we'd been in before, with the Nosoi. "We work in here," she said softly as she unlocked the door. We stepped in, and I looked around. I hadn't noticed, before, the doors that led off to the sides of the room.

"I'm trying to think of how to explain what we do. I've done this so long, I know of no other reality," Tisiphone began. She crossed her arms, studied me, thinking. "You know that the Guardians collect the souls of the dead," she said.

I nodded. "Yes. And they bring them to Hades for their final judgment, and then they come here, and the Furies carry out the punishment they have coming to them."

"That is basically how it works. Some souls never make it to us. Some, Hades sees fit to send on to the Everafter with no action on our part. Many are, actually. Our services are required of those who have done so much damage, that even death cannot redeem them. Ordinary men and women simply pass through. The monsters among us, though, come to us."

"Some have lifetimes of punishment ahead of them. Some require less. They are punished until they repent, in any case."

"Lifetimes?" I asked, staring at her.

She smiled. "That is where things get confusing. It feels like lifetimes to them. Time passes differently here, as I'm sure you've noticed. It passes quickly for us, unbearably slowly for those here for punishment. It is necessary. We'd never be able to do our job thoroughly otherwise. What feels like hundreds of years worth of pain to those we punish feels like seconds, maybe minutes, to us. While it happens, you are connected, completely, to the soul you punish. This is how we are able to punish so efficiently."

She said it all in such a calm, casual voice, as though she was discussing the weather or a newspaper article she'd read. Tisiphone caught me looking at her. "It is a sacred duty, daughter. And I've seen you work. You were made for this."

I shook my head. "So, is it just nonstop punishing, or... ?"

"If you spent all of your time in vengeance, you would lose yourself. Spend as much time as you can stomach, and then return to your loved ones. I don't remember how it felt at first, but it may be overwhelming for you. I have no idea," she finished. "The souls are not going anywhere."

She led me to a side room, unlocked it. I peered in, expecting to see a bunch of ghosts or something. Instead, it was an empty room, with just a simple bench and a chair. I looked at her. "The demon guards will bring the souls to you. Here, they have almost a corporeal form. They look much as they did when they were alive. They hurt the same, as well."

Tisiphone paused, watched me. "You will need to be careful. We are not supposed to destroy the souls, merely punish them and send them on."

"Is that even possible? To destroy a soul?"

She nodded. "Based on what I felt when you were with the Nosoi, it would take almost no effort for you to do so. Control is essential, Mollis."

I looked at my feet, remembered similar lectures from Nain, about how important control is, about how I could majorly mess things up by losing control. It was always the same story, with me. "I will be careful," I finally said.

"Good. Hades takes this very seriously. These souls are promised the Everafter once they repent. If you break his word..."

"He'll be pretty pissed. I get it," I said, ignoring the shiver that went through my body.

"You do not want Hades to punish you. I've been through it twice. It is not something I ever want to live through again," she said softly.

I nodded. No pressure. Right.

"I will leave you now. Stop when you need to," she said. I nodded and she closed the door behind her, leaving me alone in the gray room. I sat on the chair, settled my hands in my lap, and closed my eyes. I didn't know what I was supposed to be thinking about, so I just focused on punishment, vengeance. I felt strengthened as I thought the words, as if they were a verbal talisman against the trepidation I was feeling.

A few moments later, there was a knock at the door.

"Yes," I said, and the door opened. A large demon guard, wearing the typical black uniform, bowed briefly to me and shoved the form of a tall, thin man into the room. "I will collect him when you have finished," the demon said, and I nodded.

The demon left, and I was left alone with the man, who was sprawled on the floor where the guard had shoved him.

I felt a connection to him, immediately, as instinct took over, and I did what a Fury does. My soul melded with his, and I could feel and see everything I needed to know about him. There was nothing he could hide from me. Every secret he thought he'd kept so well was laid bare before me, and he whimpered when he felt me enter his soul. I knew everything.

I also knew why Tisiphone had been so sure to warn me against destruction.

The soul had been a male who had abducted and murdered seven women. I saw, in a flash of understanding, everything he'd done to the women, every thought he'd had, the emotions that had run through him as he'd tortured and killed them.

My blood boiled.

I felt fear from him, and it was good.

I also understood what my mother had meant by the soul-bond being the most efficient way to punish. I saw what he'd done, what he'd felt. And I saw what he feared. I had complete control of his mind, and I used it. I punished him with the things he feared most, even as I watched, over and over again, in slow motion, in Technicolor detail, how he'd ended so many lives.

He began to beg for mercy. I was beyond it.

His punishment continued, and I lost all track of time. I used my mind, my hands, my sword, which had appeared again of its own accord. I came just short of destroying him, drawing out his punishment, and his screams, his pain, his fear fed me.

It was glorious and sickening.

I know that my body broke out in a sheen of perspiration, that my breathing became ragged, that my entire being yearned to obliterate this remainder of human filth. Yet he still showed no remorse, so it went on.

He babbled. He begged. He screamed and cried. And still, all I felt from him was how sure he was that it was his right to do the things he'd done. I turned his mind, his memories, back on him, had him re-live every abduction, every torture, every murder he'd committed, but from the other side. I made him feel what his victims had felt, over and over again as he screamed.

And I felt it. The moment he truly repented. The moment he saw his vileness for what it was, and felt remorse. His screams went silent, and he accepted the pain, because he deserved it. And I forced myself to pull back, and I opened my eyes and saw his soul, kneeling at my feet, sobbing. Regret, sadness, flowed from him, disgust at what he'd done.

I still wanted to destroy him. I snarled at him, and he flinched away. I went to the door and banged on it, hard, twice with my fist, and the demon guard came immediately and led him away, still keening, still feeling the effects of what I'd made him feel. His time would end soon, and he would leave, repenting, and spend eternity knowing how worthless he'd been.

And I would have his memories, the images of the things he'd done, with me for the rest of my life.

"Next," I called to the guard, steeling myself against the terrors I'd see from the next soul assigned to me.

I spent as much time as I could stomach punishing the souls assigned to me. After the first man, who had been sickening, it only got worse. But I was torn between being sickened by them and enjoying punishing them, and, for a while at least, vengeance won.

My soul felt filthy from being bound to theirs. My mind could not un-see the things they'd done, could not un-feel the things they'd felt. And while their fear, their pain at my hands had been sweet, it came at a price.

As I walked past the guards, barely thinking straight enough to acknowledge them as they did their usual fist-to-chest salute, I tried to shake the disgusting feelings inside me. I didn't see anything. The amethyst sky, the demons who waved or bowed to me. I was barely there.

Instead I saw girls, women, the prey of the people I'd just punished.

Girls and women who had not been saved. I tried to

push the memories away, the visions I saw through the eyes of evil. I was sick with it, my stomach turning. At the core of the sickness, sadness, and helplessness, there was rage.

I held on to that, a life preserver to keep me from drowning.

I left the Nether, walked through the gateway into the Packard plant. Dahael and Bash were there, waiting, just where I'd left them. They thumped their chests, and greeted me with a low, "Mistress."

"How long was I gone that time?" I asked them, and it felt strange to use my voice.

"Two days," Dahael said. "Shifter has been here many times, looking for Mistress. Told him you'd be back."

I shook my head. "Time is so different there."

They both nodded.

"I need to find some lost girls. Tell me you have some leads." My rage coursed through my body, and I welcomed it because at least it deadened the helplessness, just for a little while.

"Of course," Bash said, and he and Dahael led the way out of the factory, to my car. I followed the instructions they gave me in their raspy little voices.

I hunted. I rescued first one teenage girl, then two young women, then a pair of little girls who had just been taken by a friend of the family that same night.

I destroyed their captors. There was nothing left. I stopped, just short of destroying their souls, though it meant I'd have to see them again someday in the Nether.

"Next," I said to the imps after we'd returned the two little girls to their family. After the hugs, after the declarations that I was a miracle, a servant of God himself. After I returned two little girls, when so many more had never made it back home.

"No more tonight, Mistress," Dahael said, taking my hand gently. It was caked in blood. I had not been gentle or merciful. "Enough."

"Never," I said. "Next," I repeated, more forcefully.

Bash looked up at me. "Mistress needs to go home. People who love her," he said, nodding sagely.

"Did good work tonight. Go home," Dahael repeated, pulling me toward where we'd parked my car. "We will find more for you next time. And demon Levitt helps some too."

"Does he?" I asked numbly, thinking again that I needed to check in on the demon. By all accounts, he was a valuable asset. Soon.

"Asked us how best to serve Mistress. Guards the gate, finds lost girls," Dahael said. I nodded and we climbed into the car, and I roared toward home.

It was just after three. I let myself into the dark loft, only the lights of the city illuminating the main part of the loft. I went into my room, stripped off my ruined clothing, and stood under a shower that was so hot I gritted my teeth against the pain. It still wasn't hot enough to make me feel clean again. I stood there until the water ran cold, trying not to think, and failing.

I pulled on my pajama pants and a Wonder Woman t-shirt Brennan had bought for me the previous Christmas. I went out into the dark living room, and sat in the chair Brennan usually sat in. I could smell him on it, and I curled up into it.

I felt the tears threatening, and, before long, I couldn't fight them back much longer. All those girls. So much pain. And no amount of me destroying things would save them all. Soon I sobbed harder, biting my hand to keep the sounds to myself, not wanting anyone to hear me. I could hear Shanti's stereo on. The last thing she needed was to see me losing my shit, falling apart. Not when she counted on me to be the one who chased the nightmares away.

As hard as I tried, I couldn't stop. The tears and sobs came, and I hated every second of it. So much weakness. And my anger just made me feel worse. I pulled my knees to my chest, and rested my forehead on my knees, and just tried to muffle the wracking sobs that I couldn't stop.

I heard a door open upstairs, and I tried to take deep breaths, tried not to be heard. That was stupid, I knew. They would feel me. And I could sense Brennan, awake and coming closer. I wiped my eyes angrily, trying to make the tears stop.

And then he was there, standing in front of me. I wanted to stop crying. I wanted to tell him I loved him, that I'd missed him. But I couldn't make the words come. I could barely breathe around the overwhelming emotions I was feeling.

Without a word, he scooped me up in his arms, sat down, and settled me on his lap. His arms were strong around my body, and my head rested on his shoulder. Eventually my sobs died down. He sat, calm and soothing through it all, his hand running up and down my back, his arms around me.

"I'm sorry," I whispered.

"You have nothing to be sorry for," he said softly, holding me tighter. "I'm glad you're home, but I want to destroy whatever's doing this to you."

"Life as a Fury," I said against his neck as I rested my face on his shoulder again. It was all the explanation I could give without falling apart again, and all he needed. He knew. I felt the sadness, anger in him, for me. He squeezed me tighter to him. We sat in silence for a long time.

"Why did you sit down here alone like that? You could have come to me," he finally said.

"Didn't want you to see me like this."

"Like what?"

"Weak."

He put his hands on my cheeks, pushed me back so he could look in my eyes. "Honey there is nothing weak in you. You care so much, and you take everything the universe dishes out to you, and I don't know how you do it. Being in pain is not weakness. You don't have to be such a badass all the time," he finished, gently brushing my remaining tears away with his thumbs.

"Yes I do. I need to be a badass. I need to be *more* of one. I need to protect–"

"Who? You can't protect everyone, Molly," he said, his voice warm, soothing. "Not even you. As amazing as you are, one woman, goddess, Fury, whatever you are, is not enough to save everyone."

"They need to see me as a badass. Those I need to protect and those I'm protecting them from. I can't be weak," I said. "I saved a girl tonight whose mother told me that she'd prayed to me. To *ME*. Do you know how crazy that is?"

"You give them hope," he said softly.

"And I'm not worthy. Like you said. I can't save them all." I was quiet for a moment. "I need to be a badass. I need to pretend I'm strong. It's like armor or something. I can't explain it better than that. If you, anyone, sees me weak, I feel weak."

He held me close again. "Be a badass, then. Wear your armor. But you don't need to wear it for me. I know the woman inside. And I have more faith in her than I do in the persona she tries to present. I know how strong you are, how good you are. I know how personally you take every life you can't save. Let me be the one to give you a warm place to go when everything gets to be too much, okay?"

"You already do," I murmured.

"Good."

We were quiet for a while, and, against all odds, I found myself dozing against him. He sensed it, picked me up and carried me to his room.

"Brennan?" I asked, nervous.

"Just to rest. You were gone too long, and you're in more pain than you've been in in a very long time. I need you in my arms tonight."

He reached the top of the stairs, opened his bedroom door, and kicked it closed behind us as he carried me into his room. He settled me on his narrow bed, and I watched as he climbed in beside me. On his bare chest, I could see the tattoo I'd noticed when he was sick. I traced it lightly with my fingertips, and he took my hand in his and kissed it. He pulled me close to him, and I put my arms around his waist, rested my cheek against his chest. Our legs tangled, and he rested his chin on the top of my head. My body was practically cocooned in his, and I still didn't feel close enough.

We laid there for a while, and I thought I'd fall asleep. Instead, we started talking, our voices low in the dark bedroom. We talked about nothing and everything. We compared our favorite comic book characters when we were kids, our best and worst childhood memories, toys we'd had and music we'd liked. We talked about Ada and Stone, and how great they were. We talked about Shanti, and he filled me in on how well she was doing with her training. We did not talk about gods, or demons, or souls, or lost girls. We spent the night getting to know each other's history, each other's souls, by doing nothing more than talking about the little things.

As the room brightened with morning's first light, I let myself drift off to sleep, Brennan beginning to doze beside me. I was still wrapped tightly in his arms, and I fell asleep marveling at the way he'd saved my heart, yet again, just by being Brennan. And he was mine.

◆◆◆

I woke up to Brennan's lips on my neck, his beard tickling the delicate skin there. His arms were still tight around me, and his thigh rested between mine. I blushed at the intimacy of it, but became distracted almost instantly by the sensation of his lips on my skin, the scent of him surrounding me. He knew just where to kiss me, right where the side of my neck met my shoulder, and my heart started pounding in time with his. Soon his hands were roaming my body, tracing the curves of my hips and waist, the swell of my breasts, and I gasped when he gently cupped them in his hands. He kissed his way from my throat up to my lips, and I was lost in the sensation of his lips teasing mine, his hands on my body.

"I want you," he whispered in my ear.

I kissed his throat, gently nipped the delicate skin just below his ear, and he moaned. I sucked his earlobe, and he literally purred against me.

"But," he said softly, pulling back from me. "They're all awake down there." He kissed me. "Along with my first meeting." He kissed me again. Then he looked down at me and grinned. "I want to be able to take my time with you. Without a potential audience or eavesdroppers."

"Are you anticipating making noise?" I asked, laughing a little, still breathless from his kisses, his touch.

He leaned down and kissed me again. "I'm counting on it," he said against my lips. "But," he said, pausing only to kiss me, "I think it would be rude of me to leave you this way."

"Yeah?" I asked, trembling a little.

He smiled, and his lips met mine again. I was so lost in the feel of his lips on mine, the feel of his body on top of mine, that I barely registered when his thigh forced my legs further apart, when his hand slipped under the waistband of my pajama bottoms. I gasped when his warm hand cupped the sensitive area between my legs. He held me, then his fingers parted me, and he started rubbing my throbbing, aching center with maddeningly light pressure. I whined in need, and he chuckled against my mouth as he kissed me. I arched my hips toward him desperately, his fingers only making me more needy. He increased the pressure, moving faster, and I lost myself in the growing ecstasy and desperation. I bucked against his hand, riding the edge of control. Then he slowly slid one long finger inside of me, and I came, hard, his mouth catching my cries as I rode what felt like an endless wave of pleasure. By the time it was over, I was whimpering against his mouth, trembling and breathless from the strength of what he'd just done to me.

He looked down at me and gave me what had to be the sexiest, cockiest smile ever. "That was fun."

"For me," I said, still breathless.

"For me, too," he said, still smiling. "Just imagine what we could do with our clothes off."

Then Brennan ran his hands over my body again, tracing my curves, squeezed my hip one more time, then got out of bed. I wanted to pull him back in with me, and he knew it. He threw a small grin my way before heading into the bathroom. I heard the shower start up, and I laid there for a few seconds, my body still thrumming, unable to stop picturing Brennan with soapy water sluicing down his body.

"Damn," I groaned, sitting up. But I was smiling, and he'd done what he'd intended: I was distracted from the pain I'd been feeling the night before. Maybe, just maybe, it would be enough to help me get through another day in the Nether.

◆◆◆

Over the next couple of weeks, I got into a bit of a routine, a way of steamrolling through my days ensuring that I met my obligations both in the mortal world and in the Nether. I did the Fury thing, which always filled me with sickness, helplessness, and rage. And then I'd leave the Nether and hunt. It all became this kind of never-ending cycle of avenging, then saving those who needed to be avenged, then avenging some more. My duties in the Nether only spurred me to work harder in the mortal realm. And those I saved in the mortal realm inspired me to punish the souls I dealt with in the Nether harder, more ruthlessly, than I already would have.

Of course, something had to give. And as usual, it was anything that made me feel like a normal person. Back in the old days, when I'd done everything solo, it meant that things like cooking and eating didn't get done very often. Now, with a team and a...I didn't even know what to call Brennan, because "boyfriend" just didn't seem to do him justice...now it meant that they took a backseat to my duties in the two worlds I straddled. Since he'd recovered from the illness the Nosoi had caused, Brennan had basically taken over leadership of the team, which was for the best and was what should have happened from the beginning.

I am really not a people person.

And the rest of the team followed him, happily. Shanti continued her training with Brennan, but had transitioned to an online high school to finish her graduation requirements, because I sucked so badly at keeping track of what she was supposed to do, and Brennan was stretched thin as it was without having to play teacher. Levitt kept doing whatever it is Levitt does, watched and given assignments by the imps.

How did I know all of this? Had I talked to Brennan or Shanti? Did I ever bother to ask them how their days were? Had I finally made the time to spend five minutes talking to the demon I'd taken a chance on? Hell no. My imps told me.

My imps knew more about what was happening with my friends and the man I loved than I did.

And it wasn't that I didn't care. It wasn't that I didn't want to be there. I wanted to. I wanted to sleep next to Brennan every night. I wanted to feel his hands on my body again, to have him inside me, finally. My body ached with it.

But my cravings, my needs, are nothing compared to what others need from me.

So I delivered vengeance in the Nether, and I rescued and destroyed here in the mortal world. I dozed, sometimes, at the Furies' home, and I ate whatever food the imps shoved at me, ignored their pleas to just go home and rest for a while.

I'd thought being with Brennan would make everything better. And maybe it would have, for a while. But that first morning after sleeping next to Brennan, after he'd driven me so far beyond ecstasy I thought I'd died and gone to heaven, I got up out of his bed, and I went to the Nether, and I punished the soul of a woman who had kidnapped and sold little girls and boys. She didn't care who she sold them to, though she knew why they were buying. I could see, in her mind, that she didn't know or care how many children she'd destroyed in her lifetime. She was like the scum I had been so used to dealing with back when I'd started as the Angel, but on a scale that boggled the mind. I stood there, and I punished her, knowing that I was looking at the face of evil, and that there were many, many more like her out there.

And I could barely keep up with the pieces of shit in my own city, let alone what happened in the rest of the world.

It made me feel helpless, which made me feel angry…which resulted in me coming *this close* to destroying her soul. My mother and aunts had broken into the room just in time to stop me, pulled me away, and sent me home.

Where I'd immediately started tracking down lost girls. And, because evil is equal opportunity and so I have to be, too, lost boys as well.

I hadn't been home in ten days.

I came out of the Nether, ready to hunt. My mother and aunt Megaera had given me my own set of uniforms like theirs, black shirts and tailored black pants, and I had cleaned up and changed into a clean set at their insistence. I'd tried to tell them I was only going to get them bloody again, but they'd both just stood there, blocking the door, and refusing to let me pass until I'd done what they told me to. Showered, dressed, and now thoroughly annoyed, I said good-bye to them when they finally let me pass.

I came out into the Packard plant, expecting to see Bash and Dahael waiting, as they always did.

Instead, it was Brennan. He stood there, about four feet in front of the gateway, arms crossed. Irritation, worry, frustration rolled off of him like a tidal wave, along with relief and love when I appeared on his side of the gateway. I stopped short, watching him. His gaze flicked over my face, down my body, then back up to my eyes.

"Nice to see you're alive," he said.

"The imps told you I was," I said, trying to calm the way my heart raced at the sight of him.

"I don't want to talk to the goddamned imps, Molly," he said. "I want you. You can't keep doing this. Didn't we go over this that night?"

"But I am doing it, Bren," I said.

He walked up to me and folded me into his arms. Still angry with me, still frustrated. "It doesn't have to always be you," he said softly. I put my arms around him, caught between wanting to be human for a while and wanting to hunt.

"Brennan, I have to…"

"No. You don't. Not tonight. The imps had three leads for you, and Levitt and a couple of the Grosse Pointe shifters are taking care of it. They will report to you in the morning."

"But—"

"Don't you get it?" he asked, raising his voice just a little in frustration. "This isn't just me missing you, though I do. I know you. I get it. You can't help yourself." He stopped a minute, took a breath as he stepped back from me. "But you don't seem to be able to get it through your head that you're not alone. You have a team of super-powered people who love you and want to help you. You have allies. The Grosse Pointe shifters practically worship you for saving them from the plague. They've been helping. They've been in on patrols and busts and investigations and everything else. Because of you we've basically increased the size of the team by about fifty. But you don't know any of that because you never freaking talk to me, Molly," he said, and he turned away, rubbing his face in frustration.

I stood there, silent. I watched him. Let it sink in. He was right. I didn't know any of that.

After a while, he went on. "You have to do this. I understand. Part of what makes me love you so much is that when you dedicate yourself to something, you mean it." He looked at me. "But you come home, when you manage to remember you have one, and you have a deadness in your eyes that I can't stand seeing there."

"So what do you expect me to do, Brennan?" I asked him, crossing my arms. He came back to me, put his hands on my hips, and leaned his forehead against mine.

"I want you to remember that you are not alone. I want you to keep in mind that you don't have to do everything yourself. We can do things. I bet if we asked, we'd easily manage to get a team together that does nothing but look for your lost girls."

"And boys," I said.

"And boys," he added. "Think, honey. How much more you could do if you didn't try to do it all by yourself."

"This is just a sneaky way of getting me back into your bed, isn't it?" I asked, and I was rewarded with a laugh.

"You saw straight through me. Yes. Cold showers and my hand aren't cutting it anymore."

I smacked him, and he laughed again and kissed me, and soon I started remembering what it felt like to feel something other than rage. He was still angry. I'd hurt him by staying away, and I hadn't even stopped to think about that. I kissed him back, trying to tell him without words how much I'd missed him. By the way his heart pounded, I was pretty sure he got it.

He broke away from me after a while, reluctantly. Cleared his throat. "All right. We're going to go to a restaurant and eat actual food, not that crap the imps keep stealing for you." He kissed me firmly, just once, then pulled away again. "And then I'm taking you somewhere we won't be bothered. I am turning off my phone, and you are sending your imps away. And everyone can consider themselves lucky if they see us before next week. Understood?"

I blushed, and clenched my thighs together. My body was doing its own version of persuading me to take a break. "You have a lot of nerve, bossing a scary-ass Fury around like that," I said.

He put his hand at the base of my spine and guided me out of the factory. "Yeah, well. From what I hear, the scary-ass Fury has a soft spot for me. I'll risk it." I shook my head as I let him guide me toward my car. "I also happen to know a few places the scary-ass Fury likes to be nibbled." He opened the passenger side door for me, and I got in, handing him my keys and trying to ignore the way my body heated at his words. "And I bet I could find a few more places if I tried."

He closed the door, got in, and drove. It was night. Probably around eleven, based on the moon and the fact that there wasn't a ton of traffic. He reached over and took my hand, and we drove in silence. I didn't know how I'd eat, knowing damn well what was happening after. He'd made it clear what he wanted, and I had no intention of denying both of us what we needed.

We stopped at a little Italian place we'd both liked, and sat and ate. He filled me in on what had been happening at the loft in my absence, and I told him about the Nether and my hunts. His eyes barely left me, and the desire, the need, coming from him made my heart race. Our food came, and I ate mechanically at first, then with more enthusiasm once my stomach was reminded what it felt like to be filled. I ended up finishing a lasagna dish I usually had to have bagged up, and Brennan smirked at me as I mopped up the last bit of sauce with a thick slice of warm bread.

"What?" I asked. "It was really good."

"It's been a long time since you've eaten," he said.

I nodded. "The imps think Doritos are the world's most perfect food. I am really sick of those."

He laughed a little, watched me.

"So," I said, my stomach fluttering. "Where are we going now?"

"I have a house not too far from here," he said. "It was my parents'. I don't go there much, but it's kept up and livable, and it's mine."

I nodded. He got up and held his hand out to me, pulled me up. We walked out into the empty parking lot, and my nervousness and desire was squashed when I heard a scream somewhere nearby.

"That way," Brennan said, pointing down the street to our right. We both bolted in that direction, following the sound of yet another scream that was quickly cut short. We came upon a house, where two women were fighting on the front lawn. One had a gun, the other had a baseball bat, and they were both clearly pissed.

Now I was just irritated.

The one with the gun was about to squeeze the trigger. Everything seemed to happen in slow motion. I watched her finger flex as I bolted for her, saw the terror in the eyes of the woman holding the bat as she realized she was about to be shot.

I bowled into the would-be shooter, and the gun went off. As I tackled her, I scanned both Brennan and the other woman. Both were all right; she had shot into the air.

The woman with the gun struggled against me angrily, called me several less-than-friendly names. The one with the bat, I could see, had relinquished her bat to Brennan.

Explaining. I heard the words "boyfriend" and "bitch" and "crazy" but not much else because the crazy bitch with the gun was still fighting me.

"Um… do you think she needs help?" I heard the woman standing with Brennan ask him.

"Her? Nah. She'd just get pissed off at me if I stepped in now." He pulled his phone out, I assumed, to call the police.

At that moment, I was mostly annoyed that I was muddy and that the woman I was grappling with smelled like puke. I didn't want to hurt her, but she was starting to test my patience.

I finally got the gun from her hand, kicked it toward Brennan, who stood over it and kept talking on his phone. I got the woman's hands behind her back and secured them with a zip tie, which I still carried out of habit. She shouted at me and called me names I had to admire for sheer creativity. I stood up and glanced up at Brennan who was smirking.

"I was clean for about an hour that time," I said, looking down at my muddy, ripped clothing.

He laughed. We could see flashing lights in the distance. Suburban police responded much faster than we were used to.

We explained to the officers what we'd seen, and I convinced them they'd never seen me, messed with the women's memories so they had no recollection of my freaky-ass glowing eyes. Finally, Brennan and I climbed back into my car, and he put it in drive.

"Well," he said as he pulled out of the parking lot. "That would have been much sexier if it had been me you'd been grappling with like that."

"Shut up and drive, Brennan," I muttered, blushing. He laughed, and my stomach fluttered again as we drove toward his house.

CHAPTER FIFTEEN

It wasn't a long drive to Brennan's house. It was a little brick bungalow with a neat boxwood hedge surrounding the front yard, on a quiet street lined with similar houses. It looked clean and well cared-for. The porch light was on. It looked, for anyone who didn't know better, like someone made a home there.

"I've moved out of the loft a few times over the years," Brennan explained as I looked around. "There were times I couldn't stand to live in the same house as Nain, times I just wanted to do my own thing for a while. It makes more sense to keep this up than scramble for a place if I ever needed one."

I nodded. It was all very Brennan, really. Simple furnishings, clean hardwood floors, white walls. He took me through the house, showing me where the bedrooms and bathroom were. His room, like his room at the loft, was clean, almost austere.

"Nice house, Bren," I said softly, more for something to say than anything else. He stood in the center of his bedroom, watching me.

"I like your house even better. You have all that cool vintage shit," he said. "Why don't you ever go there anymore?"

"Too many memories," I finally said. He watched me for a minute, nodded. Then he stepped closer to me, kissed me softly.

"I think it's time to make some new ones, don't you?" he asked, nuzzling my neck, his warm breath on my skin sending shivers down my spine.

"Yes," I whispered. I put my arms around him, and saw the mud on my forearm. "I am a mess."

"Don't care," he murmured, capturing my lips with his again. He pulled my top off, dropped it to the floor, then unbuttoned my pants and pushed them down over my hips, and they puddled at the floor around my ankles. His eyes swept over me, and a low sound escaped him, somewhere between a growl and a groan. He pushed the straps of my bra down, and I blushed as I spilled out of it. "I am going to enjoy this, Molly. I am going to make you forget everything except you and me, and before we're done, I am going to hear you scream my name."

My heart was pounding, and a shiver went down my spine when he undid the clasp of my bra and let it fall to the floor. He groaned and lowered his lips, pressing kisses over the swell of my breasts as he ran his hands down my arms, my waist, my hips. He squeezed my hips, briefly, then pushed my panties down my hips, my thighs, his hands following their descent to the floor, and then he stood back and looked at me, his eyes traveling my body, and I could feel my body responding, trembling, warming to the way he looked at me.

"Damn," he murmured appreciatively. "Lay down. On your stomach," he said, and I did, burying my face in his pillow. I could hear the sound of fabric; Brennan removing his clothing. I felt him kneel on the bed, then straddle my body, settling himself at my upper thighs. I felt the coarse hair of his thighs rubbing against my skin, the weight of him settling just below my bottom. He sat that way, for just a bit, and I knew he was looking at me, memorizing every curve, every dip and swell of my hips and backside. He put his hands in my hair, and started massaging my scalp. I closed my eyes, and a tiny sigh escaped my throat. He took his time, worked his way down to my neck, my shoulders, my back. His hands were firm as he massaged me, and I felt myself both loosening up and growing more needy as he worked his magic. Wherever he touched me, he followed with his lips. His hands, then his mouth, making my heart pound, making my body ache with need.

He just kept massaging, kissing, nibbling. He wanted me, and it was overwhelming how much he did. His need washed over me, hotter than flames, so strong it was almost a physical thing. But this was Brennan. He would take his time with me, give me every single thing I needed and more. Completely in control, and I was at his mercy. He worked his way down my legs, and when he ran his hands down the backs of my thighs, touched me behind my knees, I bit my lip and pressed my face into the pillow.

He gently turned me over onto my back, his eyes traveling my body as he settled me back onto the pillow. I moved to cover myself with my arms, and he shook his head. He gently took my wrists, and stretched my arms up over my head as his eyes continued to roam my body.

I looked him over, the sight of him straddling me only making me need him more. So much hotness, it almost seemed unfair — his strong chest, that tattoo, the thin line of dark hair that led from his navel down to *oh holy shit,* and I squirmed, practically panting in need. I glanced back up at his face, and he smirked, knowing exactly what I was feeling. Then he lowered his lips to mine, kissed me deeply, more firmly, his lips hungry and insistent on mine. Once I was breathless again, he licked down my throat, across my collarbone, then lower, and his tongue flicked over my breast, and I cried out as the sensation roared through my body. He did it again, then took it into his mouth and sucked and nibbled, leisurely, as if he had all the time in the world. I thrashed against him, pushed myself against his mouth, and he just kept savoring me.

When I felt like I couldn't take any more, when my breasts were aching and tender from his attentions, he kissed his way down my stomach, stopping to nibble the sides of my waist, the curve of my hips. He kissed the fronts of my thighs, nuzzled between my legs, and I gasped.

He gently spread my thighs, and all I could do was moan, beg, as his mouth drove me insane. My pulse raced, and heat spread throughout my body. I gripped the sheets in desperation, unable to withstand the torment he was putting me through. I was on the edge, when he placed one final kiss on me, then kissed and licked his way back up my body.

"So good," he murmured, then he lowered his mouth to mine, kissing me in a forceful, demanding way that he'd never kissed me before, and I whimpered against his mouth.

"Please," I begged, breathless. He chuckled and started kissing my throat. His need roared over me, through me.

He backed away so he could look at me. "Please what?" he asked, meeting my eyes.

"I need you Brennan," I whispered. "Please."

He reached over to the nightstand, pulled out a foil packet, and rolled a condom onto himself, eyes on me the entire time. I trembled as he positioned himself right where I needed him to be and I gripped the sheets helplessly in my hands.

"Say the words, Molly," he said, placing the tip of himself just inside me.

"I want you Brennan," I said, meeting his eyes, holding his gaze.

He pushed inside me, stretching me, then pulled back again.

"Are you sure?" he asked, teasing, as he did it again.

The heat in his eyes made my stomach flutter, the hungry look in his gaze inflaming me even more.

"Yes," I moaned, and he did it over and over again, entering me, then pulling back just when my body had begun to adjust to having him inside. I whimpered in my need and frustration, and he let out a low chuckle. He did it again, and again, pushing in just a little deeper each time, the unbelievable friction of him filling me and then pulling away making me almost incoherent with need.

Not enough. I shoved my hips up toward him, determined to take him deeper.

He pushed my hips down, held them firmly. "Behave yourself," he said, a tiny, insanely sexy smile quirking his lips as he met my eyes. I whimpered as he continued toying with me. I thrashed, closed my eyes.

"Look at me, Molly," he ordered, and I did. "I want your eyes on me. Understand?"

"Yes."

"Good." And then he drove all the way into me, filling me, and I felt my body clench around him, and I cried out and he captured my cries with his lips, kissed me as he started moving his hips in a slow, torturous way that had me gripping his body, my fingernails digging into his back in my frenzied need. I wrapped my legs around his thighs, and he pushed all the way into me, stayed that way, eyes locked onto mine. I was on the verge, and he stopped moving.

It was exquisite torture having him pressed deep inside me, on the verge of losing my mind, just one more thrust and I'd fall apart. I tried to push my hips up.

"No, not yet, honey," he murmured.

"Not fair, Bren."

"No?" he asked, smirking down at me again.

"Please," I begged, and he chuckled, thoroughly enjoying having me at his mercy. Then he sat back on his heels, pulled me up to him, opening me wider, pushing so deeply into me I could feel the hot skin of his pelvis against my body the coarse hair on his thighs against my ass, and I let out a strangled cry as he started moving his hips again.

He was merciless, keeping me in ecstasy, right on the edge, and refusing me release until he'd had his fill of my body. No matter how much I begged, he kept it up. It was having a toll on his control, too. I could feel how badly he wanted to let go, but he was determined to draw this out, to give me very bit of pleasure he possibly could.

He pumped against me and he caressed my body, hands running firmly over my curves in a way that had every nerve ending screaming for him.

"Eyes on me," he reminded me. "I want to see what it's like to watch you lose control."

I moaned, and looked at him, and he kept going, kept driving into me. We were both breathless, almost mad with ecstasy, and my body ached and throbbed, and he just kept torturing me. Then he placed his hand on my abdomen, pressing just a little with his palm, and he started thrusting harder.

I cried out, past any type of coherent thought, and felt myself nearing the edge again, and I moaned his name, begging.

"Yes, Molly," he said, and he thrust, hard, into me while his warm palm pressed down on my abdomen, and I went over the edge, screamed his name, over and over again, senseless, my body unable to contain everything I was feeling. I heard him groan, curse under his breath. My orgasm seemed to last forever, as he continued to do whatever it was that he was doing to me, and he watched my face the entire time. The desire coming from him was almost frightening in its intensity, and it only added to everything else I was already feeling. When I finally came down, I was limp and trembling, and he kept pumping into me.

"You're so damn beautiful," he said, lowering his body, and I reveled in the sensation of his hard, heavy body covering mine. "Perfect," he murmured. I wrapped my legs around him, and he held my hands, our fingers entwining, and he kissed me, and started moving his hips faster, harder, hammering into my aching center with an intensity that had me on the edge again, and I raised my hips to meet every hard thrust. His kisses became desperate, bruising, and I kissed him back with equal desperation. He moved his lips to my throat, kissing and biting the side of my neck as he drove hard into me, starting to lose control.

"Molly," he growled against my throat, and I went over the edge again and when I clenched around him, he exploded, grinding hard into me as he rode out his orgasm, and I trembled, aching deliciously from the hard, rough way he moved as he lost control. The emotions coming from him washed over me, bringing tears to my eyes as I came down. We were connected, in every possible way, and the connection I'd made to his soul opened him to me in a way I'd never known anyone. His heart pounded in rhythm with mine, in rhythm with our writhing, exhausted bodies and I pressed my lips to his shoulder, overcome with everything I was feeling.

When he had finished, he rolled off of me, pulling me on top of him and holding me tightly. He kissed me softly, lips warm and tender on mine, and murmured how beautiful I was, that he belonged to me, in every way.

"I love you, Brennan," I whispered, resting my head at the crook of his neck, breathing him in as my breathing returned to normal.

"I love you too, Molly," he murmured against my hair. I smiled, and we drifted off to sleep.

◆◆◆

True to his word, he did a magnificent job of keeping me distracted for the next couple of days. I'd woken once to find him talking to Stone on the phone, telling him to follow any leads on lost girls the imps gave him. He was determined to prove a point, and, just this once, maybe, I was more than happy to let him do it. I also understood, at some level, that he was doing what shifter males do when they claim a mate, shutting us up alone together until we knew each other's bodies, completely, intimately, until he'd made it clear that I belonged to him and him to me.

Considering I'd already claimed him in my own way, I could hardly fault him for doing the same with me.

Three days. Three days in Brennan's house with him, and it wasn't nearly long enough. It had been more than I could have hoped, better than my wildest dreams. I lost track of how many times we'd loved each other, all I knew was that my body ached in a way I never wanted it to stop aching. We'd gotten to know each other in every possible way, and between lovemaking and talking, Brennan fed me and just generally made a point of taking care of me. And even though it ran counter to everything I'd ever known about myself, I found myself doing the same for him. At times, it overwhelmed me how perfect it was, how his soul and mine were like two halves of a whole. In every way that I am prickly and mean and angry, Brennan is soothing, calm, and in control. In all of the ways I try to plan for the impossible, Brennan is an expert at living in the moment. When I confessed that I'd bound him to me, he simply smiled and told me he knew it, that he felt his bond to me strengthen when I'd done it. And then he'd loved me all over again.

It all felt too good to be true. Stuff like this, feelings like this, do not happen to me.

We were in bed, again, Brennan's body hunched over mine under the cool sheets as he kissed me, nibbled my throat, my shoulders. I was, as always, almost drunk on the sensations running through my body when I was with him.

I was so distracted, so enjoying his lips on my throat and his hands on my body that I barely noticed when there was a distinctive fluttering sound and Eunomia appeared in the room, at the foot of the bed. I froze, moved to push Brennan off of me, but he gave a small shake of his head and kept kissing my throat.

"Don't you people ever knock?" he muttered against my neck. I was blushing furiously, but he gave no indication that he was going to stop what he was doing.

"We do not use doors, shifter," Eunomia said.

"Start. She's busy," he said, continuing to kiss my shoulders.

"Yes, so I see," Eunomia said, and though I couldn't see her over Bren, I could hear the humor in her voice, sense it from her.

"Go away," he muttered, still focusing on me.

"Did you need something, E?" I asked, trying for some sense of decorum.

"I was trying to find you to see how you were. Obviously, you are just fine," she said.

"See ya later, E," Brennan said, and I could feel him getting irritated.

Eunomia laughed. "Oh, all right. Relax, shifter. By all means continue fornicating. I'll talk to you later, Mollis." And with that, there was that little fluttering sound again, her wings taking her into flight, and she was gone.

He shook his head and started kissing my stomach, and I smacked him on the shoulder. "That was so rude," I said. He bit me, not exactly gently, and I gasped.

"It was. Your family needs to learn about boundaries," he said. I was about to argue, but then his lips started working their magic and I promptly forgot what I was even going to argue with him about.

When it was over, he pulled me back onto the mattress with him and held me.

"You are kind of an ass," I said, still out of breath.

"Am I?" he asked, nuzzling my shoulder.

"I can't even be annoyed with you when you do that to me."

He laughed, and held me tighter. "I didn't mean to

176

irritate you. I wanted to make a point with E and anyone else who can magically appear in our bedroom. You give yourself to the world, every single day. You sacrifice, almost constantly, for everyone else. When we're alone together, you're off limits unless someone's dying. Does that seem fair?"

"Yes."

"Good." He was quiet for a while, holding me. "You're going to tell me it's time to leave now, aren't you?"

"You know me too well," I murmured.

"Not as well as I want to."

"Better than anyone else, though," I said, and he squeezed my body to his. "I am supposed to be present at a meeting Hades is having later today with a couple of other gods."

"Gods posturing is almost too stupid for words," he said, and I laughed.

"It is. It's all such a bunch of bullshit," I said, feeling my eyelids get heavy. "I owe him. Supposed to make it look like I serve him, belong to him. As if I truly belong to any of them." I closed my eyes.

"Who do you belong to?" he asked me, and I could hear the smile in his voice.

"Myself," I said, smiling. He pinched my bottom, and I laughed. "And you, even when you're being an ass."

"That's better," he said. We dozed for a while, and, slowly but surely got ready to return to real life.

I was pulling one of Bren's t-shirts over my head and I looked around. He was sitting at the foot of the still-rumpled bed pulling his shoes on. "I love this house," I said softly, and he laughed. I glanced at him, and he shook his head. "I do," I said, smiling.

"We'll have to come back here. Often," he said.

"You said 'come'," I said, and then I couldn't stop laughing, and after a while I heard him laughing, too.

"Oh my god," he said, shaking his head while I tried to get my giggles under control. "Nobody here or in the

Nether would believe me if I tried to tell them how sophomoric your sense of humor is. Or that you giggle."

"Shut up, Bren," I said, still laughing a little. "That's between the two of us."

He came up behind me and folded me in his arms. "What about the noises you make when I—"

I elbowed him in the gut, and he laughed. He kept holding me, and we stood there for a while. "I don't want to leave," he said.

"Me neither. But Stone has probably destroyed half the loft by now, and Shanti's probably running the streets eating innocents, and the city is probably being over-run with dumbass werewolves as we speak."

"You're such a pessimist. I'm almost sure Shanti wouldn't eat anyone."

I let out a small laugh, and he squeezed me tighter to him. Then he released me, reluctantly, and took my hand, and we left the house and drove back to the loft.

♦♦♦

We arrived back at the loft to find that while Stone had eaten pretty much everything in the house and was whining about how he was starving, Shanti had not, in fact, bitten anyone and there had only been a few minor issues, which the team and the Grosse Pointe shifters had taken care of easily. I kissed Brennan, then headed to the Nether to do my Fury thing and attend Hades.

I drove to the Packard plant and strolled through the gateway. The demon guards there saluted me, and I nodded to them and made my way to Hades' house. One of his demon servants answered the door and let me in.

"Your mother is in with him right now, my Lady," the demon said in a low voice.

"I'll join them. I rarely see the two of them together," I said, and he nodded, gestured toward Hades' closed office door.

I walked down the long hallway, paused in front of the office door when I heard my name.

"I am not losing her to some prophecy, Hades," Tisiphone was saying. "I won't do it. I will not allow it."

"We hardly have a say in that, now, do we?" Hades was saying in a tired voice. "She's here. She exists. It is what it is."

"How can you be this way? Are you really so cold you feel nothing--"

"Cold? Are we really going to go there, Tis?"

I raised my eyebrow at the nickname. My mother did not seem like the nickname type.

Hades went on. "We'll do what we can. Her fate lies before her, just like anyone else."

"May she be strong enough to give Fate a good kick in the ass, then," Tisiphone muttered.

"I would expect nothing less from your daughter," Hades said, and I heard a warmth, a familiarity, in his voice that made me blush. I was ready to hear more when Hades' wife, Persephone, bustled up behind me and knocked twice on the door, then opened it. I gaped at her.

"Your whelp was listening at the door, Fury," she said, glaring at me. And then she flounced off again, her skirt rustling as she walked away.

"I wasn't," I said, glaring at Persephone's back. Then I glanced at my mom and Hades. Ask them about what they were discussing, and reveal I'd absolutely been eavesdropping? Or play it off so I could get through the day and go home to Brennan?

"I am here for your meeting, Lord Hades," I said, walking into the office. Hades and my mother both looked at me for a moment, maybe trying to figure out what I'd heard. They exchanged a glance, then Tisiphone excused herself, hugging me on her way out, and Hades started making small talk about the upcoming meeting.

I managed not to lose myself to my rage, and got through my meeting without rolling my eyes or otherwise disrespecting the self-aggrandizing deities in the room. Mostly, I did so by fantasizing about getting Brennan alone again. Finally, after what felt like an eternity, the meeting was over and I made my way back to my own realm again.

As I drove back to the loft (looking forward to Brennan and a bed. Or a wall, or a shower, or a tabletop...) the imps filled me in on what had gone on while I'd been gone.

It was a little after midnight when I finally dragged myself up to the loft. Brennan was in the living room, and he got up and kissed me when I walked in. It would have gone on, except that Shanti was sitting in the dining room. I went and sat with her. I could sense that she was nervous about something, and the fact that she was sitting out in the main part of the loft instead of up in her room was definitely different. Brennan shoved a bowl of beef stew in front of me with a soft but stern, "eat" and then sat down. I stuck my tongue out at him and felt a little stab of desire from him, and I grinned.

"Behave yourself," he murmured.

"Are you two going to be like this all the time now?" Shanti asked, shaking her head.

"We could go back to arguing all the time," I said, taking a bite of the stew.

"No, we couldn't," Brennan said. "I have ways of distracting—"

"All right! Okay. Hey. Forget I said anything," Shanti said over him, and we both laughed. She laughed, too, and shook her head. I could still sense anxiety from her.

"What's going on, Shanti? You're anxious about something," I said.

She took a deep breath, looked at me. "I want to be on the lost girls and lost boys team Brennan was talking about earlier."

"No," I said.

"You can't just do that," Shanti said, raising her voice a little. "You can't just write me off that way. I've been training with Brennan. I'm fast. I'm strong. And I have more reason to want to help than just about anyone else involved."

"You're too young," I said.

"How old were you when you started finding lost girls, again?" Shanti asked, raising her eyebrow. Other than Brennan, she was the only one who knew my whole story, and I kicked myself for telling her that particular tidbit.

"I was..."

"Nothing more than a telepath who could self-heal at that point, right? I'm a vampire."

"Then you should know that you have plenty of time. Not yet," I said.

"You're not listening!" Shanti shouted, and it startled me to hear her really raise her voice like that to me. "I need to do this. I am going insane here. I have this power, and I never goddamned wanted it. But I'm stuck with it, so I'm going to make it worth something. I'm going to make myself worth something," and pink-tinged tears flooded her eyes, and I looked at Brennan helplessly. He shrugged.

I went to Shanti, knelt in front of her and pulled her into my arms. "You are worth something. You are an amazing, smart, wonderful person. I can't stand the thought of you being in danger. These are sick fucks we deal with, Shanti," I said softly, pulling back so I could look at her face. "I hate even the idea of you being near them."

"I know how they are. You rescued me from some of them, remember? I need to do this." She watched me. "You can't keep me hidden away forever."

I shook my head, and my gaze landed on Brennan. She saw. "Ask him. My training is going really well. I came close to kicking his ass a few times," Shanti said.

"She's a good fighter. Disciplined, focused. She's fast as hell, and she's not bad with a blade, either," he said.

"Whose side are you on, anyway?" I grumbled.

"Same person's side I'm always on. But I'm not going

to lie. She's good."

"Good against you. You'd never really hurt her," I said. Then I sat in my chair. "How do we know how she'd do against someone who was really trying to kill her?" I sat there, thinking. Both Brennan and Shanti watched me. Then something occurred to me, and I sent a thought at Bash and Dahael.

We sat talking for a few more minutes, Shanti trying to convince me, Brennan being reasonable. I hated it. Hated even the thought of her exposing herself to the shit we saw every day. I could admit it: I wanted her to stay safe and happy and protected and innocent for as long as possible. Never mind that she'd already seen more evil than most humans ever did. Never mind that she was now one of the most feared types of beings in existence, trained by the best fighter I'd ever known. I just wanted her to be safe.

About ten minutes later, the buzzer sounded, and I stood up and went to the door. As I'd hoped, Levitt, the demon I'd let go at the gateway, stood there.

"I received your summons," he said, bowing and thumping his fist to his chest.

"Thank you for coming. Please come in," I said to him, and he nodded and walked into the loft. I saw him looking around, noticed Shanti and Brennan inspecting this new visitor. Brennan, of course, knew about Levitt, even if they hadn't officially been introduced yet. And I'd been lax in getting to know this demon. Maybe I could kill two birds with one stone.

"Levitt, please meet Brennan," I said. Levitt walked over to him, and the two men shook hands, Levitt bowing his head to Brennan with respect. Well done, I thought. "And this is Shanti," I said, and he shook her hand and gave a small nod. I could sense Shanti, and she was nervous and confused.

I looked at them all. "Levitt, I asked you here today because I need a favor from you," I said.

"Anything you ask, I will gladly do, my Lady," he said, bowing again.

"Good. You are a formidable warrior. I've fought you myself, and remember what it was like." He was silent, though he acknowledged the compliment with a small nod. I liked him, I decided, glad my initial impression of him still held. Nothing overblown, nothing cocky, though he was confident. This would do.

"Shanti wants to join the lost girl and lost boy patrols," I said.

He studied Shanti. "She is a vampire," he said. "Young."

"Not much younger than you, demon," Shanti said, and I could sense that she was irritated.

"Looks can be deceiving, vamp. I've got half a century under my belt."

"In the Nether," Shanti said, "Which hardly counts as real-world experience."

"Think so?" he asked, raising his eyebrow at her.

"Great," I said, breaking in. "Shanti wants to prove to me that she's able to do this. Levitt, I want you to fight her. Pull no punches. Do not hold back."

Shanti was looking at him with a feral, hungry look in her eyes. "Excellent," she said. "Let's go, demon. The sooner I finish you, the sooner I can get to work."

I could feel amusement from him. "After you," he said, waving her toward the open training floor of the loft. I watched as they squared off, bowed respectfully to each other. Brennan came up next to me at the edge of the training floor.

"Are you sure about this?" he asked quietly, putting his hand on my hip.

"Absolutely," I murmured, watching as Shanti and Levitt began to circle one another. "Neither one of us could do this. He doesn't know her well enough to care, but he will do what I ask." We watched as they circled, waited for the first punch to be thrown.

CHAPTER SIXTEEN

After a few seconds of watching each other warily, of circling, of studying one another for weaknesses, Shanti ended up striking first. She hit out at Levitt with so much speed I could barely track her movements, hitting him with an uppercut, then a quick jab to his gut. I heard Levitt grunt, ready himself to throw a punch, but she beat him to it and bounced back, kicking him in the gut before he could land it.

I glanced over at Brennan, standing next to me with his arms crossed over his chest, watching. A small smile was on his lips, his attention fully focused on Shanti and Levitt. I felt for him. Pride. A bit of concern, but I had a feeling, at that point, that it wasn't concern for Shanti.

I focused on the fight again. She was impossibly fast. Light on her feet, graceful. It was like watching a deadly ballet, mesmerizing and frightening all at the same time. It took Levitt a couple of minutes, and I realized that he was not so much getting his ass kicked (which was what it looked like) as picking up her rhythms, her stance. He was already bleeding, bruising, but when I sensed for him, there was nothing but calm.

Shanti was a boiling vat of emotion: anxiety, anger, concern. I knew her. She didn't want to hurt Levitt, especially knowing how he'd served me. But she needed to prove herself. I had a moment of guilt for putting both of them in this situation, then shook it off. Sometimes, brutal solutions were the only ones you had. I was not willing to send Shanti out on patrol without knowing she could handle it. If she could handle herself against a demon who had survived the Pit, I had no reason to worry about her on the streets.

I'd worry anyway, of course.

Levitt found his bearings, started landing hits almost as often as Shanti did. The first few weren't a big deal. Then he drew back and hit her with a hard punch that had blood flowing from her nose. I started moving before I knew what I was doing, but Bren grabbed me, held me back.

"You wanted to see what she's made of, right?" he said quietly in my ear. "She's almost as indestructible as you are. A nosebleed is not a big deal."

I made myself relax, took a breath and nodded. "I had no idea she could do this." The fight raged on, both of them landing punches and kicks with frightening speed and accuracy. I'd fought a vampire once, and barely survived. I'd survive better now, of course — I didn't have full access to all of my powers back then. It's not something I had any desire to do again.

"She took to her training beautifully. At first, she just wanted to know she could protect herself. And then she wanted to be able to put the hurt on. Just like her hero does."

"I'm not a hero."

"To her? Yes you are."

I was silent in response, and he continued. "Anyway, she has been dedicated since the beginning. I don't think there's much more I can teach her. She likes swords, but I only know really basic shit with them. We might want to ask around."

I was about to ask how useful sword knowledge really was, when I remembered what had happened to the vampire I'd fought with. Beheaded, with a sword. By Nain. Since beheading was one of the only sure ways to kill a vampire, it made sense for her to know it.

Brennan seemed to read my thoughts. "I'm pretty sure she's going to specialize in bringing vampires to justice," he said quietly.

I nodded, still watching. Levitt was beginning to tire, but Shanti was still hitting, kicking, dancing as if she could do this forever. I felt frustration from Levitt, respect for his opponent. She was tireless, merciless. Her fangs lengthened in her mouth, adrenaline and the scent of Levitt's blood apparently affecting her. I was impressed with her focus.

After a few more minutes, she kicked out at him, and he fell. She was on him in an instant, rolling him over and pinning his arms behind his back, holding him down. He struggled against her, tried to get his bearings. Determined. He tried, and he failed.

After a few minutes of trying to find some way out of Shanti's iron grip, he rested his forehead against the wood floor. "I yield," he muttered, out of breath.

"Thank you," Shanti said. Then she got up and held a hand out to him, pulling him up. He bowed in respect, and she bowed back. Then, he did something I would not have expected in a million years.

Levitt pulled up the sleeve of the blue shirt he was wearing, and offered his arm, wrist up, to Shanti. She looked at him, questioning, confused.

"You defeated me. It's your right if you want, vamp," he said, though there was more warmth in his tone than there had been before.

Shanti looked at me questioningly, and I gave a small shrug.

She was unsure. Worried. Tempted. Hungry. The fight had taken a lot of energy. I knew she worried about hurting people, still, even though she'd been around all of us for nearly six months now and had been good about managing her bloodlust. She was worried about losing control. Then I saw the moment she resolved to stay in control. She nodded, and took Levitt's hand in hers, brought his wrist the rest of the way to her mouth.

She kept her eyes on Levitt, I knew, to gauge any signs of pain or fear. Then she breathed a few breaths against his skin, and sank her fangs into his wrist.

Levitt stood, quiet and calm, as she drank. I watched, knowing this was a defining moment for both of them, for all of us. Building trust, building bonds. I stayed in tune with Shanti, felt her become calmer, more peaceful, less hungry. After a few more moments, she withdrew from Levitt's wrist, licking the puncture wounds to heal them. Levitt pulled his wrist back and nodded, and he and Shanti watched each other for a moment.

"That was so much better than bagged blood," Shanti said, then immediately ducked her head, embarrassed. "I mean...yeah. Good fight, demon."

Levitt grinned. "Good fight, vamp. I think you probably proved your point. Who the hell trained you to fight like that?"

Shanti smiled and nodded toward Brennan. "He taught me everything I know," she said.

Brennan grinned. "I showed you what I know. I can't take credit for vampire reflexes, though."

"I don't suppose you're taking on new students?" Levitt asked, laughing.

"Anytime, man," Brennan said. Then he looked at me. "So?"

They were all watching me. I could feel the expectation, impatience from Shanti. I still didn't like this. Hated it, in fact. But she had proven, beyond a doubt, that she could handle herself. And who the hell was I to tell her she couldn't do her part?

I nodded, slowly. "Okay. You win." Shanti let out a

little squeal, and clapped a couple of times. Levitt smiled, and Brennan walked up to her and they bumped fists, and then she pulled him into a hug, and he laughed.

"But," I said, and all three of them turned to look at me. "You need a partner." My gaze landed on Levitt. "Any chance you're looking to join us officially?"

He looked dumbstruck. He stared at me, then glanced around the room. Shanti was watching him expectantly, and she laughed. "Duh. You're surprised by this? Haven't you already been helping?" Then she put it together. "Oh. Wait. You want him to be my partner?"

I nodded.

"Why not you? Or Brennan?"

"Because I never know when I'm going to be around, and because Brennan has seven million things going on already and when he does hunt, he insists on hunting with me."

"Obviously," Brennan murmured.

"And," I went on, "because you want to take on the lost girl duties, and Levitt has already been doing it. The imps have been working with him. So if you're determined to find lost girls, you and Levitt should work together."

"You were letting him find them alone, though," Shanti said. "Double standard much?"

"Levitt, awesome as he is, is not as near and dear to my heart as you are. It has nothing to do, especially now, with believing you're weak or unable to do this."

"Or because I'm a girl?" Shanti said.

I raised my eyebrows and gestured at myself. Brennan laughed. "I'm the last one on Earth or anywhere else who's going to pull the 'you're just a girl' card, Shanti."

"I know. Sorry," she said.

I sighed. "Look. I love you, you little pain in the ass. Humor me in this, all right? Work with Levitt and the imps."

She nodded. "Okay. Um," she glanced at Levitt. "You need to join the team now or I'm gonna kick your ass again."

Brennan snorted and I bit back a smile. Levitt watched her with a bored look. "I was going to join anyway, vamp. It's an honor that the Angel considers me worthy." Then he looked at me. "Thank you."

"Thank you for all of the hard work you've already put in, and for doing this tonight. You're welcome to move in. We have an empty room. Lots of food, as long as you beat Stone to it."

He stared at me. "Here? I could live here?"

"Yeah. I need to apologize to you. I should have asked you before this. The imps told me you were making do, but..." I shrugged. "I am sorry I let you go and then left you to fend for yourself."

He shook his head vehemently. "No apologies are necessary. You gave me a second chance. I was squatting in an abandoned house. I was comfortable enough. It was much better than what I came from."

"Well. Nonetheless, if you'd like a home here, it's yours," I said.

He bowed and thumped his fist to his chest. "Thank you."

"You can have the room next to Shanti's," I said, and Shanti walked off to show him where it was.

"Those rooms have a connecting bathroom," I said to Brennan, grimacing.

"Please tell me you're not getting all protective over your baby girl," he said, laughing.

"She is attracted to him."

"Let her deal with it."

"So you're not going to hammer a bunch of boards over his side of the bathroom door for me?"

"You could give him Nain's room if you're that worried about it," he said, watching me.

I shook my head. "No."

"So, what? Are we going to keep it there as a shrine forever?"

I glared at him, felt my shoulders tense. "We'll keep it there, the way it is, until I feel up to going through all of his clothing and other stuff. When I'm ready, I'll deal with it."

He watched me. I could sense irritation from him. "Yeah? When are you going to stop wearing that?" he asked, gesturing at my finger, where I still wore my ring.

"Do you seriously want to do this now?" I asked him, meeting his eyes, and I could hear the snarl in my voice. He didn't answer. "Why are you acting like this now?"

He shook his head, wiped his hands over his face. I felt his irritation draw back, just a little. "I'm sorry. This...bringing people onto the team, watching this fight to see Shanti prove herself...this just all reminds me of him, and thinking of him inevitably makes me think of him and you. And he's gone, but in some ways, it's like he never left."

I didn't know what to say. Nothing he said was inaccurate. Our day to day life was still imbued with Nain's memory, traces of him still affecting every day of our existence. "Timing probably has something to do with it, too," I said quietly.

He nodded. "A year tomorrow." Then he turned his gaze to me. "I'm guessing you won't be around much the next day or so."

I gave a slight shake of my head. Knew it was selfish, that he was grieving in his own way, and I was leaving him to it. He took my hand.

"It's okay," he said softly, pulling me into his arms. "Do what you have to do. I'm sorry I acted like an ass."

"I love you, Bren," I said softly. I rested my cheek against his chest and closed my eyes.

"I love you, too," he said. "I feel like I'm constantly competing with a ghost, and there's no way I can win."

"You're the only one who sees it that way, babe," I

said. "Believe in us. I do. It's the only thing that keeps me sane sometimes."

He held me tighter, and we stood in silence. I could hear his heartbeat, hear Shanti and Levitt talking in Levitt's new room. I stood there, and my mind was flooded with memories of the man who'd brought us all together.

◆◆◆

The next morning, Brennan was up and out of the loft before I was even awake. He knew me well enough to know that things would just be weird between us, considering what day it was. One year, to the day, since Nain's death. And we both knew I was still carrying around a shitload of guilt, anger, confusion...just about everything it was possible to feel about a person, that was what I felt for Nain, a year later.

So I got up, and I tossed on my Fury uniform. I had no idea what Brennan thought I'd be doing all day, but it didn't involve sitting next to the spot Nain had died and crying. I had two meetings to be present for with Hades. And then, to honor my dead husband and try to assuage some of my own guilt, I was going to seriously start hunting the fucker who'd sent Astaroth after me in the first place. I'd lost Nain to them. Losing Brennan....losing Brennan was something I would not survive. Period.

I had some ideas, now. Time spent in the Nether had not been wasted, and even though most of my time was spent punishing the wicked and attending to Hades, one hears things. And when someone, like me, who can sense emotions, is around enough, you get some ideas. There were gods who very clearly did not like me. That was one thing. My existence was the one threat in the entire cosmos to their own. I understood their dislike, their fear.

Then, there were others. Others, who I felt active, strong hatred from. Those, who got a rabid look in their eyes every time they passed me in the streets of Hades' city. There were not many. Dionysus, in his two visits to Hades so far, had been one who seemed ready to leap up and stake me through the heart. The Nosoi, as a whole, hated me, especially after one of their own had been punished severely. By me. I was less worried about them, though. They were being watched closely by my mother and aunts after that little fiasco, and I don't think any of them even moved without one of the Furies knowing it.

There were others. Hades' wife, Persephone, hated my guts and had never hidden her feelings on my visits to their home. Hermes. Apollo. The gods from the Aether, especially, seemed to hate me. All the indications we'd had, though, were that my pesky god was from the Nether. He or she had contracted a demon to destroy me. Had contracted the Nosoi to target Brennan.

I thought as I drove the Barracuda to the Packard plant. Bash and Dahael were subdued as well, riding in the back seat. The thing was, the Nether were my people. Gods. Whatever. Some of them didn't like me, but I was theirs. It was like being part of some huge dysfunctional family. Everything in me told me that my enemy was not actually of the Nether, though they'd worked very hard to make it appear so. Which meant that I was probably dealing with a god from the Aether. Or a terrestrial god, like my father. So far, though, they seemed to keep to themselves. Including my father, who still hadn't bothered to contact me.

Maybe word traveled more slowly to mountain gods.

I slowed the car and pulled over to the curb. "Guys," I said softly to the imps. They both looked up at me, ears perking up at my voice. "I'm going to let you out here. I should not have brought you with me today."

"But…" Dahael began.

"I need you to do something more important than wait outside the gate for me."

They both watched me, waiting. "Keep an eye on Brennan today. Okay?"

"Is wild man in danger?" Bash asked in his hoarse little voice.

"I don't think so. But I just...I would feel better if you two watched over him. Today is making me jumpy, I guess." They both nodded, thumped their chests, and left the car, slamming the passenger door behind them.

I drove away, now feeling completely alone. The imps were my constant companions. I trusted them completely, which meant they needed to be with Bren. The feeling of dread that had been settling on me since I'd opened my eyes that morning was now a raging sense of foreboding. I pulled up outside the abandoned factory and made my way inside, through the crumbling doorway, into the rubble and litter-strewn interior. The graffiti was easy to see in the cool morning sunlight, and the smells of the factory, decay, urine, and dust, surrounded me.

I hated it there.

That hadn't changed. I walked toward the gateway. I had told myself I wouldn't do the stupid grieving thing here in the factory, but as I passed the spot where he'd died, I ended up going back and crouching next to the scorched concrete.

"You left me that letter, remember? Telling me this was the only way. I wonder how much you knew. Whether you suspected any of the shit that would follow your death. How much of a joke is it that I practically became invincible because of your death, but if I'd been invincible in the first place you wouldn't have had to die?" I took a breath, sat down. I was glad now that the imps were not with me. How crazy did I look, talking to an empty factory?

"The Fates had a field day with us, didn't they? Put us together, take you away from me, all to unlock my powers, undo the spells that hid me. For what? If I could find those three old hags, I'd love to know what they were thinking." I sat in silence for a few minutes. At least I wasn't crying.

"I love you, I guess. Maybe not in the same way. Sometimes I suspect we were a farce, Bael. The gods played their games, and we were just two pawns in all of it. I'll avenge you. Somehow, I'll make whoever played this particular game pay. Then, maybe I can let you go. Maybe I'll stop talking to you as if you can hear me. Maybe I can be the woman Brennan deserves. Probably not, but I hope so." I paused, looked up at the broken windows.

"I feel guilty about him. I shouldn't, but I do. I love him, and I know he is meant for me, in every way. I feel guilty that I didn't feel the same thing with you. And I feel guilty that I still think about you, when I have him beside me. Maybe my Nether side loves you, and my nature-god side loves Brennan."

I heard a distinctive "crack" and Eunomia landed beside me, then crouched down and put her thin arm around my shoulder.

"There you are. I figured today might be a hard one for you, my friend," she said quietly.

"I am so confused, and angry, and just....this is all so stupid," I said, and now the tears did threaten.

She hugged me tighter to her. "It is. The Fates are jerks."

I laughed, a little. "You sound like me now."

"Well, sometimes you make sense, demon girl."

"I miss him."

"Of course you do. I suspect he was the first being you ever really loved. Yes?" I nodded. Hadn't really thought about it that way, but, yeah. She was right. "So it's okay to miss him. And I heard part of what you said at the end. You shouldn't feel guilty, either for loving and missing him, or for loving your shifter now. This is life. Things happen."

"Because of the Fates," I said.

She looked thoughtful. "Yes, and no."

"Meaning?"

"The Fates put the pieces into place. They may put two

people in the same city, but they don't determine whether those people love or hate each other, should they meet. They put the game pieces on the board, but we decide how to play the game. They may put someone on the track toward early death, but that person's actions determine whether they succumb or survive. The Fates make us decide who we are, how strong we can be."

"And who am I supposed to be, E?"

"You are supposed to be Molly."

"Not Mollis Cithaerus?" I asked, hearing the sneer in my voice.

"She is part of who you are. She is not all of you."

"I hate her. So much shit has happened because I'm a god, Fury, thing."

E gave me one of her knowing little smiles. "Yes. So much has. You've met and fallen in love with not one, but two amazing men. You've made friends you wouldn't have made, had you just remained a simple vigilante. You have an adopted daughter. You are friends with me, which should be enough to make it all worthwhile," she finished, and I laughed.

I stood up, and she rose as well. "Don't hate yourself. Not any part of you."

"Who I am puts the people I love in danger, though," I said.

She studied me. "Then eliminate the threats against them. It's not like you are powerless."

"Doing that will only piss more gods off," I said, walking toward the gate. "Where does it end?"

"Are you becoming cautious in your old age, demon girl?" Eunomia asked, laughing.

I shrugged. "I have a lot to lose." We walked through the gateway, and we chatted as we traveled the already-bustling streets toward Hades' home. Demons saluted me, and I greeted them in return. The demons, to a one, adored me. That made me smile for some reason, maybe because of what day it was.

Eunomia seemed to guess what I was thinking. "They admire you. A god who really is more like them. A god who bonded with one of their own. That just isn't done. Most gods, even those of the Nether, aren't comfortable around demons."

"Because demons are the gods' biggest failure, or so they say. Thriving on fear, anger and, pain," I said.

She nodded. "Right. One almost wonders why they were created in the first place, no?"

"Probably with the intent to be used by someone, or several someones," I murmured.

"You have learned a lot since you've been here," E said, a bit of humor in her voice.

I snorted. "Except that they probably didn't anticipate how stubborn demons can be."

"True." As we walked, I looked around, at the buildings, the sculptures that dotted the main avenue. "Can you tell me something?"

Eunomia glanced at me. "I will try."

"What's with three? I'm always noticing that three of something appears just about everywhere here. Three eyes on that sculpture. Three birds painted on that mural. Sets of three windows, on all of those buildings over there. Three lights on each lamp post…"

She nodded. "Three is an important number. Haven't you ever read fairy tales? A genie grants three wishes. Say Rumpelstiltskin's name three times. Make a wish and turn around three times."

"Superstitious bullshit," I muttered.

"Except that it's not. The number three has power, just as our true names do. Anything, done three times, has power in our world."

Something tickled my psyche when she said it, but I couldn't quite put my finger on it. "But not always. Not accidentally."

"No. Intent is important. There must be a reason to do whatever it is three times. For example, you might pray to

Asceplias to heal. Once might do it. But three times..."

"Hades came to me after I said the plea to Asceplias three times," I said quietly, remembering.

"Of course."

We reached Hades' home, and she turned to me. "You'll be okay?"

"I'll be fine. Thanks for the company, E."

She nodded. Hermes walked past us, into Hades' home for his upcoming meeting, and, instead of sneering at me as he usually did, he gave me a bright smile and a wink. I glared at him. "Time to go play enforcer for Hades," I muttered.

"Try to think happy thoughts," E said, laughing.

"I will try." Then I headed inside, through the door Hermes had just walked through.

CHAPTER SEVENTEEN

I made my way into Hades' home. It was large, but not gaudy. It was a more modern-looking building than many in the Nether, and my mother had once explained to me that Hades appreciated architecture and often changed the look of his home. Currently, he was in a Frank Lloyd Wright appreciation phase. As I walked in the front door, I was greeted by one of the demons who worked for Hades. The demon thumped his chest once as he approached, and I gave him a small nod in return.

"Lord Hades is speaking with his wife right now," the demon said. "Do you mind waiting a bit? Lord Hermes is in there if you'd like to sit with him," he said, pointing toward the living room.

I shook my head and grimaced. "I think I'd rather drink acid."

He grinned, though to his credit, he did try to hide it. "What is your name?" I asked him.

"Elsoloth," he said, surprise coming from him.

"Nice to meet you, Elsoloth," I said.

"And it is an honor to meet you as well, my Lady," he

said, bowing a little. "Can I get you anything?"

I shook my head. "No thank you." I studied him. He was tall, around six foot six or so, with dark gray skin and red glowing eyes. He wore the black uniforms many denizens of the Nether wore, not so different from my own. The guards, house servants, and Furies all wore pretty much the same thing. He caught me looking, and I looked away. "I'm sorry," I said.

"No apologies are necessary, my Lady," he said.

"There are not many demons in my world. And most there wear human skins. I am still getting used to seeing demons in their true form."

He nodded. "You were bonded to a demon though, yes? I can feel demon blood in you. It calls to my own."

"Yes. I was. My mate was trapped in a mortal body, though, so I was never able to see his true form. Unfortunately," I said, and meant it. Nain must have been a spectacular demon, given the human skin he wore.

"I am sorry for your loss," Elsoloth said softly.

"Thank you."

He cleared his throat, looked around. "I would like you to know, my Lady, that should you ever need anything, the demons of the Nether are here for you. You don't know us, but we consider you one of ours, maybe even more so than these gods do," he finished, his voice low enough that only I could hear.

"Why?" I asked, genuinely curious. "You don't know me."

"We demons are not exactly the warmest, kindest creatures in existence, maybe," he said with a wry grin. "But we take care of our own. And the blood in your veins makes you one of us."

I watched him, tried to fight back the tears that threatened at his words. "That means a lot to me, Elsoloth. More than you know, today."

He bowed his head. "Don't forget. Trouble is coming," he said.

A shiver went up my spine, but I tried to keep myself calm. "I won't. If there is anything I can do for you, please let me know," I said, holding my hand out to him. He took it, his huge hands enveloping mine, and he shook my hand gently. "Thank you."

"My pleasure, my Lady," he said softly. And he gave me a small bow and walked away. I stood for a few minutes, watched Persephone come out of Hades' office, and Hermes walk in. Persephone glared at Hermes' back as he walked into Hades' office, then she turned toward me.

Persephone never failed to make me feel small. Not so much in stature; she wasn't much taller than me. But in the way she carried herself, in her beauty. And in her obvious disdain for me.

She swept into the entry hall, wearing her customary green satin gown, multicolored jewels sparkling among her fiery tresses. "Mollis," she said in a voice that made it seem as though she might as well have been addressing a slug.

"Lady Persephone," I said, bowing my head to her. This was Hades' wife, and he had done me a huge favor. He adored her, and, from what I'd seen of them together, the feeling was mutual, even if there was a bit of an undercurrent of anger there. I figured, a few thousand years or so, they probably had a whole lot to be irritated with each other about. They argued, but, for the most part, they were practically saccharine when they were in the same room. Kind of like me and Brennan lately, I thought, feeling myself blush a little. Would we be the same way a hundred years from now? Two hundred? I pushed thoughts of Bren back. Distracting, gorgeous man. Right now, I had a pissy goddess to deal with.

Her sweetness definitely did not extend to me. I would show her respect, no matter how much I wanted to do the bitch act right back at her.

She stood there, watching me, lip curling in distaste. "Listen to me, Fury," she said, and I looked at her more closely. Not only was she talking to me, but the urgency in her tone surprised me. She was afraid, and angry. "You must be alert in there."

"With Hades?" I asked, raising my eyebrow.

"With Hermes. Listen. Pay attention both to what he says and what he doesn't. He and my bastard of a son are up to something. I can feel it."

"Your son?"

"Dionysus. Zeus's. You've heard the story, yes?" she asked impatiently.

"Oh. Right," I said, embarrassed.

"Something's happening. The entire Nether is restless. Can you feel it?"

I stared at her. She'd never said more than two words to me, and usually with a sneer. I couldn't disagree with what she was saying, but I'd thought it was me and my mood. Elsoloth's warning echoed by a goddess. Fuck.

"Do you think Lord Hades is in danger of some kind?" I whispered.

She looked at me, her gaze fierce. "The only one he really needs to fear is you. Remember that."

"I would not hurt him," I said.

"I should think not," she muttered, glaring at me again.

"Is there something you want to say to me, my Lady?" I asked, losing a bit of my patience.

She glared at me. "Are you really so clueless? How can you spend so much time in his company and not know?"

"Know what?"

She let out a breath, irritated. "It is not my place to say."

"Says who?"

"Your mother and my husband." She looked at me, studied me. "Where is your father, Fury?" she asked, and I was startled by the change of subject.

"I...don't know. On his mountain, I guess. Why?"

She muttered something that sounded like "idiocy."

"What? Just spit it out, whatever it is." Well. There went my attempts at "nice." I suck at this kind of thing.

She glared at me. "Your father is no mountain god. 'Mollis Cithaerus,' my foot."

I gaped at her. "Uh. Yes he is. My mother—"

"Your mother is doing everything she can to protect you, to keep the horror of what you truly are a secret. And since everyone knows your mother is sleeping with Cithaeron, it is convenient. However, if your father was a mountain god, he would have known you existed. He would have felt his own blood upon the earth, as many times as you've been injured, and he would have found you long before this. That is how they work."

I stared. "Okay. So....?"

"Consider the fact that he's done favors for you that he'd never do for anyone else," she said, and continued. "Consider how often he requests you attend him. And then consider the way your blood undoubtedly responds to his," she finished, meeting my eyes, and after a moment, I caught the gist of what she was saying.

"Uh. No. No. Nuh-uh. Not even possible. He can't create life. Everyone knows that," I said, balling my fists. My hands had become ice cold.

"Well," she said, glaring at me. "Accidents happen, don't they?" She let her eyes sweep over me, making it clear who and what she considered an "accident." Then she swept past me. "Protect your father, Fury. With your insignificant life, if you must," she said as she walked away.

I didn't know how to handle what Persephone had just said. Didn't know whether to believe her, or even begin to figure out why she would lie about something like that.

I walked into Hades' office to see Hades and Hermes already sitting across from each other, Hades' black stone desk between them. As always, the desk was piled with a crazy assortment of things, from newspapers and an old typewriter, to skulls and what looked like the bones of a small animal. Maybe a bird. Candles in iron sconces lit the perimeter of the room, and, as always, anywhere Hades was the air was permeated with the not-unpleasant scent of smoke. I went and stood in my customary place, behind and to the slight right of Hades' large leather chair.

I tried focusing on his blood, mine, and my response to it. My blood did call to his, and his to mine, but I'd always figured it was because we were both creatures of the Nether, and that his blood called to me more strongly because he was Lord of the Nether. I didn't know what to believe.

"Mollis," Hades said in greeting.

"Hades," I said. "Please forgive my tardiness. I apologize." *Dad*, I thought at him.

He barely reacted, though I did note a tiny grimace. *My wife talks too much. We will discuss this later.* "Not a problem, my dear. Hermes here was early."

Who else knows? I need to know. Now.

I settled my gaze on Hermes. I would heed Persephone's warning. I didn't like her, but she was shrewd, and if she saw fit to warn me against him....

Me, my wife, your mother, Cithaeron, and you. That's it.

Cithaeron knows?

Your mother had some explaining to do. As did I with Persephone.

I sighed and tried to focus on Hermes again. My life was one fucking soap opera after another.

Messenger god, was how most people thought of Hermes. They forgot the rest. He is also a trickster, a troublemaker. And more. Gods really are not all that fond of traveling between the Nether or Aether and the mortal world. It wears on them, depletes their power for a time. They are at their most powerful, and most comfortable, in their own realms. So, when Asclepias and Hades came to me in my world, that was a big deal, and I'd had no idea at the time what I was asking of them. That type of thing is not often done.

Hermes, though... Hermes was different. He could easily cross into my world with no problem. He was the first of the Guardians, and Eunomia and her sisters were the continuation of what he'd begun, taking the souls of the dead to the Nether for their final judgment. He easily traveled from Aether, to the mortal realm, to the Nether.

I stared at him now, my own suspicions and Persephone's warnings ringing in my ears. He was a beautiful man. Dark hair, dark eyes, tall, with a slight point to his nose and a strong jaw. It was a cold beauty, though. One got the sense, looking at Hermes, that he didn't love anything or anyone as much as himself. He felt me staring at him, and gave me a small wink as Hades made small talk the way he did at the beginning of every meeting. I didn't react, kept my eyes firmly on him. Hades was talking, but I wasn't listening to the words. I was sensing for Hermes.

And I couldn't feel a thing.

Suddenly the room got quiet. I glanced at Hades, and he had turned to look at me.

"I'm sorry, my Lord. Did you need something?" I asked, trying to keep myself under control. There was not a being in existence who had been able to hide him or herself from me. What the hell was this now?

Hades raised his eyebrows. *You are throwing off all manner of crazy power right now, my dear. Are you all right?*

"I am surprised the Fury has come in to work today," Hermes said, a small smirk on his lips.

"Why is that?" Hades asked, glancing from Hermes to me.

Hermes just smiled. "Seems to me, one would want to be with her loved ones on a day like this," he said, and the threat in his voice was only heightened by the smug smile on his face.

Before I knew what I was doing, I had leaped over Hades' desk, my sword appearing in my hand. I held it up to Hermes' throat, and he held his hands up, laughing.

"Something you want to tell me?" I growled. All he did was laugh.

"Mollis!" Hades said.

"Why can't I sense you, Hermes?" I asked. "What have you done to make it possible to hide yourself from a Fury?"

Now Hades was looking between the two of us, and Hermes let out another small laugh. "Maybe you are not as powerful as you thought you were, little Fury," he sneered.

"Answer her question, Hermes," Hades said, standing up. "Why can't she feel you?"

Hermes just sat there, looking at me with that smug smile on his face. "You probably want to run home now, don't you?" he said. "Never know what might be happening to those mortals you love so much while you're here, playing enforcer for Hades."

I gripped my sword tighter, tried to dampen the terror rising in me.

"Of course, you're here already. And you've been gone for hours, yes? Anything could have happened."

I tensed, and he laughed. "What are you going to do, Fury?"

"You're saying all of this in front of Hades. What is your game, Hermes?" I asked, hating the tremor in my voice and realizing, sick as it was, that the lives of a few mortals meant nothing here. Not to Hermes, not overmuch to Hades. The only importance mortals had here was that they could be used, and my friends were being caught in the crossfire again, because the gods wanted something from me.

I shook with rage.

He smiled. I pressed my sword, just barely, against his skin, and heard his flesh sizzle against the flaming blade. He let out a low whimper, then composed himself, though he had at least stopped smirking. "Are you going to kill me, Mollis?" he asked.

"That depends on what you've done," I said, forcing my body to calm, my nerves to become ice. I'd linked my mind to my mother's, my aunts' as soon as Hermes had taunted me. My mother and aunt Megaera were on their way to the loft to check on everyone. My aunt Alecto was on her way to Hades'. All I could do now was try to understand.

"Abomination," he said, as pleasantly as if he was calling me a friend, "going to start a war over a mortal or two?"

"Hermes," Hades threatened, but I cut him off.

"A war? Is your worthless existence worth all that?"

He laughed, even though my blade cut deeper and blood began to drip down his neck. "Mine? Maybe not. But if you kill me, you do exactly the thing they all fear. You prove that they are not as immortal as they thought. They will come after you."

"So they'll kill me. If you've done the things I suspect you have, them killing me is worth it, as long as I get to kill you first."

He laughed again. "Silly girl. This is so much bigger than you."

God, I wanted to kill him. Just on principle. Hades stood next to me, arms crossed, staring daggers at Hermes. Rage rolled off of him, reminding me that though he was a god, he was THE demon. I'd thought I'd felt demonic rage before. It was nothing compared to what I was feeling now. My aunt arrived, and stared at me, with my sword at Hermes' neck, then came and stood across from me, drawing her own sword.

Which she then pointed at me.

"Lower the sword, Mollis," Alecto said quietly.

I stared at her. Hades was looking from me to Alecto, then back again, clearly as confused as I was. "Fury?" he said.

"Withdraw the sword, Mollis," Alecto repeated, and I lowered my sword, staring at her.

"Now, be a good girl and do away with Hades, will you?" Hermes asked, standing up and straightening his robes. Then he went and stood next to my aunt, putting a hand on her hip. I gaped. "Quickly now. Wouldn't want your mother and auntie to walk in on this."

"I'm not going to kill Hades," I said. I could feel Hades' rage, his confusion.

"It's really quite simple," Alecto said, continuing to hold her sword on me. "Either you kill him, or we kill you and then destroy the lovely shifter we've captured. After I have a bit of fun with him, maybe."

I stared at her. Sensed for my connection to Brennan. Fuck.

He was close. Way too close. My connection to him when I was in the Nether was usually pulled thin; there, but just barely. And now...I hadn't noticed in the stupidity with Hermes.

I could barely breathe. *Hades.*

"I have always wanted a panther rug, though," she said, smiling. "Maybe we'll kill him anyway."

This makes no sense. Keep them talking.

"Of course you will. The same way you helped kill my husband," I said. They both smiled at me.

"Oh, no, darling. That was all you. Don't fool yourself."

"Astaroth," I said.

"Oh, Astaroth was a fool. He was mine, but he was a failure," Hermes said. I tried thinking at my mother, and I couldn't reach her.

Alecto laughed. "She's not close enough to hear you. She's off, chasing down mortals."

I could have screamed. Forced myself to calm down. "Is he still alive?" I finally asked, trying to buy time.

"He is. If you behave, he'll go home."

"And what about me?"

"Well. Either the gods will hunt you down and kill you for the crime of deicide. As powerful as you are, you are ultimately nothing more than a mortal, after all. Or, we'll manage to keep you hidden away until we have use of you again. One or the other," Hermes said, grinning.

"I'd tell them you made me do it," I said, still stalling.

Hermes laughed. "As if they'd believe you. Who are they going to believe? Me, a god. One of them, who they've known for eons? Especially if a Fury backs up my version of the story?"

"Or you? An abomination, something that should never have been. Someone who maybe, just maybe, wanted a bit of power for herself. It's a lovely story, really, and I'd spin it beautifully. About how you believed you deserved a place among the gods, about how you saw yourself as a better judge of souls than Hades, and how I stood here in fear of my life and watched you murder him, and how poor Alecto arrived just in time to see you do it, but too late to save Hades. How she subdued you, just in time."

"Persephone and the servants are all here," I said.

Hermes just grinned. "Dionysus is keeping his mother busy for us. As for the servants… it's not as if a few demons really pose any threat to me. Should one happen to hear too much…" he just smiled again and shrugged.

"You won't get away with it, Hermes," Hades said. "Tisiphone…"

"Will be the next being to die. Right after you," Hermes said, still smiling.

"And she'll deserve it, too," Alecto sniffed. "For bringing this abomination into the world."

"I am so tired of you guys calling me that," I muttered. I sat, and they all watched me. I tried reaching my mother again, to no avail. *What the actual fuck, Hades?* All I got from my father was anger and confusion in response.

"What is your game, Hermes?" Hades said after a while. "You are a bastard, but this is a bit much even for you."

"My Lord Hades," Hermes said with a sneer. "This isn't about me, or her, or even you. I am here in the service of another. A favor granted, which, I'll admit, I am happy to give."

"Who?" Hades demanded.

Hermes just grinned, refusing to answer. I worked at his mind, but trying to force your way into a god's mind is nearly impossible, and I was rewarded with a pounding headache for my efforts. He watched me. "So many pieces in this game, little Fury," he murmured. "We are like the Hydra. Destroy one of us, and another will take its place."

"Why?"

"Because we tire of wasting away in the Aether and Nether like relics," a strong, cold female voice said, and I stood again, glanced toward the door to see a tall woman with short black hair walking through. She was dressed in armor, head to toe, and her eyes glowed blood red. "Because while Zeus and Hades' rules have kept humanity safe," she said with a sneer, "they have also made humanity forget us."

"Enyo," Hermes said pleasantly, giving her a small nod.

"Messenger. You may go now," she said.

"Oh, I want to see how this all plays out," Hermes said pleasantly, returning to his seat.

"Do it, abomination. I tire of waiting," Enyo said, standing a few feet away from me. "And we have a date in the Aether."

I was screwed either way, I realized. They had no intention of letting me die here. They would use me. They needed me. Enyo had tipped her hand. But I had two options for the time being: Kill my father, and trust that they'd keep their word and let Brennan live. Not to mention that Hades' death would be a bad thing, for reasons I could only begin to comprehend. Or, try to overpower, and possibly kill, two gods and a Fury, and pray that I could not only survive it, but also stay free and alive long enough to find Brennan and take out whoever they had guarding him before it was too late. If I succeeded, I was dead. Killing a god would mean an immediate death sentence for me, no matter what they'd done to push me to it.

"Yeah, okay. I'll do it," I said softly. "You swear you'll let Brennan go?"

My aunt and Hermes smiled. "We swear. The Guardians have been instructed to free him the moment they feel Hades die." My stomach rolled. The Guardians. E and her sisters. "Get this over with," Hermes said.

"Yes, yes. We promise. Do it." Enyo said, impatience, worry clear in her voice. She put her hand on the pommel of her sword, red gaze tracking my every move.

I nodded and raised my sword, meeting Hades' steadfast, angry gaze.

There is one lesson I should have learned sooner:

Never, ever trust a god.

CHAPTER EIGHTEEN

Hades got ready to fight me. I saw it; the way his body tensed, his posture changed. I met his blazing white gaze, held it. I raised my sword, flames leaping between us.

Duck, pops, I thought at him.

I started to swing, toward him. Felt elation, excitement from Enyo, beside me. Hades ducked just in time, and my sword went through where he should have been, and I kept swinging, toward Enyo, the long, thin blade of my sword sizzling, flames leaping.

Like I said: Never, ever trust a god. Or the child of one.

Her head hit the floor before she even realized what was happening. Hades leapt for Hermes, tackling him to the floor. He landed a good punch right in Hermes' pointy little nose, and I felt satisfaction from him. Demon god.

I turned to my aunt, who raised her own flaming sword toward me. My father was keeping Hermes out of it so I could concentrate on the threat I could more easily dispense with. Couldn't hurt to have some help, though.

ELSOLOTH and demons of the Nether. You are needed, I thought, with as much force as I could. Not all of them were telepaths, of course. But there had to be at least a few among them.

My aunt and I circled each other. Rage flowed from her, hot, sticky. Fear. I fed on it.

The fear of a Fury. Oh, hell yes.

I smiled, and swung, and she ducked back just in time, hissing at me. "He's dead, you know," she snarled. "The only thing keeping him alive was your obedience."

I tried not to think about it. I just had to get to him before she or Hermes could send word to the Guardians.

Backstabbing bitches. I got angrier the more I thought about it. Eunomia and her sisters. Lies. My entire fucking life was lies. And then I felt it: pain. Brennan's pain, through our connection. It built, unrelenting, and I tried to stay calm in the face of it. I had no chance of saving him if I lost my mind now.

I swung again, in an absolute rage fueled by my mate's pain, and caught Alecto's arm, heard her flesh sizzle, and she screamed.

We come, my Lady, a thought came to me, loud and clear. Demon.

Much appreciated, I thought at the demons who answered. *Find the shifter the Guardians are holding.*

My aunt and I continued circling each other. I tried to focus despite the pain coming through my bond with Brennan. I tripped once over Enyo's body, and Alecto nearly took my arm off, but I kicked out and tripped her, and she stumbled away. I jumped up, leaped toward her, and our swords came together in a fiery, sizzling glare of pure bluish white light. In the background, I heard the door of Hades' office crash open, and the room soon swarmed with demons. They roared a single word, a battle cry: *Mollis!* and surrounded Hades and Hermes.

I felt my aunt panic. More fear for me to feed on. I was ready to burst with my power, in the same room with Alecto and her fear, Hades and his anger, and the energy and anger provided by all of the demons now filling the room at my call. My sword burned brighter in my hands, dwarfing Alecto's, bathing the room in eerie light. She was staring at the blades as she swept mine aside again.

"Don't feel bad. Size isn't everything, I hear," I said, swinging at her and catching her shoulder. She screamed in pain and anger. "Though that hasn't been my experience."

She tried now to take flight, and I pulled her down by the ankle, yanked her to the ground and punched her in the face. My fighting style never has been pretty.

I was about to hit her again when I felt a presence enter the room.

My raised fist started trembling. My heart raced.

No way. Not possible. Someone was just fucking messing with me now.

I put my hand around Alecto's throat in an iron grip, keeping her down, barely noticing the way she struggled against me. My gaze jumped around the room, barely taking in the chaos surrounding me. Where?

The part of my soul that had felt empty for the last year flared back to life.

I scanned the chaos in the room, and my gaze landed on a demon. Huge. Over seven feet tall, easily. Hulking. Reddish-black skin that absorbed the light around him. Glowing blood-red eyes.

I could barely breathe.

Later, Molls. Kick her ass first. A voice in my mind I thought I'd never hear again. My breathing escalated, my body trembled. My pulse raced, and I badly wanted someone to hit me, just to prove I wasn't hallucinating. *Don't lose your shit now. Fight.*

They have Brennan. Focus on the most important thing. Try to focus on concrete shit. Because thinking about anything else right now is impossible.

Not anymore. Eunomia got him out, right after she freed me. He's safe.

How?

Later, Molls. Let's take care of this first.

I made myself focus. Alecto shoved at me, freed her sword hand from my grip and I had to jump back to avoid her blade. We began our deadly dance again, though Alecto was weakening, blood pouring from her thigh, her arm, and her shoulder. She would heal, but not as quickly as she needed to, facing another Fury.

"Abomination," she hissed.

"Liar," I growled. "I know which of the two I'd rather be, bitch." She swung at me, and I deflected easily. "How does it feel to sell your family out? He doesn't give a damn about you, you know."

She snarled and swung again, and it gave me the opening I wanted. My blade swept up and across. Instead of meeting her blade this time, though, the flames of my sword met flesh, and her arm was severed at the elbow as I swept the blade upward. Her lower arm and sword fell together, and she screamed. I put the point of my sword to her throat.

"Kneel," I said, kicking her arm and the sword away. Without her energy suffusing it, the blade disappeared completely; just the hilt rested in her severed hand.

She knelt, angry, in complete agony. Her body would be focusing on healing now; no strength to fight me. "I don't care about him. All I wanted was to see the stain upon my family eliminated. Your existence is a filth upon us all," she hissed.

I glanced across the room. Hades had made quick work of Hermes, who was now kneeling, face bloodied from the fight. The demons guarded him, on alert for any new threats to me or Hades. The beautiful thing was, Hermes was in a lot of pain, and it seemed to feed every demon in the room. Including me.

I glanced around the room, spotted him.

Not even possible.

Nain was talking to a group of demons. Giving them instructions. He finished, and they saluted him sharply.

I remembered everything, memories assaulting all at

once. His death. Veronica's death. Holding a box of George's ashes in my hands. Attempt after attempt after attempt on my life by Astaroth and his crew. All at the behest of one god.

My gaze landed on Hermes, who looked up just in time to see me focus on him, and he was afraid and it was perfection.

I raised my sword again, the flames burning high and bright, in tune with the energy coursing through my body.

"No!" he screamed.

"I'll see you in Tartarus, bastard," I said, and I drew back as he tried to scramble away, not quickly enough. I stabbed, my sword going straight through his heart, sizzling along his flesh, sparking and spitting as flames met blood. I watched his eyes as he died, watched the last light of this god who'd caused the deaths of innocents in his hunt for me, finally go out.

I pulled my sword from him and his body fell over, landing at my feet. I kicked it away. Insignificant garbage. Then I looked up.

The room was silent as my father and the demons stared at me. Hades' mouth was hanging open as he looked from me to Hermes' body, then he composed himself, focused on me.

"We need to get you out of here, Mollis," Hades said. "Before they learn about—"

At that moment, my mother and Megaera swooped into the room, their huge black wings sending a draft through the area, fluttering the papers on Hades' desk. Their eyes were on Alecto. My mother landed and punched her sister in the face, hard. She was pulling Alecto up by the hair, ready to punch her again, when Megaera pulled her back, gently.

"Mom," I said. And then I felt it. Brennan was in pain. Worse, now. Terrible, agonizing, nauseating pain. I screamed as it fell over me through our connection. The adrenaline and power running through my body was only adding to the agony. I could barely breathe. I could feel it spiking. "Oh, god," I said, gritting my teeth against the pain.

"Demons out!" I heard Nain shout. Then he ran at me, shoved me down and covered my body with his huge, hulking one.

"Too much. I can't... Fuck!" I screamed.

"Let it go. You can't hurt me. Do it."

I screamed, felt my power explode inside me, felt my body burning, from the inside out. Everything was white light, and heat, and pain, and Nain's voice in my mind, reassuring me, telling me it was all okay. His body was cool over mine, soothing me even as I burned. I opened my eyes, and my entire body crawled with flames that did not burn me, or him.

"Breathe, baby. Breathe," he said, and I felt a sob escape along with the breath I tried to take. I would not fucking cry. Not now. Not when there were asses I needed to kick. Answers I needed. I breathed more, saw the flames eventually sink back into my body.

"Okay. Okay. I need to get up," I said, saying words that meant nothing, just to say them because they were real, and they kept me from freaking the fuck out. I couldn't afford to lose my mind right then.

He got off of me and pulled me up. I stood, determined to stay upright of my own volition. Stared at him, meeting his blood-red gaze as I'd done hundreds of times before. I tore my eyes away from him, and looked around. My mother and aunts, Hades, were staring at me.

"We need to get you out of here, Mollis," Hades said.

"I need to know—"

"You need to get back to your world," my mother shouted, and I could feel her fear. "You killed two gods. They are going to start calling for your head, and nothing we do or say will stop them."

"She was plotting to overthrow Hades. She wanted me to kill someone in the Aether next. And he caused the deaths of three people I cared about, hunting for me, on her behalf," I said. "They–"

"It doesn't matter!" Hades shouted. "All they'll see is that you did what they're most afraid of. I'm still alive. Zeus still lives. But Enyo and Hermes are dead, at your hand."

I stared at him. "What difference does it make? They'll hunt me there, won't they?"

"Molly," Nain started to say, and Hades shook his head.

"We'll keep them back."

"They'll fight."

"Yes."

"War, then," I said, and both Hades and my mother nodded. "you could just turn me over. Brennan is safe, right?" I asked my mother.

She nodded. "Eunomia brought him back to your home. I met her en-route. They are both injured, and the Guardians and Hermes' people did their best to make a mess of him, but he is alive and he will recover."

"But we're not turning you over. You must survive. At all costs." Hades watched me, shared a long look with my mother. Then he glanced at my aunt Megaera and Nain.

"We can trust Meg," Tisiphone said.

"And who is this demon, who has powers that seem very unlikely in one of his kind?" Hades asked me, gesturing at Nain.

"My husband," I said, the words wrong, strange in my mouth. Those words were meant for Brennan.

He raised his eyebrow. "I thought your mate was dead."

"That makes two of us. All kinds of crazy shit is happening today," I said, feeling exhausted after my crazy burst of energy.

"Can he be trusted?"

"Yeah," I said, starting to tremble again. Nain put his hand on my arm, and my body calmed at his touch. I shook my head, and he pulled his hand back.

"The secret is out, Hades. It's not as if Hermes' death will go unnoticed," my mother said, glaring at Hermes' still form. I heard footsteps outside the door, and Persephone appeared. Her hair was disheveled, her dress askew.

"Are you all right, darling?" Hades asked.

She went to him and took his hand. "Yes, thanks to the demons. They have my son in custody. They are bringing him here for you to deal with."

Hades nodded. I glanced toward Persephone and saw her watching me. "You did well, Fury," she said grudgingly, and, for once, there wasn't absolute hatred coming from her.

"I may have made a bigger mess," I said.

"War," she said, nodding. "Yes, war is coming."

"Why can't you just turn me over? I started saying again. "I'm fine with dying."

They all watched me. "But *I* am not fine with you dying," Hades said. "And your world needs you."

"Why?"

"Do you really think a war between the gods will contain itself to the Aether and the Nether?" Hades asked. "We will fight. Immortals, vying for power, getting out old grudges here in our world. This may have begun with Hermes and Enyo and their schemes, but it will not end there. Your world will suffer with our power. Storms, earthquakes, famine…just for a start."

"Then let them kill me now. Or kill me in front of them, if you're afraid of them using me. Take their reason for war away, *now*."

"It will happen, no matter what. Their plots have been exposed. Overthrow me and Zeus, using you. Put whoever they've deemed more worthy in our places. Now that they've failed, they'll make it about you. War was brewing already. It has been for the last twenty years."

"They'll do this? They'll let innocents die, over grudges?" I asked, sickened.

Tisiphone gave me a grim smile. "They're gods. What do you think? Have you ever known one of them, except for those few in this room, who gave a damn about humanity?"

"Enyo said they wanted to be revered again or something," I said.

She nodded. "A war of the gods would be an excellent way to remind humanity that we exist. Never mind the fact that all it will do is make them hate and fear us."

"Hate is better than apathy," I murmured.

"To some, yes," Hades said.

"Well. This is my world that's going to pay. What can I do to stop it?" I asked.

My mother, Hades, and Persephone exchanged concerned glances.

"You can fulfill your destiny," my mother finally said, and I felt one thing from her.

Mourning.

◆◆◆

"What? What do I do?"

"We can't. The Fates need to be the ones to tell you," Tisiphone said. "We don't know the whole story. They do," she said, when she saw that I was about to protest.

"Okay. Fine. Where do I find them, so I can take care of this?"

"We don't know," Hades said.

"Oh for the love of fucking god," I growled. I felt humor from Nain, and he reached over and squeezed my hand.

"Relax," he said.

"Yeah. Of course. You are not getting out of this either, you bastard," I said, turning on him. "You are going to explain this to me, and then I am going to kick your ass for letting me kill you, and then…"

"I know," he said, his voice, just as I'd always thought,

like two stones rumbling against each other. "I will. And you can do all the ass-kicking you need to do. Later."

"Things are not the same," I said, meeting his eyes.

He just smiled. "So I hear. But nothing lasts forever, baby, except for you and me."

I rolled my eyes and shook my head. *And cocky goddamned demons,* I thought at him. He laughed.

"You have to be able to tell me something," I said to my mother.

She looked uncomfortable.

"There is a prophecy," Hades began, and I sensed the same sorrow, nervousness from him. He made a face. "Ugh. This is exactly why I've always been so good about keeping it in my pants. Unlike Zeus."

"Yes, the fact that you only cheated on me once is quite admirable," Persephone murmured, irritation rolling off of her. Hades took a small step away from her without seeming to realize he was doing it. Smart god.

"Well, seriously. Zeus can screw anything that moves and it's fine. Me? I have a roll in the sheets with one goddess other than Persephone—"

"The one goddess you never should have been with!" Persephone said, glaring at Hades.

"We've been over this, dear," he said.

"Can someone explain this to me before I lose my mind?" I snarled, and they all looked at me.

"The prophecy is that one day, there will be born the child of the avenging Fury and the lord of the dead," my mother began.

"And that child will embody the full terror of death," Hades intoned.

"And that on the day of her birth, that child will herald the destruction of our world," Tisiphone said.

"While saving the world of Man," Hades finished.

"Oh, damn," Megaera whispered, falling back onto the chair behind her. "She's not Cith's?"

My mother shook her head.

"Why would you do such a thing, Tisiphone?" Megaera asked.

"We were foolish. And too full of our own power. Cithaeron had hurt me, and Persephone and Hades were arguing again. We comforted each other."

"One time," Hades said, raising a finger to illustrate. "Once."

"That's all it takes," I muttered.

"You knew about the prophecy..." Megaera said.

"Everyone knows he can't create life," Tisiphone said. "And I didn't think anything would be born of my body, either. Cithaeron and I loved each other for years, and nothing ever grew in my womb. From an *earth* god, which says something."

"And we were attracted to each other. And we were both kind of alone, at that time," Hades said.

"It was foolish," Tisiphone said. "But I wouldn't change a thing." Hades nodded.

"How can you stand there and say that?" I asked in disbelief. "I'm supposed to be here to destroy your wold. I'm bringing war to mine. How can you say that?"

Hades watched me, and all I felt from him was warmth. "Because you have been worth knowing, my dear. Tisiphone and I, two beings who deal only in death, created something beautiful and good in you."

"Something destructive," I said.

"You'll ultimately save your world. At this point, the lives of thousands of innocent mortals is worth more than the lives of gods who have lived far too long. Look at how ready they are to battle," Tisiphone said. "They grow bored, restless. Useless."

"They forget what it is to truly be gods," Megaera agreed, starting to get over some of her shock. "They forget that what makes us great is service of that which we have created, not the other way around."

"You will remind them not to take mortals for granted," Hades said. "Though it will be too late for them to put that lesson to use."

"I don't want to destroy anyone," I said, forcing tears back from my eyes. This was not the time to be weak.

"You exist. Your path lies ahead of you, daughter, whether you want to follow it or not," Hades said.

"Sometimes, you have to destroy something in order to make it stronger," Nain said. I looked at him, met his eyes. He still stood there in his demonic form. He was definitely stronger than he had been, and I could feel a lot of my own power echoed in his. I saw what he was trying to say.

"Okay. What now?" I asked.

"We get you to the gate and into your world. And then we guard the gateways with everything we have, to keep them from hunting you. You must survive, Mollis," Tisiphone said.

I nodded. At that moment, the demons brought Dionysus into the office. Hades turned to my mother and aunt. "Will you take them into custody? Keep them locked well away."

"I will, my Lord," Tisiphone said. She grabbed Alecto and took flight. Megaera followed, with Dionysus. They flew out the large window behind Hades' desk, toward their home and the cells where the souls of the wicked were kept.

I glanced toward Hades. He was studying Nain. "Explain yourself, demon," he said to Nain, finally.

"I resurrected here in the Nether after my death."

"How?" Hades asked, interrupting Nain before he could go on. I looked between the two of them; my father and my mate (former mate, whatever), as insane as it seemed that either thing was possible.

"Three times bonded to a daughter of gods," Nain said quietly.

"The number three is magical in our world," I whispered, repeating what Eunomia had explained about the significance of threes.

Nain watched me. "I didn't know this would happen. I didn't plan on three times. I would have bonded more with you if I could have. I just wanted to give you as much of my own strength as I could, before you faced Astaroth."

"You knew it would kill you, when I finished him," I said quietly.

"Yes."

I curled my hands into each other to keep myself from hitting him, remembering the way I'd mourned, the emptiness inside me that had just only now been filled, being in his presence again. There would be time later. I just shook my head.

"And what happened when you resurrected here?" Hades asked, trying to hurry things along before I lost my temper.

"I woke up. And I tried to get back to her, but I couldn't get through the gateway. I tried, but the guards kept me back. I knew there were other demons getting through to her world, and I wanted to be there, with her, to keep her safe. To let her know I was alive," he said to Hades, though his eyes were on me. "I drew too much attention to myself, and the gate guards called on the Furies. Alecto was the one that took me into custody. And when she realized what she had, she and the Guardians kept me locked away, figuring they could put me to use eventually."

"And you were freed by one of the Guardians?"

"Eunomia," Nain said, and I said a silent prayer to who knows what in thanks that E had not betrayed me. "She didn't know. The Guardians knew Molly was her friend. I think they planned to try to use E eventually, too."

I nodded, and so did Hades. "And the shifter?"

"Tossed in the cell with me. That was an interesting reunion," Nain said, watching me. "And then I guess things started going bad for Hermes and his people here, and a few of the Guardians and Alecto came to us, started punishing Brennan. There was a huge fight, and then Alecto had to come here, and then E showed up and between the three of us we managed to overpower enough of them to get free. E took Brennan away, and I came here, because I could feel Molly."

"You will return to your world and aid my daughter in any way she needs, demon," Hades said. I could feel dislike from him. He knew what I'd been through. Who knew Hades would be a protective sort of dad?

Nain bowed to Hades, then glanced at me.

"Uh. So. You're coming home with me?"

He nodded.

"Well. This is going to be interesting."

He grinned. "Always."

"Mollis, we need to leave. Now," Hades said, and I nodded. We walked out of his office. The army of demons that had assisted us in the fight against Hermes lined the halls and they all bowed to Hades, briefly, then saluted me, fists to chests, and stood there that way. Hades studied them, and me.

"You are all free of your bonds to the Nether, should you swear allegiance to the Fury Mollis Eth-Hades in the mortal realm. Should you bind yourselves to her, you will serve her with your lives. Choose. Now."

Not a single demon moved. They kept their fists over their hearts, their red glowing gazes on me.

"You're sure?" I asked them. "Things are about to get bad."

"We were made for bad, my Lady," Elsoloth, said, and the rest of the demons, males and females, nodded.

"Oh," Persephone said, and Hades, Nain, and I looked at her. "This was another part of the prophecy."

"And she shall rally an army of the Nether,

And the heavens will bleed in her wake." She said softly. A chill went down my spine.

"That is just fucking creepy," I muttered.

"Agreed," she said, raising her eyebrow at me.

"Let's go," Hades said again, and we left, my army (Jesus Christ...) flanking me as we walked out of Hades' home.

"Why couldn't I be part of Christian mythology?" I asked as we marched. "I could be surrounded by happy angels eating Philadelphia Cream Cheese on fluffy white clouds or some shit like that."

Hades laughed, and I heard Nain snort behind me.

The streets of the Nether were mostly deserted. We marched toward the gateway, and as we approached it, I could see why.

"Damn," Hades muttered beside me.

I looked. Several gods were coming toward us, from one of the other gateways.

"Run," Hades shouted, and my army moved me along, toward the gate. A few beings blocked the gateway, and my demons cut them down like they were nothing, then they turned to watch me. I looked toward Hades. A group of gods had gathered around him and another. The other god had a flowing white beard, white hair. He was huge, and a golden lightning bolt adorned the front of his white robes. He was shouting, and pointing at me, as were several other gods. Nain's hands on my shoulders held me back.

The conversation went on, getting more heated. Hades was saying several things that were pissing the other god off. As it went on, some gods went to stand behind Hades, some stayed behind Zeus. I looked at individual gods. That there, behind Zeus, had to be Ares, god of war. I'd killed his sister, and, by the way he was staring at me, he knew it. Yeah, he wouldn't be joining Hades' side in this fight. Athena, however, had stood with Hades and Persephone immediately, and, as I looked at her, she gave me a nod of acknowledgement and respect. Aphrodite, as well, had gone to Hades' side, along with Asclepias, Artemis,

Demeter, and Hestia. The Nosoi sided with Zeus, as did the remaining Guardians, Hera, Hephaestus, Apollo, and a few gods I couldn't figure out.

The shouting got louder. Things were getting heated between the two groups of gods, and I heard my name several times.

And then Ares let out a wild shout, and struck at Hades, and Hades struck back, and Persephone stabbed Ares with a long blade that just seemed to appear from nowhere, and Zeus threw a lightning bolt toward the Nether's group of allies.

"Time to go, Molls. Earth is going to need you," Nain said behind me, and I nodded numbly. I glanced at my demons.

"Last chance. You're sure?"

They all nodded. I faced the gateway, and started to walk though, with my army and my very alive demon mate at my back.

CHAPTER NINETEEN

We walked through the gateway, the demons, Nain and I. When we came through, I saw that my entire imp army, as well as Shanti, Levitt, and several shifters from the Grosse Pointe pack, were there. They were all armed to the hilt, ready. Waiting.

There was nearly a bloodbath when they saw the demons come through, but I shouted, and everyone froze. "They're with me," I said. "They are allies."

My Earth-bound allies eyed my Nether allies, and vice versa. Dahael and Bash stood right near the front of the group. Bash looked up at Nain, who was still beside me.

"Demon," he said in greeting.

"Bash. Dahael," Nain said, looking at my two imp captains. Bash just nodded. Dahael stared daggers at Nain, undoubtedly remembering everything she'd seen me go through after his death. She didn't say anything, but her ears twitched in irritation. Had to love her.

"Okay. Things are about to get messy," I began.

"Messy already, godslayer," a creaky, crackly voice said from behind the group of very armed Earth allies.

Everyone turned, and three women stood there. Dressed in flowing white robes. One looked ancient. One was a woman in the prime of her life. And another was a young woman, a maiden. They each wore an amulet around their neck.

"Fates," I murmured, and my stomach turned.

They walked toward me, through the group that had parted. "Messy. Bad times. Your parents told you about the prophecy."

I nodded.

"They didn't tell you everything," the maiden said.

"They are gods. That doesn't surprise me."

The three Fates laughed, their laughs ranging from a ringing tinkle to a cackle, but coming together harmoniously. "Smart girl," the woman said.

"They said I can save this world," I said. "How?"

The Fates stood a moment, so still they could have been statues. "By being you, mostly," the maiden said.

"That doesn't help a whole lot," I said, trying to be polite.

"You have everything you need. Except the knowledge, which we can give you," the ancient one said.

"Your home, this city, will be hit hardest by the war of the gods. Punishment for being the place you call home," the woman said.

"And if I move? If I go where they can't find me?"

"They will still punish this area, because your memory lives strong here. People here who love you. People here who pray your name in the long, cold night."

I swallowed. What a goddamn mess. People were going to die, again, because of me and my stupid lineage. "What can I do?"

"First step is to keep the gods where they belong," the ancient one said.

"Meaning?"

"Make it so they cannot cross into your realm, godslayer," the maiden said.

I bristled. Already hated "godslayer" as much as I'd hated "abomination."

"But....they need to be able to come here," I said.

"Why?" all three asked at once.

"The Guardians have to escort the souls of the dead. And the Furies need to come here sometimes. And what about the Earth gods, like Poseidon and Cithaerus? What happens to them?"

"The earthly gods will simply become the elements they once ruled. Cithaeron will be nothing but a mountain. Poseidon is currently in the Aether, and he will remain trapped there," the woman said.

"As for the rest. The Guardians are no longer of use. Compromised," the ancient one said.

"Yes," I said.

"Old days, ravens escorted the dead. They can do so again," she continued. "The Furies have no reason to come here."

"So, I can keep the gods away from this world. Can I go back to the Nether?"

They were silent, and their silence was all the answer I needed.

"But... my mother. My father..." I stared at them, and Nain took my hand.

"They survived eons without you," the woman said.

"But I just found them," I said quietly, knowing I sounded like a child, and, for once, not caring.

"We must all pay a price," the ancient one said.

"And how much is she supposed to keep paying?" Nain said, finally losing his temper enough to break the calm facade he'd been showing. "She gives, over, and over, and over again, and it's never enough with you people. Why does it always have to be her?"

"With great power—"

"if you say, 'must come great responsibility' I am going to scream," I said.

The Fates stayed silent.

"So I won't see my parents again. What else will it cost?" I tried to focus, Brennan's pain duller, but still present. I needed to get to him.

"There is no telling," the maiden said. "It takes a great amount of power to close a realm off from the gods. Only the child of prophecy could do it."

I felt the gate shaking, trembling. They were trying to come through. My parents were fighting, just beyond the gate. I looked that way.

"I didn't get to say goodbye," I said quietly.

"Goodbyes mean nothing to immortals," the maiden said.

"It does to me," I said. "Can you tell them I said thank you? As crazy as they are. I'm glad I had them."

"We will convey your message, godslayer," the ancient one said.

The gateway shook again, and everyone readied themselves for a fight.

"If they get through, your life is forfeit, and there is no protection for your city. Is this what you want?" the Fates asked.

"Fine!" I snarled. "What do I do?"

"Mortals. Leave. All of you," the Fates said, and, after I nodded, everyone, Nain, demons, imps, and shifters alike, left. Shanti gave me a fearful look before Levitt took her arm and led her out.

"You are closing a doorway, a gateway. The demon taught you how to build a doorway in your mind, to protect it from those who would breach it, yes?" the woman said, and I nodded.

"Yes."

"This is the same process, on a much, much larger scale. You are building an impenetrable threshold between here and the Nether and the Aether, one that can never be breached. You will put all of your considerable power behind it. Once it exists, it is forever."

"It has been foretold," all three Fates intoned, which was creepy as fuck.

I shook my head. "So, just think it? How does that make sense?"

"The gateways only exist for the gods. A strong enough god, one who was destined for this particular task, is the only one capable of keeping the gods in their own world. The time has come."

"I won't be the same when this is done," I said softly.

"No," they said after a pause. "But not even we can tell you how this will change you, Mollis Eth-Hades," the maiden said.

"So... we won't feel the effects of the war here, right? This saves them from that."

They shook their heads. "Wrong. The world of the gods and your world are still tied together, even if the planes between them can no longer be crossed. Zeus's anger will still cause storms, and the gods of Famine, Strife, and War's influence will still be felt. Your world needs your gifts. This region will be hit hardest by the effects of the gods' war, and there is no telling even to us, how long it will go on."

"Is there any way to stop them?"

"No. This was destined."

I wanted to scream. "So all this does..."

"Is keep you alive and keeps the gods out of your world, where they can cause even more harm than they can from their own realms. Now are you going to do it or not, girl?"

"Fine!" I shouted.

"Good. Focus. Give it everything you have. We will speak with your parents." And with that, the three women disappeared, and I was alone.

"Focus," I muttered to myself. The first thing I had to do was clear my mind. I almost laughed at how ridiculous that sounded. Clear my mind of the fact that the love of my life was in pain and I had no idea how badly. The fact that the gods think I'm a child of some prophecy, that Hades is my father, that if this works, I'll never see my parents again. I'll never see the amethyst sky of the Nether again, feel my soul sing as I step through the gateway, into a world that I recognized as "home." Try to clear my mind of Nain, and the demons I was now responsible for. Clear my mind of the fact that, right this moment, the gods waged war on each other, because of my actions, and my world was already beginning to suffer. I could hear thunder, sirens, from beyond the factory.

Try to clear my mind of the worry that I was not up to the task, and people would die because of it.

Right.

But I tried. I tried to find my cold, empty place, the place I'd so often retreated to in the early years of my life, before I'd met Nain, before I became a Fury, a god, a slayer of deities. Back when I hadn't known what love was, or how much it cost to lose it. Back when I was nothing more than a lost girl, finding lost girls.

I cleared it all, and tried to ignore the way the gateway trembled as they fought on the other side.

"Bye, mom and dad," I murmured, and then I cleared them from my mind as well.

When I was cold, and empty, it was just me, and my power, and the gateway. This gateway, every gateway between this world and the others. I could see them all, and I started building, walls of slick black metal, like nothing I'd ever seen before. Seamless, perfectly smooth, thick and unbreakable, unbendable, impervious to fire, water, or any other force a god could throw at it. No spaces around or underneath, no way to sneak past.

I felt my body break out in a sweat from the effort, my muscles beginning to tremble.

The pounding from beyond the gateway became more frenzied as I built. They could feel it, and my parents' adversaries fought harder to get through.

I focused harder, making it real, making it strong,

stronger than anything in any of the realms I'd known. My head began to pound as my power increased, and I was soon full. My nose bled, and I could feel wetness coming from my ears, my lips. My skin felt like it was about to split. I gritted my teeth against my power more full now than I'd ever been, more than the night Nain died, more than the night I'd nearly died in the explosion that sparked more of my powers to life, more than I'd felt when Nain shielded me in my father's home. The pain was nothing. I pictured Brennan, knew I would go through any amount of pain to keep him safe.

I opened my mouth.

"Make it so," I said, and I felt my power surge harder, higher, and I screamed in agony as my power snapped, making the barriers I'd built real.

I could no longer feel the Nether.

I could no longer hear the pounding, feel the gateway trembling.

There was no gateway.

And the whole world went black.

EPILOGUE

My name is Mollis Eth-Hades.
Fury.
Abomination.
Godslayer.

I killed a god and a goddess, started a war between the gods, and resigned myself to exile, by my own choice and actions, in the mortal world, cut off from my family, from the beauty of the Nether. It was the price of peace for the innocents of the mortal realm, as well as my penance.

Why am I so cold? And where is that shouting and crashing coming from? I flex a leg, an arm, feeling as though I am waking from a long, numb, deep sleep.

I know this. I know that I am the only child of Hades, lord of the dead. My mother is the Fury, Tisiphone. I know that I killed Enyo, the goddess of war and Hermes, the god of thieves and messenger of the gods, because they caused the deaths of innocents and plotted against my father. I know I have seriously pissed the gods off, though they craved war, and I gave them all the reason they needed.

I sit up and look around. I am in a barren, rocky place. Amethyst sky above me, black stone below. I flex my wings, stretching them.

Wings?

"What the ever loving fuck is this now?" I groan, throwing my head back. I try to shake my groggy mind awake.

I'd been on the Earth side of the gateway. I'd closed it. I remember not feeling it anymore. And then I felt nothing.

I look around.

This was definitely the Nether. I could feel it surrounding me, suffusing me with its power. I look down at myself, and see my body, naked, unmarked. Even my tattoo of Mjolnir was gone. Nain's ring, gone, emptiness in my soul again where I'd felt him, for a few crazy minutes, before I'd closed the gateway.

Glistening black-feathered wings, like my father's, sprout from my back.

I can feel my power, roaring within me.

I sit, and think. If I am here, there is only one way it could have happened, one way I could be here, when I know for sure I'd been on the other side before everything went black.

The cost of closing the gate had been a high one. It had cost me my life, ultimately. Except that I am not all that easy to kill.

I'd died.

And come back.

Here.

Cut off from just about everyone I love.

Unable to protect their world the way I am supposed to.

Tossed into the one place in existence I should not be.

The one place I would be hunted.

I want to scream. I want to hit something. I want to

destroy the next being I see, just on principle.

I take a breath, look around. And then I smile, and there is no joy in it.

Fine. If I am here, somebody is gonna pay for taking my life away from me.

I walk across black jagged stones. I can see a small cave several yards away. I'll wait, and plan, and figure out how to keep myself alive. There will be peace between the gods, one way or another.

My world will not be allowed to suffer because of my brash actions. I will protect those I love, even if I can't be with them.

And then, I'll figure out a way to get home.

THE END

Keep reading for a sneak peek of
HIDDEN BOOK THREE: HOME

HOME: CHAPTER ONE

What doesn't kill you makes you stronger.

So far, this was true for me. I'd had my soul shattered when my first husband, Nain, died. I'd teetered on the brink of death after a demon tried to blow me up. I'd watched the man I love waste away from a plague sent to my realm to punish me.

Each time, I got stronger. I got angrier. So strong and angry that I'd sometimes been afraid of myself.

But what about the things that *do* kill you? What does it do to you, to die and come back?

I guess I'd find out soon enough, I thought as I made my way across the rocky ground toward the cave I'd seen after waking.

When I entered the cave, I was pleased to find that it was not only empty (gods knew what weird creatures I may have found there) but also that the opening was just big enough for me to get through, crouched down, and then opened into an only slightly larger space. Large enough for me to stand up, to sleep on the floor, but not much bigger than that. The black stone that the mountains were made of was the same stone I'd seen throughout the Nether, in homes and sculptures, tabletops and other items. I'd never thought to ask the name of it.

I sat down, leaning my bare back against the rough wall of the cave. I'd never thought to do a lot of things. At times, I hadn't thought much, period. I frowned, thinking. I leaned my head back and closed my eyes, more tired than I expected to be. The short walk from the place where I'd revived to the cave had taken a lot of energy. Not quite up to peak form yet, I guessed.

Coming back from the dead, regenerating a body, apparently takes a lot out of you. Which was a whole crazy thing I really didn't want to think about too closely. I'd never even considered that it could work that way, that, as a god, or the child of gods or whatever, I could lose my body completely and re-form in the Nether. Nain had done it, thanks to my blood in his veins. I was starting to suspect that it was more than blood, that it was life, or energy, or the soul or whatever the hell you wanted to call it.

Freaky shit.

I started to feel myself doze, and kept ruminating on what I'd do differently this time around. Before, my trademark had been smashing first and asking questions later. I'd thoughtlessly charged into buildings, not knowing what waited for me. Thoughtlessly destroyed beings whose deaths only came back to bite me in the ass. I tried to tell myself that action was necessary, but the fact was that I just hadn't been smart enough. I'd charged headfirst into my relationship with Nain, when I knew, now, that everything I'd ever wanted in a relationship, Brennan had been all along.

My eyes shot open. Brennan. Oh, no. Was he mourning me? I put my head in my hands. Damn it. Would he know I was still alive, somewhere?

I hadn't even been able to see him that last day, after E had dragged him from the Nether. Was he okay? Had he made it? My gut clenched at the thought. I closed my eyes, and focused, then I breathed a sigh of relief. My connection to Brennan, the one I'd made after he'd been healed from the shifter plague, still existed, bright, warm, soothing. Once again, I couldn't feel my connection with Nain, but remembered it well enough to know that it felt more to me like a searing inferno. I'd stupidly believed, in the beginning, that that inferno, the passion, meant that Nain and I were supposed to be together, that two beings of the Nether, bonded, just made sense.

I knew now, that what makes sense is being with someone who makes you happy, who feels like home. Nain being back had, strangely enough, only made me more sure that Brennan and I were the real thing. With them both alive and well, the only one I wanted was Bren.

I laid down, curled up on myself. It was a moot point, now, unless I figured out a way to get back to my own realm.

I need clothes, I thought blearily as I dozed off again.

◆◆◆

When I opened my eyes, it took me a while to remember, again, where I was and how I got there. And it just depressed me and pissed me off all over again. My eyes adjusted to the dark interior of the cave, and I saw something move.

I froze.

I continued to look, as my eyes adjusted more, and, eventually, I could make out the dark shape of what looked like some kind of huge animal, so large it blocked most of the meager light coming in the cave entrance. It sat. Dog? Wolf? Its round eyes glowed a dark, stormy blue.

I barely breathed. It looked like it would really hurt if it decided to start attacking me.

I sat up slowly, readied myself to throw flames if I had to. Gods I hoped my powers still worked the way I remembered them.

The animal cocked its head, inspecting me. In that moment, it reminded me of Eunomia, and I thought of her with a pang. She was trapped in my world, much as I was trapped in hers. I watched the creature, and it watched me. The more my eyes adjusted, the more sure I was that it was some kind of large dog or something. Then, it turned and padded out of the mouth of the cave, leaving me alone.

I got up and walked toward the cave entrance, trying to see the animal better, but my foot hit something on the floor, near where it had been sitting. Something soft. I bent down and touched it, timidly, half expecting it somehow to turn into something that would rip my arm off.

Cloth.

I picked the bundle up, and found that a long sleeved top, a pair of pants, and a soft pair of some kind of leather boots had been left.

As nice as it would be to not walk around with all my parts on display, I felt more than a twinge of apprehension. Somebody knew I was here. And if somebody knew, then the element of surprise I was counting on was lost. I picked the shirt up, fumbling with it, and noting that it had two large slits in the back, which I was able, after some maneuvering and quite a bit of swearing, to push my wings through. I eyed them, warily, as I pulled my pants on.

How the hell was I going to walk around in my own world with these goddamned feathered monstrosities?

I pulled the pants on, then the boots. Everything fit like a glove, as if they had been made for me. The shirt had some kind of built-in corset thing that I managed to awkwardly lace up, and the pants almost fit like a second skin, which was definitely not something I'd gone for in my clothing choices back home. The boots went up to just below my knees, fitting my calves and ankles perfectly. The leather was supple, almost velvety.

A knife might be nice, I thought, but then I remembered that I had no need of mortal weapons in the Nether. At least, I hoped not.

I extended my hand, focused on bringing my sword into being. It appeared, effortlessly, but it, like too many things, was no longer the same. The hilt was still dark black metal, but the blade, the one that had leapt with blue flames, was different now. The blade itself was longer, thinner, and the flames were black.

"Well, that's creepy," I murmured. "We're going for a very angel of death type look here, aren't we?" And then I realized I was talking to myself and that it probably wasn't a good sign. I looked at my sword again, at the black flames leaping along the blade, then I shook my head and focused on making it disappear. It did.

From inside my cave, I could hear the sounds of battle raging in the Nether, as it had since I'd revived. Booming, crashing. Distant shouts. Almost constant thunder and lightning. Every once in a while, the sound of a horn blowing. The occasional scream. Really, it was stupid. The gods couldn't actually kill each other. I guessed that, when they were injured badly enough to die, they just regenerated the way I had. The only being who could actually kill a god and make him or her stay dead, was me.

I'm special that way.

I crept out of the cave and looked around. Everything looked the same as it had when I'd awoken. Amethyst sky overhead, sharp black mountains behind me and cutting the western horizon. I looked up at the millions of whitish-purple stars that dotted the sky. They were always there, no matter what time it was. When I'd first started coming to the Nether, I'd purposely tried coming at different times, trying to get a sense of day versus night. Eunomia had finally explained to me that there was no difference, that the Nether was endless night, and I'd smiled. Night had always been my time.

Looking up at the sky now, I just felt empty and lost. I missed the sky back home, even the gray clouds that Detroit wore in November like a cloak. But every once in a while, you'd get a brilliantly sunny, bright blue sky, and you'd remember what beauty was.

I shook my head, and looked around. I could see the city in the distance, where Hades' palace and everything else was. The Nether was vast, but few ventured beyond Hades' reach. The mountains, the eerie forests that surrounded the city, were inhabited by creatures great and small, creatures I'd only ever read about.

I glanced around again, looking for the mysterious creature that had, I had to believe, left the clothing for me. Not a trace of it. I racked my still-groggy brain, trying to guess, from my stupidly limited knowledge of mythology, which of the gods might have a giant dog thing at its command. It wasn't Cerberus; I'd seen that beast outside of Hades' home. Even if it had been, I wouldn't have felt any better.

I knew I needed to be smarter now. And the smart thing, at this point, was to trust no one. My father had lied to me, about pretty much everything. My mother wasn't much better. I wondered if they'd known closing the gateway would kill me. If they had… then they won for shittiest parents EVER. My aunt had tried to kill me, and I had to wonder how much the other aunt despised my existence, considering how much venom had been spewed my way. Every god, now, had a reason to want me dead for closing the mortal realm to them, weakening them.

Well. Dead again, I guess.

I wondered if I'd come back from a second death. I didn't intend to have to find out.

The only thing I knew is that I'd have to be careful. I'd have to think instead of smashing first. No more taking things on faith. No more prophecies, family bullshit, or entangling alliances. All I wanted was to end the stupid war and figure out how to get home.

There had to be a way.

READ MORE IN
HIDDEN BOOK THREE: HOME
AVAILABLE NOW

Visit http://www.colleenvanderlinden.com/hidden
for news, updates, and more

Never Miss an Update!

Sign up for the Hidden Newsletter.
http://bit.ly/hiddennewsletter

For backstory material, news, and upcoming events
be sure to check out
http://www.colleenvanderlinden.com/hidden

ABOUT THE AUTHOR

Colleen Vanderlinden is the author of the *Hidden* and *Soulhunter* urban fantasy series, as well as the *Copper Falls* paranormal romance series. The third *Hidden* novel, *Home*, was a finalist for *RT Book Reviews' Editors Choice Awards* for best self-published urban fantasy novel of 2014.

Her books have consistently received positive reviews, and *RT Book Reviews* has called her storytelling "electrifying."

She lives in the Detroit area with her husband, kids, demonic Basset hound, and two lazy cats. You can find out more about Colleen's books at her website, colleenvanderlinden.com, or follow her on Twitter, where she's @C_Vanderlinden.

Website: http://www.colleenvanderlinden.com
Facebook: facebook.com/colleenvanderlinden
Twitter: @C_Vanderlinden

FICTION BY
COLLEEN VANDERLINDEN

The Hidden Series
Book One: Lost Girl
Book Two: Broken
Book Three: Home
Book Four: Strife
Book Five: Nether

Hidden Novellas
Forever Night
Earth Bound

The Hidden: Soul Huter Series
Book One: Guardian
Book Two: Betrayer
Book Three: Zealot – Coming 2016

The Copper Falls Series
Shadow Witch Rising
Shadow Sworn

The StrikeForce Series
A New Day

www.ingramcontent.com/pod-product-compliance
Lightning Source LLC
Chambersburg PA
CBHW070553130626
46556CB00001B/139